A NOVEL BY FREDERICK HARRISON

AN
OPAQUE
WAR

An Opaque War is a work of fiction, all characters and events the product of the author's imagination. Any resemblance to actual events or persons (living or dead) is purely coincidental.

March 2007   FHE Trade Paperback Edition

All rights reserved under International and Pan-American Copyright Conventions. Published in the United States by Frederick Harrison Enterprises (fhentp@aol.com)

ISBN 978-1-4276-1626-5

Cover: Cindy Wokas

Formatting: Charlotte A.M. Gallagher

Printing: Peggy Irvine, Kirby Lithographic Co.

Cover Photo: JupiterImages Corporation

For Charlotte

The hotel room in Karachi was so dimly lit that the men sitting at the small table could barely be seen, wreathed as they were in dense tobacco smoke. There were three of them, two young with jet black hair and beards that were holding droplets of sweat glistening in the light of the single bulb that hung overhead. The third man was much older; his hair and beard were streaked with gray, and he wore an Afghan-style headdress. All were wearing dishdashas, loose-fitting gowns designed to accommodate the endless heat. The older man was speaking, the others listening attentively.

They did not seem to hear the first noises at the door, but then it crashed open and six uniformed security policemen stormed into the room and were quickly upon the men, throwing them to the floor and kneeling on their backs while binding their hands. This was done so quickly and efficiently that the two additional men following behind had only to stand by and watch. They were not in uniform, but dressed all in black and wearing ski masks. Finishing, the officer in charge turned to them and said, in English: "We will take them to the bureau and see what we have caught." It was said as a statement, but its tone requested concurrence. One of the men nodded, and the captives were hustled out of the room.

When they were gone, both men immediately tore off their masks. Underneath, their faces were bathed in sweat, hair plastered flat against their skulls.

"I hate these fucking masks," one of them, called Sid, complained. "You would think they could afford to provide us with something more suitable to the climate. But, instead, they buy these woolen things from a sporting goods catalog."

The other man, whose name was Jed, nodded sympathetically, and began looking around the sparsely furnished room.

"It's in the nature of the business," he replied. "There's lots of money and attention for things that seem big and nothing for the little things that really matter to the grunts on the ground. I'll tell you what, though. Next time we give a couple hundred K to some warlord for god-knows-what, we'll slip him some extra and get him to order us some better masks on the Internet."

Jed pulled a canvas bag from under the table at which the three men had been sitting and dumped it on the table. Bundles of used U.S. banknotes fell out, along with a satellite telephone handset.

"Shit," his partner exclaimed. "There's got to be fifty grand here. There's more to these guys than we suspected."

"The bag probably belongs to the older guy," Jed reasoned.

"The other two looked like they're renting the clothes they're wearing." He began searching the room more carefully.

"Did you notice anything unusual about him, specifically at the time the cops were manhandling him and his dishdasha got pulled up around his waist?"

"I've always wondered what they wear under those things," Sid replied, "but I don't think I noticed anything unusual. Did you see something?"

Jed and Sid were members of CIA's Clandestine Service assigned to the Agency's Karachi station. They had known one another, on and off, for many years under a number of different field names, and were both entering the twilight of long careers.

"Did you happen to notice the long scar on his left knee?" Jed asked.

"No. What about it?"

"I've seen one like it before. It's unusually long and curves around his kneecap."

"Where would you have seen something like that?"

"In the files at Headquarters," Jed replied. Last home assignment, I worked in the AGWOG."

"The what?"

"The Al-Ghabrizi Working Group: about a dozen analysts dedicated to finding out all there is to know about Anwar al-Ghabrizi and following him until he is killed or captured, which seems like never."

Sid was incredulous. "You think this threadbare jamoke is al-Ghabrizi the kingpin of the international terrorist movement. You've got to be out of your fucking mind!"

"I don't really think he's al-Ghabrizi, but that scar is interesting."

Sid appeared mollified. "If you were even to mention his name in an EMail back to Headquarters, all hell would break loose. You know how hard up they are for some good news from this area."

"I know," Jed replied. "Let's go over to the police station and see what the Paks are planning to do with these guys." He took a final look around, picked up the canvas bag with the money and the telephone, and shut the door behind them.

The small, windowless lounge was stifling hot, a slow ceiling fan struggling against the heavy air. Jed and Sid, sprawled across worn waiting room chairs, had been there for almost five hours. Once, Sid had dozed off and rolled off his chair onto the floor with a crash loud enough to bring the desk officer in from the outer office.

"I hate this fucking business," he announced.

"So you are always telling me," Jed responded, annoyed to have been awakened by Sid's fall.

"They pay us shit to spend our lives waiting around in places like this for things that never happen and people who never show up. I'm fucking tired of it."

"So why do you keep doing it? If you like so much being out here at the ass end of nowhere, you could become a contractor and make almost three times what the Agency is paying us."

"I've been thinking about that more every day," Sid admitted. "But, I've got only six years to go until I can retire. While I'm sitting around in a sweatbox like this, I'm not someplace where I might get my ass shot off."

"It would be a lot more bearable, if we could do something clearly useful every once in a while," Jed observed.

Sid looked at him sharply. "You're not thinking about that al-Ghabrizi shit, are you? Forget it! You open up that can of worms and we will get dumped on by Headquarters for the rest of our careers."

"Yeah, but what if it is him. It could mean promotions maybe, and cushy jobs back home."

Before Sid could respond, the Security Police captain in charge of the station came into the room.

"I'm sorry for the delay, gentlemen, but we had to check the suspects' papers and interrogate them. The two young ones have Egyptian passports and claim to be just passing through Pakistan on their way home. The older man has Afghani papers. Although we suspect they are terrorists, we have no specific evidence of it, and they are foreign nationals. So, unless you gentlemen wish to take custody of them, we will release them until a hearing before the magistrate next month."

"They'll be long gone by then," Jed observed.

"That sometimes happens," the Major admitted.

"Let them go, Jed," Sid argued. "What they could know is not worth bothering with. The young ones are just kids, and the old guy looks too worn out to be anything."

Jed thought for a moment, then turned to stare at Sid. "We'll take them," he said. "If you would be kind enough to hold them until transportation can be arranged, we would appreciate it." Sid saw the look on Jed's face, and said nothing. Jed was Chief of Station.

The plane, a Gulfstream with nondescript civilian markings, made regular courier runs between Karachi and Bagram Airfield west of Afghanistan's capital Kabul. In addition to mail and supplies, the plane carried a strange mix of passengers, ranging from diplomats to military personnel, to suspicious looking civilians, to shackled prisoners wearing now-tattered dishdashas and bags over their heads. Jed checked on them as the descent into Bagram began.

"You'd better stop going back there to stare at that guy's knee," Sid laughed. "When he turns out to be a highly respected clergyman, he could accuse you of being a pervert. What are you going to do with them?"

"We'll have our own interrogators go over them. And, I'm going to ask Headquarters to fax me the picture of the scar from al-Ghabrizi's file."

"Is it a photo of the actual scar?"

"Unfortunately, not. As I recall, it's a drawing of the scar made from memory by an Agency source, a family doctor, I think."

"Shit! That ain't what you would call prima facie evidence."

"I know, and I'm beginning to have second thoughts. You are probably right about the reaction from Langley, even though I intend to weigh my message down with caveats."

"While you are having your second thoughts," Sid said cooperatively, "I'll figure out how we get rid of these guys, if we decide not to do anything with them."

CHAPTER TWO

The seventh floor of the CIA Headquarters Building, in a fenced and guarded compound off the George Washington Parkway in Langley, Virginia houses the office suites of the Director of the Central Intelligence Agency and his principal deputies. It also holds a number of much smaller offices assigned to special assistants who serve as the Director's immediate connection to major threats and targets on which the Intelligence Community is focused. One of these rooms was home to Hannah Crossman, who spent more time there and in the operations center on the floor below than she was willing to admit. Her portfolio was international terrorism, which meant that she got called every time an intelligence or law enforcement service somewhere in the world turned up an indication that the bad guys might be up to something. It was not always clear who the bad guys were or whether the threat was real, but some determination had to be made about it, if only that nothing was to be done.

As the gatekeeper, in her area of cognizance, for the Director, Admiral Philip Bergen, it was Hannah's responsibility to decide whether newly arriving intelligence or a developing situation needed to be brought to his immediate attention or could wait until the regular 7 AM briefing. Since she was but one of a number of specialized gatekeepers, competition for Bergen's attention was often fierce, and not infrequently got Hannah and her counterparts in trouble when the boss rebelled against being chivvied by his ankle-biters, as he called them. He knew, however, that they were just doing their jobs, and that the greater danger was that he would not be chivvied enough and something significant would be missed.

Hannah also needed to be careful to avoid being squeezed between Bergen and his deputies, who wanted to know everything the Director knew before he knew it. When she acquired information from the web of sources she had developed within the Agency, or from someone in another organization, Hannah needed to make sure that the appropriate Deputy Director was clued in before Bergen was, so that no one was caught flat-footed when the boss asked a question or demanded to know what was being done. They were grateful for that service, and subtly vindictive on the rare occasions it was not rendered. Sam Glover, a Deputy Director, was particularly sensitive to such things. His baronetcy included the Clandestine Service, the people deployed undercover all over the world to collect intelligence on a broad range of subjects of interest to the United States Government. He also commanded the paramilitary agents who worked with guerilla groups in countries like Afghanistan actively supporting U.S. military forces. Much of Hannah's support to Bergen came from Glover's intelligence assets and areas of responsibility, and he resented that she did not work for him, the more so for knowing that it was deliberately set up that way.

However, Hannah's lot was made easier by Glover's awareness that she too was a member of the Clandestine Service, her current assignment being the first in her ten years with the Agency that she was not posted to a foreign country or preparing to go to one. Her parents were Lebanese who immigrated to the United States during the nineteen-sixties and settled in an agricultural region of California, changing their surname to Crossman (the name of a nearby town) to signify their commitment to America. However, they remained practicing Muslims and, although Hannah and her brothers grew up as ordinary American kids, their home remained a part of the old country, much as any first generation American household. As a result, Hannah spoke fluent, colloquial Arabic and understood Islam and the extremes pursued in its name. She won a scholarship to Stanford, took a degree in Middle Eastern Studies then, on the eve of 9/11, paused belatedly to see what she could do with it.

Not much, it appeared. Aside from a number of small colleges looking to start a Middle East area studies program, there was only the CIA. Her talents and training could have been very useful to the international financial institutions and oil companies operating in the Muslim world, but she was a woman and her ability to be effective in conservative Islamic countries was severely circumscribed. Beyond that, she was beautiful, even when all but her face was concealed by an abaya. This would have created another big problem when the local potentates, whose good will was indispensable, began hitting on her.

But, Hannah liked the idea of working for the CIA and moving to Washington, which effectively put an end to her parents' plan to arrange a marriage for her. She thought she would become a translator, perhaps an intelligence analyst, but the Agency had other ideas. Its offer of a position in the Clandestine Service came immediately upon completion of the indoctrination courses required of all new employees. Hannah accepted without really knowing what was involved, but was soon finding out down on The Farm, the Agency's training area in southern Virginia, and at other out-of-the-way locations. When it was over, she was designated for overseas assignment.

The name Hannah, given at birth, reflected her Lebanese parentage and a genealogical history that provided a wonderful foundation for her "legend," the backstory created by the Agency for each of its undercover agents to provide them a plausible life and history. According to her legend, Hannah was the daughter of John Crossman, now unfortunately deceased, and a Lebanese woman who had left the two of them almost twenty years earlier to return to Lebanon. The history of her youth and education was, not surprisingly, identical to her real one. Hannah's permanent cover was as a mid-level administrator in the State Department office that managed passports and visas. Since every American embassy and consulate deals in passports and visas, Hannah could go plausibly on short - term assignments anywhere in the world. For longer term missions, she used her given name and "legend." When dialed, the phone number on her business card provided a message in Hannah's voice asking callers to leave a message. The calls were monitored continuously by the Agency's Cover Staff, which notified Hannah of them, including those from her mother wondering why her daughter was still unmarried.

Hannah had just returned to her small office from the morning briefing when Steve Hammel, a junior AGWOG analyst, stuck his head in the doorway.

"We got a back channel message from Jed at Bagram last night wanting us to send him that sketch of al-Ghabrizi's knee scar that we have in the file."

"Who is Jed and what does he want with it?" she asked, testing her coffee and finding it cold.

"Jed is Bob Berke who was in AGWOG a while back. He's now station chief in Karachi, and his field name is Jed. His message was very vague and defensive, but apparently the Paks grabbed up a guy who has a scar in the same location as does al-Ghabrizi. Jed has him up at Bagram and wants to compare scars.

Most of the message was taken up by assurances that there is probably nothing to this."

"I shouldn't wonder. Does Sam Glover know about this?"

Hammel was astounded. "Do you think we're crazy? We told Sam long before we told you. He said to send Jed the sketch and to tell him to report his findings immediately for Glover'seyes only."

Hannah was not surprised. "The question is: Who has Glover told, if anyone? Does the Director know?"

The analyst smiled conspiratorially. "I was told to say nothing to nobody. My life is in your hands." He disappeared from the doorway.

Hannah was in a quandary. If Bergen didn't know, and she mentioned it to him, Glover would find out and burn her informants in the AGWOG (a cardinal rule in the intelligence business is that you always protect your sources). However, should Bergen hear about it from someone other than Glover or herself, he would suspect that they were not as infallible as they would like him to believe. But, she couldn't check to see whether Glover was going to tell the boss because she wasn't suppose to know about it herself. This was daily life at the CIA, but Hannah wasn't really concerned: there was little likelihood that Jed would come up with anything.

Jed and Sid were waiting around the CIA compartmented facility at Bagram for the response to his message. Both knew that the request would not be refused, but were anxious about the fallout it would cause. Jed had tried to make the request as innocuous as possible, but he knew that the name al-Ghabrizi alone was sufficient to set off alarms.

"Our guy has not said a word since we grabbed him," Sid reported. "He doesn't bother to pretend that he doesn't understand English, but when we ask him questions, like do want to go potty or are you hungry, he will only grunt or shake his head."

"What about the other two?"

"They're singing like birds, but claim not to know anything, and I believe them. They're Egyptians just out of a jihadi training camp in the mountains, and were given walking-around money and told to come to Karachi for the meeting with Knee Scar. He was supposed to tell them what it's all about, but didn't get a chance before the raid began. What are we going to do with them?"

"Since they've got Egyptian papers, let's put them on a plane to Cairo," Jed replied. "The Egyptian security service will find out whether they know anything useful. When we get the sketch from Headquarters, we'll put Knee Scar in the shower to clean him up while we compare scars. If he is al-Ghabrizi, we don't want him to suspect that we're on to him.

"I think he would be the most surprised of all of us to be al-Ghabrizi," Sid observed dryly.

Just then, the suspect's satellite telephone, which was sitting with the confiscated currency on a nearby table, began to ring. The men stared at it, but neither made a move to answer. Jed glanced at his watch, and made a note of the exact time of the call.

In Paris, John Balthazar held the handset to his ear a few moments longer, then turned it off and tossed it on the bed in his hotel room, and resumed knotting his tie. It was early evening, and he was dressing carefully for a very important dinner with clients. His suitcase, from which he had removed little, was lying open on the floor ready to be secured for his departure. If all went well at the dinner, he would be off for New York in a few days.

Looking at himself in the mirror, Balthazar saw a handsome, dark-eyed man in his late thirties. His black hair was cut in the latest fashion, and the tie he was knotting was one of Hermes's finest, a subdued pattern befitting the serious business he would undertake that evening.

He contemplated his handiwork then, checking his watch, dialed the room telephone, listening impatiently to ring after ring. Finally, a recorded voice cut in to ask him to press 1, if he wished to continue in French, and 2 if he wished to do so in English. Balthazar didn't care which, but pushed 2: he could use the practice for New York. The voice returned in English, telling him that he had reached the Caspian Sea Trading Company, but that both the Paris and New York offices were closed. He did not want to leave a message, so he hung up. Tomorrow, when the last detail was in place, would be a better time to call.

For a moment, Balthazar paused to listen to his body, and was proud that he was so calm and confident, just as he had been at every critical moment of his spectacular career so far. At the beginning, he had attributed it to luck and desperation. But, he had quickly discovered that he liked his calling and was good at it. Now, fear came only in fleeting moments before the operations started, in the form of concern that his plan had an undetected flaw rather than that he would be hurt or killed.

Balthazar was the professional planner and manager of a lengthening series of attacks around the world targeted principally against the United States and other Western countries. He worked for factions of the Islamic jihad or, more specifically, for certain powerful and wealthy individuals who supported them. But that his current patrons kept him well supplied with cash and assignments, Balthazar would have provided his specialized expertise to any one who would meet his terms. Had he real confidants, he would have told them that the CIA could save itself a fortune by paying him to take out Anwar al-Ghabrizi, rather than offering multimillion dollar rewards to mere snitches.

Each of Balthazar's operations was grander and more imaginative than the previous one, and cost a lot more to prepare and support. His revenue was more than sufficient to maintain his cover as an international businessman and to keep him in the two thousand dollar suits, super luxe hotels, and first class airline seats that he enjoyed so much and, indeed, comprised his cover. He gave his tie a final tug and smiled at himself in the mirror, looking over his shoulder as he left.

Jed stalked into the room where Sid lay sprawled on a settee reading a tattered copy of Playboy.

"We're fucked."

Sid looked at him calmly. "Surprise, surprise. He's not al-Ghabrizi."

"Not exactly."

"You mean he is al-Ghabrizi?

"Not exactly. Our guy's scar is in the same place as the one on the sketch. It looks to be the same length. But his seems to zig in a couple of places where it looks like the one on the sketch zags. Bottom line: inconclusive."

"You're right. We're fucked. Now, Glover has got to decide what he wants to do, that is, in addition to keeping us from ever coming back to the United States. I don't see how he can bury this, when there's even a remote possibility that it really is the AGWOG's pin-up boy."

"He can't," Jed agreed. "That's why I told the guards to get Knee Scar ready to travel. I assume they'll send a plane out from the States to carry him back."

Sid jumped to his feet and began to leave the room.

"Where are you going?"

"I'm going to send an EMail back to see if the guys at the AGWOG can get the flight crew to bring us a couple dozen jelly donuts."

Balthazar sat at the end of a low table covered with dishes containing Middle East delicacies of broad variety. Every time he or one of his three companions at the table ate something from a dish, using his fingers, a waiter would come to replace it. Only Bathazar, who was anxious for the meal and the business it accompanied to be over, noticed. The others were fixated by the girls in flimsy costumes dancing in the center of the room. They were dressed for the occasion in expensive, Western-style suits that appeared to Balthazar's discerning eye to be ill-fitting. At home, they wore the more comfortable garments appropriate to the climate, and were so dressed this evening because they did not wish to call attention to themselves. The one closest to Balthazar was a Deputy Petroleum Minister and junior member of the ancient family that ruled his country. The others were businessmen with huge international interests prominent in other countries in the Middle East.

At last, the display on the table dwindled down to sweets and small cups of thick, black Turkish coffee. The room was crowded, smoky, and buzzing with conversation, now that the floorshow was over and the diners no longer had to race to keep up with the servers. When the Sheikh spoke to Balthazar, he turned his head only slightly so that it was not apparent to anyone watching. His voice was modulated, and his lips barely moved.

"Your plan is very ambitious, Mr. Balthazar."

"Yes, it is, Excellency. But, I am sure you have noticed that audacity multiplies the effect of a successful operation many times."

"That is true. But, it also multiplies the risk."

"I find risk exciting. A great part of my reward is the opportunity to be smarter, quicker, and more powerful than the enemy and, of course, have the world acknowledge it."

The Sheikh smiled. "I don't pretend to understand your motives, but I must admit that it is refreshing to deal with a man who is not dedicated to blowing up everyone and everything just for the glory of God."

"But, you need to remember," he continued, "that your usefulness to us depends on your remaining unknown to the world's intelligence services and police forces. Should they discover who you are, and put a price on your head, we will not be able to support you."

"I understand, Excellency," Balthazar replied. "But, the new operation involves no risk that I will be exposed. When it is over, all those who have executed it will be dead, and there will be no documents to be found and traced. I am going to New York because I want to be there when it happens, to see the effect it has on the city and on the American government. That will be a special reward."

He knew they had arrived at the showdown, the moment at which he would be told whether or not the funds he had asked for would be made available. In anticipation that they would be forthcoming, he had already expended a substantial amount of his own money to obtain needed resources, something he had never done before. The Sheikh selected a dried apricot from a dish on the table, and Balthazar had to wait patiently while he slowly chewed it, prolonging the suspense for his own amusement. The others knew what was happening, and studiously ignored the conversation at Balthazar's end of the table.

At last, the Shaikh patted his lips with a napkin and turned to look squarely at Balthazar. "We have decided to give you what you have asked for," he said. "But, we are concerned that our business relationship has begun to diverge. We are not primarily interested in how big the explosions are or how many people are killed. We need you only to create and sustain a belief among the Americans and Europeans that the future will be much worse if they fail to fully support my government and those of my colleagues here. For us, crusaders for democracy are almost as big a threat as al-Ghabrizi's extremists."

Balthazar tried to look mindful, but inside he was exultant.

"I understand, Excellency."

"I know that you understand," the other noted, "but will you comply? You must know that, should you become a liability to us, we will pretend to be shocked by your actions and devote all of our official and unofficial resources to tracking you down and killing you."

Balthazar smiled contritely and, a short time later, was deposited in front of his hotel. The limo driver removed a heavy, expensive suitcase from the trunk and left it when the car drove off. Balthazar had a bellman take it up to his room.

Sam Glover signaled Hannah to stay as the Director's conference room emptied after the morning briefing. She guessed that he was about to tell Bergen about Knee Scar, and reminded herself that she was not supposed to know about him, although she was sure that Glover assumed that she did. By including her in at the beginning, he astutely assured that she would be part of whatever conspiracy needed to be hatched to handle this business in Washington. Aside from that, Bergen liked and trusted Hannah, who had the same access to him as Glover did. She took a seat in the background, and waited for Glover to begin.

"Our people, working with the security police in Karachi, have captured a man who has a superficial resemblance to Anwar al-Ghabrizi."

"What the hell does that mean: superficial?" Bergen exploded. He was not a career intelligence officer, and the constant use of weasel words drove him crazy. Of course, this did not prevent him from using them in reporting to his own superiors.

"It means that this guy is about the same build and age as AG, and he has a similar scar on his left knee."

"Does he look like al-Ghabrizi?"

"We can't really tell," Glover replied. All of our photos of AG show him with long hair and beard that obscure everything. He's like one of those poofy show dogs that's really the size of a rat. Our guy's hair and beard are much shorter, and he seems much less gaunt than AG appeared to be in that last video they gave to al-Jazeera."

Bergen scratched his head and looked at Hannah. "How could al-Ghabrizi be in Karachi, and what would he be doing there?" he asked.

"The odds are very strong that it's not him," she responded.

"So, what are we doing about it?"

"I've sent a plane to bring him back for DNA and other testing," Glover reported. "He'll be arriving late tomorrow at Langley Air Force Base. We'll stash him in the stockade there."

"Good. Please keep me informed," the Director said, dismissing them.

But neither of them moved.

"What?"

"Sir," Glover explained, "I think you need to provide the DNI and the White House some carefully caveated indication of what is happening. If we don't, and it leaks out or suddenly becomes a big deal, we'll catch major grief for holding out."

Bergen looked at Hannah, who nodded.

"Okay. Put something together for me this afternoon. I'll catch the DNI before the President's intelligence briefing at the White House tomorrow morning."

As they turned to go, Bergen signaled Hannah to stay behind.

"Hannah, I want you to stay with this thing all the way. Mr. Glover has been here a lot longer than I have, and thinks he owns the place."

CHAPTER THREE

The small group waiting for the President's intelligence briefing was gathered in the anteroom outside the Oval Office. Previous Chief Executives had gone downstairs to the Situation Room, which was equipped with state-of-the-art audio-visual facilities and instant worldwide communications. But, this President was uncomfortable with what he called whizbang electronics, and believed that their use made the briefing unnecessarily longer. He had also changed the briefing schedule from daily to every other day, claiming that, most of the time, there was really nothing new.

Admiral Bergen arrived with Glover and Hannah in tow, although neither of them would actually attend the briefing. He saw Director of National Intelligence, Albert Bierschmidt, in a corner talking with the two earnest-looking young men who would do the briefing, and went over to him.

"Good morning, Al. Can I have a word with you, please?"

Bierschmidt was not happy to have his last minute instructing interrupted, but signaled his people away. Bergen had gotten his position after the DNI's office had been created and Bierschmidt appointed. He was not part of the CIA that existed prior to that time, and so his relations with the DNI were civil and collegial, if not friendly. The structural change in the Intelligence Community pecking order mandated by Congress, ultimately a reaction to the World Trade Center calamity, had destroyed the dominance that CIA had exercised since its establishment in the post-World War II era. By law, the Director of Central Intelligence, who was also Director of the CIA, had been the President's principal intelligence advisor. His people conducted the daily briefings and manned the Situation Room; his staff prepared and administered the Intelligence Community budget. Although he was never quite able to bully the Department of Defense, which actually owns the bulk of the country's intelligence resources, his control of the Intelligence Community's management and coordination infrastructure enabled the CIA to effectively prevent or at least retard developments that could result, deliberately or accidentally, in diminution of its clout. The transfer of that clout to the new DNI had left CIA adrift, searching for a new definition of its mission and authority. Installed at Langley as the new broom, Bergen was instructed by the White House to clean out the old guard and to help Bierschmidt succeed.

The problem was that no one, least of all Bergen and Bierschmidt, was sure what that meant. The country's intelligence establishment had operated the way it had for almost sixty years, its dysfunctional elements growing worse following the end of the Cold War and disappearance of the benefits that having a clearly defined enemy bestowed. As a result, Bierschmidt was proceeding slowly, too slowly for his growing number of critics on Capitol Hill and in the public watchdog committees that had sprung up after 9/11. As the pressure increased, he became more suspicious of the motives and loyalties of the many department and agency heads with whom he had to work. Thus, his reaction to Bergen's news about Knee Scar was predictable.

"You're telling me this NOW, Phil?"

"I just found out about it myself last night, Al. Since it's such a wildly improbable long shot, I didn't want to bother you with it at home. But, we've got to assume that this could leak to the media and, if it does, we will be in the deepest shit for either not knowing about it or for not having told the President."

Bierschmidt looked dubious, but grudgingly agreed. "The problem is," he said, "that telling the President means telling that asshole Norton, which guarantees that it will leak."

"I know," Bergen replied, "but I don't think we have a choice."

The DNI thought for a moment.

"I agree with you, but I don't want to have anything to do with this. You can tell the President. We'll do it after the briefing is over and everyone else has left."

In Paris, the business day was ending, and Balthazar returned to his hotel room to rest and dress for dinner after a successful day. The suitcase he had been given was, as he anticipated, filled with neat packages of American, large denomination currency. He had done only a cursory count, determining quickly that there was more than enough to meet his needs. This morning, he had taken the suitcase to the small mercantile bank that managed his finances, which would distribute the funds to his various accounts from whence they would be disbursed to support both his legitimate import-export business and the growing number of offensive operations he had in varying stages of development around the world. The critical requirement, with respect to the latter, was that, when the money reached the point at which it would be spent, its origin needed to be unknown.

Balthazar retrieved his satellite phone from a briefcase and punched in the same number he had called the previous day. Again, there was no response. On the room telephone, he dialed the number for the Caspian Sea Trading Company, continued in English, and, it being midmorning in New York, was rewarded by a response:

"This is Omar Khalid. How may I help you?"

"Canary Export Corporation calling," Balthazar responded, making no attempt to disguise his voice. "The cases of sardines you ordered have been prepared, and will be delivered to you next week."

There was a momentary hesitation, then Khalid replied in a voice that reflected surprise: "Thank you very much. We shall be looking for them."

"You intelligence people are always telling me the same thing, which is nothing," President Tucker complained, looking around the group gathered in the Oval Office.

"We can't find the damned terrorists, we don't know what they're up to, and every time they blow something up somewhere we're surprised. That's not satisfactory!"

He was almost shouting.

"Why haven't we been able to catch this Al Gabrichi or at least keep him from running operations all over the world. I know that he's hiding in the mountains, but I would be willing to take the heat, if we could sneak a special ops team in to kill him."

The DNI looked hard at Admiral Bergen.

"I don't want to see you here again," the President continued, "until you can bring me some useful information. It doesn't have to be good news, although God knows we could use some, but it should at least show that we know what the hell is going on."

He turned away, and John Cook, his Chief-of-Staff began herding the attendees out of the room. Bierschmidt caught his eye and told him that he and Bergen needed a moment of the President's time.

"Mr. President," Cook called as the last of the attendees was leaving, "Directors Bierschmidt and Bergen would like a word with you." The last person was Roger Norton, who quickly sidled away from the door. Norton was officially a Counselor to the President, but his sole duty was to keep the President's political rear end covered and to make it smell as good as possible. He had been doing that with obvious success since Tucker's first run for state office many years earlier, and was never far away from his boss. He equated the nation's security with that of the President, sometimes giving Tucker the edge. As a result, he had earned the dislike and unyielding suspicion of the White House senior staff and the Cabinet by his willingness to skew policy and operational decisions toward what made the President look good, often at the expense of what they considered to be good governance. But, Tucker loved him and, as his Presidency came under increasing criticism and poll numbers dropped, relied upon him more and more for advice and comfort.

The President turned toward them and Bierschmidt hesitated, hoping that Norton would leave. But, Tucker noticed and waggled his finger at them.

"Whenever you intelligence guys have something private you want to tell me, I've learned that I need to have John and Roger present. What's up?"

Bierschmidt stood aside for Bergen, an anomaly that only Cook noticed. Since the establishment of his office, the Director of National Intelligence had been more than zealous in claiming his prerogative as the new principal intelligence advisor to the President, at the same time assuring that the former Director of Central Intelligence, now the Director of CIA alone, no longer enjoyed the access and influence of his former position. Cook was, therefore, surprised when Bierschmidt pushed Bergen forward in what was obviously going to be an important matter. Bergen took a deep breath and began.

"Mr. President, I need to start by heavily caveating what I'm about to tell you. Our information here is fragmentary, unverified, and most probably false." He began to repeat that warning, but the look on Tucker's face stopped him. The President was already pissed, and his level of expectation was so low as to make him totally intolerant of even the slightest imposition. It also made him more vulnerable to the potential impact of what he was about to be told. Bergen sighed. "We are fucked," he told himself.

"Mr. President," he continued, "our people in Karachi have captured a man who might possibly be Anwar al-Ghabrizi."

Norton shot his arms skyward as though a touchdown had been scored. "Yes-s-s," he hissed. Tucker was more restrained.

"What does "might" mean here? Obviously, he might not be what's-his-name. Which does it look like?"

"On balance," Bergen replied, "the probability is that it is not him. There are just too many anomalies."

"So, why are you bothering me with this?" The President was even more pissed than before.

"Because the man we're holding bears a general physical resemblance to al-Ghabrizi and has a very similar scar on his knee. We are flying him to the United States for DNA and other testing."

"Does he look like al-Ghabrizi?" Cook asked.

"He's the same approximate age, same build, a little stockier, perhaps," Bergen replied. "Our problem is that all of the photos we have of al-Ghabrizi show him with the huge hair and beard, so it's hard to tell what's underneath. We did a computer comparison using some photos our people sent ahead, but the results were inconclusive. We'll just have to wait and see when he gets here. The testing will take two or three days because we want to be absolutely sure, yea or nay."

Norton's eyes were shining as he conjured up the headlines the news would generate. "This could really save our ass," he told the President."

Bierschmidt was alarmed. "Mr. President, please let me reiterate what Admiral Bergen told you. There is the highest probability that this man is not Anwar al-Ghabrizi. Physical characteristics aside, the circumstances in which he was captured do not in the least correspond to the intelligence and understanding we have regarding al-Ghabrizi's whereabouts and operations."

Cook stepped in here. "If the White House should release anything about this, either overtly or by leaking it, the impact of having to later deny it would be devastating. The public has been wondering for years why we can't seem to catch al-Ghabrizi. To tell the world that we think we've caught him and then have to admit we were mistaken would kill what credibility we have left."

"We need to keep this matter extremely close hold until we determine who we have," Bergen added.

Norton looked frustrated and resentful. "I don't why you are looking at me like I was some kind of traitor or something. I agree that we can't talk about this thing now. But, I need to get ready for when we can talk about it. Because, if it comes to pass that it is al-what's-his-name, our poll numbers will head for the sky."

The President smiled indulgently.

Bierschmidt and Bergen met with Cook afterward in his office. "I have no confidence that the son-of-a-bitch is not leaking the story even as we speak," the Admiral declared bitterly.

"I wouldn't bet against you," the DNI agreed.

Cook shook his head. "I think he's too smart to be that obvious, and he recognizes the deep shit we'd be in, if the story turned out wrong. It'll be hard for him, but I think he'll wait a while."

"Let's hope." Bergen prayed. "Until we know for sure whether or not this guy is al-Ghabrizi, we need to keep all of this well below the radar, particularly here at the White House.

He beckoned to Hannah, who was standing in the background. "This is Hannah Crossman, my special assistant for counterterrorism. I'm going to assign her as my day-to-day point of contact to work with your staff on this business. She's junior enough that no one will get excited if they see her wandering around here."

"Good idea," Cook agreed. I've got a young, fast track FBI agent name of Jerry Ogden interning in my office. He'll be Hannah's immediate counterpart. I'll have him contact her immediately."

As they were leaving the building for the Director's car, the Admiral turned to Glover and Hannah: "We're screwed, you know. That asshole Norton will find some way to leak this and, when it all turns to you-know-what, who will they blame: the good old CI of A."

Hannah got back to her apartment late that evening after a series of meetings the Admiral called to make sure that everyone was in sync regarding the handling of the growing furball. Included was a teleconference with Jed, who was still at Bagram. The plane had picked up Knee Scar earlier, and was now en route the United States with several refueling stops and crew changes, ETA sometime tomorrow. Nothing new had been learned about him, in the interim: he still was refusing to speak, but displayed no other indications of resistance. Cairo Station had reported the arrival of the two young men who were with Knee Scar when he was taken. They were turned over to Egyptian authorities, and the station would immediately forward any feedback received. The Admiral had closed the conference by praising Jed for his initiative in pressing the Knee Scar case, even knowing the uproar it would cause.

The apartment that Hannah was renting was as small as it was expensive, in one of those high end buildings with the fitness centers, party rooms and concierges that one somehow never gets around to using. Its great virtue was that it was located ten minutes from CIA Headquarters in a burgeoning commercial area that featured a full range of shops and restaurants. Often, she realized, on the way home at ten p.m., that she had not eaten lunch or dinner or, waking in the morning, that there was nothing in the apartment for breakfast. When Hannah was assigned to the AGWOG, and pulled frequent all-nighters, her male colleagues conspired to remind her that she had no life. Whenever she was in the cafeteria, day in day out, one or another of them would contrive to come up to her and recite the old line: "What's a good looking girl like you doing in a place like this." All of them, including Hannah, got a big laugh out of it. But, she did, in fact, have no life.

Having no life, she had no relationships with men and no sex, both of which bothered her a great deal. The failure of their aging daughter to bring home a suitable husband bothered her parents, and they let her know it through increasingly unsubtle reminders of their own mortality and interest in grandchildren. Hannah, however, had no time for a life and, even if she did have time, the system was working against her. Most people who work for intelligence agencies can acknowledge that fact, and are restricted only in that they cannot discuss the specifics of what they do. This, to many people, is a great boon, insofar as being, for example, a computer programmer for the CIA or NSA will seem a lot sexier than doing the same thing for an insurance company or a bank. And being prohibited from talking about it effectively precludes having to admit that it ain't necessarily so.

But when, like Hannah, the intelligence officer has two lives, and must move between them without overlap or connection, establishing and maintaining successful personal relationships becomes very difficult. The divorce rate in the Clandestine Service was higher than that of the general population. There were foreign assignments to which a husband and wife could go as a couple, but not many. When one or the other spouse was not an Agency officer, there was no choice but to split up for two or three years, with intervals of home leave or rendezvous at resorts, perhaps in the Mediterranean or South Asia.

The casualty rate among deployed Agency operatives was low, but that was because the vast majority of them were assigned to embassies and consulates. For field agents like Jed and Sid, and others spooking around the mountains of Afghanistan, it was another story. Their success was measured in ability to work with the local population and power centers, sometimes spending weeks in cold huts on windy plateaus. On such assignments, the agents' best protection was often their ability to dispense large numbers of American dollars.

Hannah had an additional problem. If she met a man she liked and decided to take him home to meet the folks, he had to be knowledgeable enough of her dual life, "witting" as they say in the business, to avoid subjects about which they had no need to know and to do it without exciting suspicion. Of course, the only men Hannah was likely to meet who could qualify were other intelligence officers, and she had seen and heard enough about the downside of office romances to be scared off. So, as she prepared for bed, Hannah forced herself to think about the day's proceedings at the White House. She set the clock radio for five AM, turned out the lights, and got into bed. Living only ten minutes from the office, she could afford to sleep in.

CHAPTER FOUR

John Balthazar was pissed. He had thought that the business part of his stay in Paris was done when his benefactors came through with the suitcase full of cash. But, he had been advised the next day that the people for whom he was mounting his operation were putting a hold on it, because two of the men earmarked to participate had been taken into custody by the Pakistani police, and it was not clear that the plan could be executed without them. He had checked, but no one seemed to know what the men were doing when arrested, but they had apparently been turned over to the Americans.

In addition to cash, the jihadis provided two things that were invaluable: people and cover. He had realized early on that his operations were easier to design and execute if the people who were carrying them out were willing to sacrifice their lives. It eliminated the need to provide for escape and made it almost impossible for the target to do more than limit damage once the operation was underway. Once suicide bombers don explosive vests or enter an explosives-rigged vehicle, only instantaneously mortal bullets or technical failure can prevent them from blowing up themselves and those around them.

Much of Balthazar's success was due to the quality of the people provided him by his employers. They quickly grasped what they were supposed to do and when to do it. Some of them were university trained and knew more about the technical aspects of the operation than he did. But, they were also utterly convinced that killing themselves for the greater glory of the jihad was absolutely the right thing to do. He personally did not believe that any cause was worth sacrificing oneself, and did not understand how these people could be trained and indoctrinated to do that. But, none of them ever let him down.

The two men arrested in Karachi were chosen and qualified specifically for his next operation. But, Balthazar believed that it could be managed without them, and that the opportunity should not be allowed to slip away. He spent almost the entire day on the telephone with his employers' representatives explaining how it could be done before he got the go-ahead. Balthazar didn't resent the fact that he was apparently not trusted by his employers because the wall between them protected him as well as them.

Another useful thing about having your people kill themselves, from Balthazar's perspective, was that there is no one to be interrogated and gotten to implicate others, such as him. No effort was made to conceal the identities of the proclaimed martyrs, who were significant only because their names and nationalities were congruent with the claims of responsibility that their sponsors posted on the Internet and Middle East satellite television channels. The impact of Balthazar's spectaculars around the world enhanced the claimed omnipotency of Anwar al-Ghabrizi, who was said to have pulled the very long strings from his unlocatable lair in the mountains of Afghanistan. To the eyes of a scared and very impressed world, John Balthazar was invisible.

When Hannah left the morning briefing, she was told by one of the Director's secretaries that an FBI agent named Jerrold Ogden was waiting in her office. She found a tall, serious-looking man about her age examining the Islamic hangings decorating the walls, while trying to not spill his coffee. He turned as she came in and looked her over carefully.

" You certainly don't look like a Hannah Crossman."

"Well, you don't look much like an FBI agent," she replied.

"I'm Jerry Ogden. We talked on the phone."

"Yes, I remember. Welcome to the CIA."

"This is my first time here. I've been at the White House only three months. I was in Chicago before that."

"I'm very sorry," Hannah said.

"I'm a bit disappointed. Inside it looks like any other government office building."

She leaned toward him, lowering her voice. "That, Jerry, is because you don't have the proper security clearances. If you did, the building would look entirely different to you."

Jerry stared at her, then realized he was being had, and smiled sheepishly. "If you're going to mistreat me," he said, "I'm going back to the White House and ask the President to tell your boss how mean you are."

Hannah laughed. "Truce," she said. "I've set up a meeting with the analysts and techies on the Knee Scar case. Grab your coffee cup and follow me."

She led him to a small conference room on the floor below where five young people were already gathered in loud and animated conversation.

"People, this is Special Agent Jerry Ogden of the FBI. He's assigned to the White House and is my counterpart on the Knee Scar business. I'd like you to brief him on what we know, think we know, or suspect at this point."

After introductions, the senior person in the group outlined the salient points. Knee Scar was, as they spoke, on the final leg of his journey to the United States, scheduled to arrive sometime that afternoon. He was in good physical condition, not making trouble, but still had not uttered an intelligible word. The doctors who examined him at Bagram and during a refueling stop in Germany had found no reason why he could not speak, if he wished. The satellite telephone that Knee Scar had with him when arrested, on the other hand, was sounding off regularly. The calls weren't being answered, of course, but more would be learned when the telephone handset itself, which is on the plane with Knee Scar can be examined in the lab. He had been exchanging calls with people all over the Middle East, many of the numbers known or suspected to be associated with terrorist activity. But, the largest volume of calls had been exchanged with numbers believed to be in Damascus, Syria.

"What's in Damascus?" Jerry asked.

"Actually, we think it's an automatic relay that takes in satellite calls and shoots them out over landline or microwave to prevent them being tracked to their destination or point of origin. Either that, or it's an insomniac who stays up 24/7 talking with his buddies around the world"

"We think the relay is used primarily for calls going to and from the West," explained another of the techies. "The bad guys know we can do the kind of forensics we just told you about. So, they would be particularly concerned to keep us from locating their people in places like Europe and the U.S."

"So, Knee Scar has a whole rolodex of telephone buddies all over the world," Jerry observed. "Doesn't that tend to support the hypothesis that he actually is al-Ghabrizi or, at least, someone important?"

"It could," Hannah responded. "But, the bigger question is what would a kingpin like al-Ghabrizi be doing in a cheap hotel room in Karachi meeting with a couple of scrubs? While we've been unable to keep close tabs on his whereabouts over the years, all of our information indicates that he's in the mountains somewhere in the Pakistan-Afghanistan border region, a helluva long way from Karachi."

Jerry looked around the room. "So, what do you guys think?"

They looked at one another, then to their senior who answered: "We think that it's not him. But, we hope that the DNA tests are going to prove us wrong."

"How do we do that, by the way?" Jerry asked. "Do we have a sample of al-Ghabrizi's DNA?"

"No, we don't," Hannah answered. "But we have his brother's and sister's. While we can't look for an exact match, we will be able to verify a close familial relationship, which should be good enough. As far as we know, the al-Ghabrizi family has no deadbeat cousins wandering around the Middle East."

Roger Norton's office at the White House was cramped and hot. But, it was almost as close to the President's desk as the bathroom, and Roger resisted all efforts to get him another one. As a Counselor to the President, he was an official member of the White House staff and payroll, but he had no official duties and functions. Other staff members called him the Punka Wallah, the title of the young boy who pulled the cord on the ceiling fan that cooled his master in the day of the Raj in India.

But, Norton was not to be trifled with or underestimated. He fulfilled his mission extraordinarily well because he could uncannily channel the rank and file voters who made up the President's base, and who had elected him and were, he hoped, going to reelect him the next year. Norton knew instinctively the things Tucker needed to do, the attitudes he needed to display, even the kind of clothes he needed to wear to keep his public believing that he was their man. Tucker trusted Norton absolutely, and shielded him when his activities exceeded the boundaries of Presidential decorum, good taste, and occasionally the law. To Norton, Tucker and the Presidency were indistinguishable: anything that helped Tucker automatically helped the United States of America.

On this morning, Norton was speaking to three of his aides, whose status and mission were similar to his, but without the access and perks. Within the White House, they were called The Clones because they closely resembled one another in dress, grooming and manner. Most of them were recent college graduates taking their first steps toward a career in politics and what they called public service. Their principal job was to circulate through the many nooks and crannies of the Executive Office of the President keeping their eyes and ears open for anything that could be built upon and ballyhooed for the greater glory of the President and, much more important, looking for lurking alligators that could rise up to bite him. Their score with Norton depended on what and how much they brought to him, and one or more of them were always waiting outside his office for a moment of face time.

"The CIA may have al-Ghabrizi," he announced suddenly, primarily to see their reaction. He was not disappointed. They leaped to their feet and, forgetting decorum, began to babble enthusiastically.

"This is classified information," he told them, "and I expect it to not leave this room." He knew that the secret was safe, because it gave the three in the room an edge over their peers.

"How good does it look that it's him, sir?" one of them asked.

"Actually, the Agency is downplaying it, saying that the odds are great that it's not him. But, at the same time, they're flying this guy all the way back here from Afghanistan. I suspect they're more confident than they want to let on."

The aides were now standing at attention in front of Norton's desk. "What would you like us to do, sir?" they said almost in unison.

"Breathe," Norton laughed, "and keep your eyes and ears open. Also, think about what we should do with either outcome: if it is him or if it turns out not to be al-Ghabrizi. He's supposed to arrive at Langley this afternoon, and I plan to go down to take a look at him."

When they had gone, Norton checked to ascertain that the President was still at his desk (and not loose somewhere), then sat back for a moment with his feet propped on an open drawer. Despite his best efforts, things had not been going well. It was May, the election would be in November of next year, and their approval numbers were headed down the toilet. The public was unhappy with the Administration over a number of things, but one of the key issues was terrorism, specifically the growing feeling of insecurity and ebbing confidence that the Government would be successful in preventing another major attack on the United States. The capture of al-Ghabrizi would be a total restorative easy to exploit. What occupied his thoughts were possible schemes for benefiting from the situation even if it turned out not to be al-Ghabrizi.

In Paris, the business day had ended, and Balthazar felt better. His immediate business was progressing, and he was in Paris. That evening, freshly groomed and expensively dressed, he escorted Elodie Marchand to dinner and the opera. She was a lawyer with the Ministry of Justice working with the Surete, France's national police agency. Balthazar knew of this, but never sought to gain advantage from it and she, in turn, showed no interest in his import-export businesses in Marseille. Elodie came from a prominent family, and paparazzi photographed them out on the town, the pictures appearing later in Paris Match and international publications. Balthazar reveled in how handsome and distinguished he looked, and was particularly gratified when he began to be recognized in public places, like hotels and airports, and to receive special treatment. He greatly enjoyed knowing that he was the world's first celebrity terrorist, even though he could unfortunately tell no one else.

The small passenger jet, with undistinguished markings, taxied into the hanger where several groups of people waited along with a squad of armed, uniformed air police. When the engines had been shut down and the door opened, Jed climbed out first and recognized Hannah standing with Jerry Ogden and several Agency personnel. Roger Norton and one of his aides stood by themselves off to the side.

"Hello, Hannah. I didn't expect to find you here. I'll bet the old AGWOG is buzzing."

"We're all very excited about your big find, Bob, or should I call you Jed?," she responded. "This is Jerry Ogden. He's an FBI agent working with us on this."

After the two shook hands, Jerry asked him what his latest view was. Jed shook his head. "I've spent a full day staring at this guy on the plane and I feel even more doubtful that he's al-Ghabrizi. He still hasn't said anything, but he conveys the impression of a beaten man rather than an arrogant leader. When I sent my first message into Headquarters, I threw in every caveat I could think of, trying to make sure they understood that the scar was the only thing I was going on. Even his physical appearance doesn't really fit. The last photos al-Ghabrizi posted on his web site show him to be skinny and ascetic-looking. This guy's about the same size, but he's well fed and has clearly not been living in a cave."

They turned to watch a pair of Air Police lead their subject off the plane. His face showed no interest or emotion, and he stared straight ahead until eased into a waiting van. Norton and his aide had photos which they were comparing to the man passing before them. From the look on their faces, it was obvious they were unhappy with the results.

"Are you planning to stay in Washington, Jed?" Hannah asked.

"Only to visit with my family for a few days and to go shopping for Sid. He let me leave only after I swore to bring back jelly donuts. He knows they'll be pretty old by the time I get there, but says he doesn't care. I'm beginning to suspect that we're going to need to have him evacuated."

"Won't you be needed here?" Jerry asked.

"They pretty much already know everything I do. And, I don't want to be close at hand, if the shit hits the fan around here.

"What happened to the money that Knee Scar had when you grabbed him," Hannah asked.

"It turned out to be the price we paid for him and his two buddies. But, I got to examine it before it disappeared. It was all used bills in packets held together by rubber bands. There were no packaging or serial number sequences that could be traced.

Hannah was only slightly disappointed, since she hadn't expected that they would be so lucky. "How about his telephone?" she asked.

"Right here." He handed her a plastic bag with the markings of an airport Duty Free shop.

"I see that you started your holiday shopping early," she smiled.

Balthazar and Elodie Marchand returned to her apartment after midnight, even though it was the middle of the work week. She considered days that Balthazar was in Paris to be holidays, and did not concern herself with being fresh and alert at work the next day. She never considered visiting him in Marseille, something a Parisian would not do willingly. Balthazar actually spent more time in Paris than at the official home of his companies; it was just that he wasn't spending all of it with Elodie. The sometimes long intervals between their meetings and couplings served to increase anticipation and prevent boredom for both of them.

Elodie had discovered, through Balazar, that she was capable of multiple orgasms, a blessing she ranked equally with her superb mind and her family's wealth. Her body was extremely sensitive to touch, and not just in the obvious places. In their sexual adventures, which had achieved the level of ritual, he would slowly undress her, applying fingers or tongue to the right spots as they were exposed. By the time he actually entered her, she had usually experienced at least two orgasms and could feel her body anticipating the final one which, when it came, was the most spectacular of all. As she lay there on her back, her legs resting on his shoulders, she invariably tried to decipher the expression on his face, deciding that it was ecstasy, although she wasn't sure that she really cared.

This evening, Balthazar was mentally reviewing the check list of things that needed to get done before he could be on his way. He had gotten a go-ahead from the employers, and the people he would need (with the regrettable exception of the two men taken in Karachi), as well as the materiel, were on their way. Preparations for the London operation had been completed two weeks earlier, and it was completely in the hands of the locals. Finally, all of his flight and hotel reservations had been made and reconfirmed. He thought a moment longer, then unceremoniously dropped the startled Elodie and padded out to the living room where he had left his jacket. He fished his satellite phone from a pocket and punched in a speed dial number, listening as ring after ring went unanswered.

The sudden ringing startled the group of people in the room, who were deep in discussion and not paying attention to the telephone lying on a workbench with its back plate removed and wires alligator-clipped to its circuit board. This was Knee Scar's phone that Hannah had brought back to the lab attached to the suite at CIA Headquarters housing the al-Ghabrizi Working Group, locally known as the AGWOG. It was after normal business hours, but everyone was still there, although not because of the telephone. Al-Ghabrizi had apparently struck again, this time in London. Hannah had been busy coordinating the acquisition of information from the scene and from listening posts around the world, funneling it to a voracious White House. Not unexpectedly, there was shocked reaction in almost every city in the United States, one of sympathy and concern for local safety.

They stared at the ringing phone, but no one made a move toward it. A lab technician dialed another phone and, when the ringing stopped, told Hannah that they would able to determine the origin of the incoming call, but obviously not who was calling. She returned to the interrupted conversation.

"Have we had a claim of responsibility?" she asked.

"Not yet, but it's a bit early."

Terrorist groups were usually quick to take credit for their deeds, first because they needed to demonstrate to supporters and potential recruits how powerful and effective they were and, second, taking immediate credit in Central Asia for an event that occurred in Europe or Indonesia, the Americas or Africa created an illusion, for the unsophisticated and scared, of instantaneous worldwide reach.

"What's the latest from London?"

"Preliminary, but it looks like the same MO as Madrid and Moscow," one of the analyst present reported. "It's not very elaborate and requires no special equipment. You just turn someone into a walking or driving bomb, then send them to the target to blow themselves up. If you've got a willing supply of mules, it's a cinch. You can probably find the bomb plans on the Internet."

"That's a comforting thought." It was Jerry Ogden standing in the doorway. He had gone back downtown when he and Hannah returned from seeing Knee Scar's arrival, and was now wearing around his neck the shiny new badge that allowed him access to the building without an escort.

"John Cook told me to come out and not come back until I had more information than your guys in the Sit Room are giving us."

"Well, we'll show you where you can sleep. The cafeteria begins serving breakfast at 0530," Hannah told him helpfully.

"Thank you very much," Jerry responded. "But, Cook says that the President is getting ready to crawl all over your boss tomorrow morning, if all we've got to report is the same old bullshit."

"I'll warn him. But, I'm sure he won't be surprised. We're waiting now to see whether al-Ghabrizi issues the usual claim of responsibility."

"How does that work?" he asked.

"They deliver an audio tape to the Arabic satellite TV channels and also post it on a number of terrorist-associated websites along with a photo of al-Ghabrizi. We think the voice on the tape is really him."

"So, if the guy we've got is al-Ghabrizi, we should not be hearing from him, unless the recording was canned a while back."

"A logical conclusion," Hannah agreed. "But, this is not a logical business."

CHAPTER FIVE

The Tremont Grocery Supply Company was a small business located in the South Bronx a short distance from Yankee Stadium. Its premises, in a rundown industrial neighborhood, comprised a fenced yard containing a storage building and a bungalow used as an office. The yard had room to house the firm's trucks after closing, since leaving them out on the street was tantamount to giving them away. It also had space to store several large steel containers of the kind used for intermodal shipping of large quantities of merchandise. Tremont's main business was supplying small stores and bodegas throughout the Bronx and upper Manhattan with non-perishable goods, such as canned and packaged food items. Because many of the neighborhoods it serviced housed large ethnic populations, much of merchandise in which the company dealt was imported through the Port of New York and delivered to Tremont by truck right from the dock.

Tremont was a subsidiary of the Caspian Sea Trading Company, a much larger firm, headquartered in lower Manhattan, owned and operated by Said Ghoravi, whose father had founded the firm after fleeing Iran just ahead of the Shah. The company had immediately prospered because its founder had simply transferred its base of operations from Tehran to New York, retaining all of the business contacts and relationships needed to conduct a successful international business. In fact, the elder Ghoravi had subsequently negotiated a deal with the new theocratic government in Iran that gave him exclusive importation rights to a particularly famous and hot selling brand of Iranian caviar.

Said, who was a teenager at the time of emigration, went to work in the company immediately after college, and had succeeded his father five years earlier, whereupon the old man went off to a huge mansion in California where the climate was more pleasant and he could be near his expatriate buddies. The acquisition of Tremont was the son's initiative, although he never visited it and left its operation almost entirely to his manager Omar Khalid, a Palestinian emigre who had come to him looking for a job. Ghoravi's plan was to use Tremont as the foundation for a high margin outsourcing operation, where the company would provide its clients full service management and operation of their dining and provisioning facilities, in addition to food provisions. He had succeeded, the year before, in obtaining the contract for servicing the snack bars on the boats of Big Apple Tours that carried tourists on a sightseeing circuit around Manhattan Island. This was not big business, but it was a start.

Khalid was relieved that Ghoravi had not seriously checked his references before giving him the job, verifying only that he had a Green Card that permitted him to be legally employed in the United States. However, the identification was not, in fact, his, the real Omar Khalid having returned to the Middle East to join Hamas. The current Khalid had been urgently dispatched from Gaza in the middle of the night when Hamas determined that Israeli intelligence was about to assassinate him. Since his arrival in New York, he had been preoccupied with getting used to his new life and doing his new job to his boss's satisfaction. Khalid liked Ghoravi, and was grateful to be allowed to work without oppressive supervision. His rare contacts with his former life came through cryptic messages sent and received through an Islamic website based in Damascus, Syria. Khalid had gotten himself a laptop computer and, when he checked into the website, it was from a different public library or coffee house in scattered locations throughout the city. During one of those sessions, he was alerted to a coming call, which came over the dedicated line that Caspian Sea Trading maintained with its Paris office. That was the first time he had talked with Balthazar.

The President's voice, proclaiming his frustration, followed Bierschmidt out of the Oval Office into the anteroom where Hannah and Jerry were waiting. Cook and Norton followed quickly behind.

"I've never seen him so angry," the Chief-of-Staff observed.

"It's no wonder," Norton shot back, "the man is tired of fighting with ghosts and losing. He's the friggin President of the United States and he can't find anyone who can do something about this terrorist son of a bitch. Every time something happens, like in London yesterday, everyone in the country wants to know if it can happen here. Then some smart-ass 'terrorism expert' goes on TV and says that the correct word is 'when' not 'if'."

Cook turned to Hannah. "Have we had a claim of responsibility yet?"

"Not yet, sir."

"I guess that's good," Norton volunteered. "When will we know the DNA findings on what's-his-name?"

"Tomorrow afternoon sometime, I think, sir. The Director is keeping the whole thing very close hold," Hannah replied.

"I'll bet he is."

"Is there anything at all that's new?" Cook asked.

"Cairo Station reported that the Egyptians believe that the two guys who were with Knee Scar when he was captured don't know anything, neither about him nor about what he was supposed to tell them. They were recruited in Aqaba, by someone they didn't know, for a mission that was supposed to make them heroes of the jihad known throughout the world. They were sent to a training camp in eastern Pakistan and, afterward, were told to go to the meeting in Karachi where they would get instructions and money."

"What kind of training did they get?" Jerry asked.

"The usual: some small arms and explosives. Mostly it was political and religious indoctrination about the joy of dying for Allah. It appears that they were intended to be killed performing their mission. But, however important that mission was, it's hard to believe that al-Ghabrizi himself would come all that way to brief them."

"Is what's-his-name saying anything to us?" Norton demanded.

"Not a thing. He still refuses to speak."

"So, we continue to have nothing new," he groused, and stormed off.

After checking in the Situation Room for newly arrived information (there was none), Hannah and Jerry left the White House grounds through a rear gate and walked out onto the Ellipse, a very large, grassy field used mostly for athletic competitions among teams fielded by Government offices. It was a warm, sunny Spring day, one of the more pleasant times of the year in Washington. There were no ballplayers out yet, as they crossed the field toward the Potomac, running high from heavy rains upriver.

"You know, when you're in there," Jerry mused, indicating the White House behind them, "you get so wrapped up in everything that you forget that there's a world outside or even whether it's night or day."

"Tell me about it," Hannah replied. "You've never served in a 24/7 ops center environment when something big is happening and you're sitting there waiting for people in the field to tell you what's going on, while the people you're working for are climbing your back because you don't know it already. The belief that "Intelligence" knows or should know everything, as it does in the movies and Cold War thrillers, ignores reality. Unless we are really lucky, which we rarely are these days, the threat situation is highly ambiguous. You don't really know who's planning to do what to whom, when or how. Often, you don't know whether or not any of it is real. Because we can't afford to ignore any potential threat, we're vulnerable to being hoaxed, spoofed, and deceived."

"So, what do we do?" Jerry asked.

"The first thing you do in such situations is try to get more information to resolve at least some of the ambiguity. Tasking satellite intelligence collectors and other so-called national technical means is often helpful, but where you are dealing with a terrorist threat being mounted by a handful of individuals hiding in the general population, they are not much help. What you need to do is to go look: send out a plane or cutter to check out a suspicious boat or ship; board it, if it remains suspect. You need to send cops and agents to eyeball things, like foreigners taking flying lessons without interest in learning how to takeoff and land. Virtually none of these resources belong to Intelligence. Many don't belong to the federal government, and you can't just order them about the way you order up a satellite image."

"Is this the intelligence sharing problem we're always hearing about?" Jerry asked.

"Part of it. Another part is that we've had difficulty agreeing about what constitutes intelligence. To me, it's simple. Any information that helps us do our jobs successfully is intelligence. I don't care whether it's a list of the people who entered the country, visa applications, wire transfers of large amounts of money, whatever. The devil is always in the details and, if you don't deal with them effectively, you never find him.

Jerry looked at her strangely, and she blushed, realizing that her voice had become insistent, mirroring her frustration.

They had come to the edge of the greensward, and paused before turning.

"How long have you been doing this?" he asked.

"On and off, about ten years," she answered. "And you're going to tell me I need a break."

"No," he replied, "but there are people who will say that what you're advocating will lead to the erosion of our basic civil rights."

Hannah nodded. "I know. But, I've never subscribed to the "thin edge of the wedge" belief that, if you give the government an opportunity to screw you, it will. Certainly, there will be abuses, but it bothers me a lot when people say, in effect, that they consider the terrorists a lesser risk than our own intelligence and law enforcement officers."

They were now walking back toward the White House. Hannah smiled at Jerry apologetically. "I'm sorry about the sermon. Don't ever get me started on the Redskins."

"It's not a problem," he replied. "How much of the ten years did you serve overseas?"

"Most of it, in bits and pieces. This is the first real Headquarters assignment I've had; the others were basically rest periods between deployments. The Agency doesn't have many native Arabic linguists, particularly female. A number of the things I did involved living on the local economy, outside the protection of our embassy. I probably spent most of my time overseas wrapped from head to toe, with only my eyes showing.

"A great loss to the world," Jerry noted. Hannah bowed her head.

"Did you go through the clandestine service training down at The Farm?" he asked, referring to the facility at which the CIA trains its spies.

"I did the whole nine yards: parachute jumping, hand-to-hand combat, weapons training, everything. When I finished that course, I felt like the Warrior Princess."

"Wow! I'm impressed," Jerry admitted, pretending to cower.

"Were I you," Hannah told him. "I would try not to piss me off."

When Balthazar awoke, it was well past noon. He was lying between Elodie's satin sheets; her body, back turned, fitted into the curve of his. He raised his arm to look at his watch and she made a small noise to show that she was awake. He ran his tongue along the ridges of her spinal column and was rewarded with a shudder and another small noise.

"I was going to leap out of bed to face the day," she said, "but I've just changed my mind."

"You are going to have to go back to the world sooner or later," he observed, kissing the nape of her neck and running his hand, fingers pressing slightly, up the back of her thigh and onto her buttock.

"There will be time enough tomorrow," she sighed. "You are leaving Paris?"

"I have business in New York."

"Another woman, probably. At least one."

He hesitated for a moment, rubbing the palm of his hand gently against her nipple.

"Do you think for a moment, cherié, that I would dare come to your bed unpracticed?"

She rose suddenly and threw herself on top of him with a squeal of laughter.

CHAPTER SIX

The conference room at One Police Plaza, headquarters of the New York City Police Department, was rapidly filling with men and women in a variety of uniforms, as well as in civilian clothes. Outside the room was the City's Emergency Operations Center, a cavernous, electronics-filled room that was not dissimilar to those to be found in various subbasements around Washington and inside a mountain in Colorado. This was the location from which the City government coordinated its response to any major event, foreseen or not, that affected the populace and its ability to live safely and comfortably. Over the years, the City had experienced massive blackouts, snowstorms, demonstrations, and terrorist attacks, such as those against the World Trade Center. As perception of the seriousness and continuity of the terrorist threat to New York grew, so did the level of continuous manning at the Center, which was under the supervision of the Deputy Mayor for Public Safety Richard Caplin.

Caplin, a former FBI agent, held a regular weekly meeting to review the status of ongoing concerns and operations, and to plan for anticipated security challenges . This was in addition to an almost continuous chain of ad hoc meetings convened at all hours of the day and night to address time-sensitive issues, some real, others the result of a seemingly permanent level of tension created by the events of September 11, 2001. Caplin's office was on the floor above the OpCenter, and was equipped with remote monitors. After seeing little of him for two years, his wife had left the City with their children, so he had little reason to stray far from his office, where he had a cot installed in the file room.

This week's meeting, for which people were now gathering, was particularly important because Fleet Week was to begin the following Monday. Every May, New York City hosts visiting naval ships from all over the world: modern warships, tall-masted sailing ships used for training seamen, and auxiliaries of many descriptions. Some of the visitors anchor in the upper bay and in the Hudson River, while others dock at Manhattan piers. The festivities last for a week, and are hugely popular with both the locals and tourists who flock to the City. All of the docked ships are open to visitors, and boats ply between the shore and the larger of the anchored ships carrying visitors out for a tour. At night, there is fireworks, and almost everything is strung with red, white, and blue bunting or colorful signal flags.

For Caplin and his associates, however, it was a security nightmare in which the theoretical possibilities of a terrorist-instigated catastrophe are endless. Protecting the City from terrorist attack and coping with one, should it occur, was difficult enough at normal times. But, when many thousands of people converge on lower Manhattan from all directions, coming by car, boat, and subway, the points of vulnerability are glaring. On the face of it, Fleet Week was the ideal terrorist target, not only because of the potential for spectacular infliction of mass casualties, but also because its focal point was the same area of the City in which the World Trade Center had stood.

Spiritually, emotionally, and economically, New York City could not afford to be cowed by the terrorists' triumph and the prospect that they would someday seek to repeat it. Fleet Week had been held every year despite the events of 2001, each one bigger and grander than the last. The extent and elaborateness of attendant security precautions had grown with it, as each year's preparatory "what if" exercise uncovered a new potential vulnerability. Their cost was enormous, but no one ever mentioned it.

The span of control that Caplin enjoyed, at least theoretically, was very broad. Aside from the NYPD, the transit police, and the Port Authority police, who patrolled the bridges and tunnels connecting Manhattan with the other boroughs and New Jersey, his operations center housed representatives of the street and highway bureau, the water and sewage people, even the taxicab overseers. Beyond the City government subdivisions, public safety in New York City involved the FBI and the Department of Homeland Security, which have large local field offices, the Coast Guard, responsible for guarding the harbors and seaward approaches, and the Federal Aviation Administration which controlled the crowded airspace over the City and the approaches to its three busy airports. On this day, attendance at Caplin's planning meeting was expanded further by the presence of several Navy liaison officers and a senior officer of the New York State National Guard, who had been specifically requested to attend.

As he called the meeting to order, Caplin considered the paradox represented by the variegated crowd before him. While the number of organizations, jurisdictions, and bureaucratic competitions represented was the largest he had ever dealt with, the prospect for operational confusion and dysfunction was relatively low because the tasks and responsibilities of each were distinct and reasonably well defined. The Coast Guard, for example, knew that it had to patrol the harbor and potential lurking places along the shore. The NYPD Harbor Patrol knew that it needed to cover those areas outside Coast Guard jurisdiction. Both organizations were represented at all times in Caplin's ops center, and he and his watch commanders knew where to turn for immediate reaction and assistance. Overarching was the knowledge that they could not afford to be found wanting and, should that happen, the certainty that the world would know that they and their services had failed.

There was a potential joker in the deck, however, that could confound Caplin's planning and the relatively smooth implementation that had been experienced in previous years. American officials on all levels of government watched closely the activities of Anwar-al-Ghabrizi seeking insight into the strategy and tactics he and his lieutenants might employ. The targeting of subways in Europe was particularly alarming in New York City, given its sprawling system. But, whoever was masterminding al-Ghabrizi's operations was very inventive, and predicting the future on the basis of the past could be self-deceiving.

In the absence of tangible indication that a threat actually exists, there is little alternative to the worst-case scenario, whereby counterterrorism and public safety officials hypothesize the threat, then take precautions to forestall or combat it. Caplin's assumption was that an increased threat to New York City, whatever it was, would end when Fleet Week did because of al-Ghabrizi's penchant for synchronizing his operations with symbolic dates or occasions, and because the casualty potential would be significantly lower when activity in the City returned to normal. But, what if a terrorist attack was mounted the day after Fleet Week ended to take advantage of reduced security? While, perhaps, causing fewer casualties, it would show the world that the Americans could be outsmarted.

Another problem with responding to worst-case scenarios is that it is inordinately expensive and debilitating, like keeping a warship perpetually at general quarters. After a relatively short while, particularly if nothing eventuates, the extra precautions become wearisome for both the protectors and the public being shielded. When it inevitably becomes public that there is no verified, imminent threat, the criticism and second-guessing always in the background rises to a crescendo.

But Caplin and the Mayor knew that, notwithstanding the costs and criticism, they could not avoid pursuing a worst-case scenario. If a terrorist attack occurred that could have been forestalled or prevented by better preparation or smarter management, the effect would be devastating, not just in terms of casualties and destruction, but in shattering the fragile confidence of the American people that their government could protect them. Therefore, in protecting the City during Fleet Week, they would go balls-to-the-wall. What bothered Caplin most was not knowing whether his worst-case scenario would be the one the terrorists would follow.

Jerry Ogden left FBI Headquarters after his weekly get-together with Assistant Director James Detwiler, the purpose of which was to brief him about what was going on in the White House. He disliked these meetings because they made him feel guilty, as though he was somehow betraying John Cook's confidence. On the other hand, Jerry recognized that his White House internship would eventually come to an end, and he would be hoping for a desirable assignment within the FBI, thoughts that made him feel even more guilty. He had, of course, briefed Detwiler on the Knee Scar business and about his assignment to work with Hannah and the CIA. The AD was very interested, telling Jerry to inform him of developments immediately and not wait for the next weekly meeting. The Bureau's overseas contacts had been excited of late, which was assumed to reflect the London incident of the other day. Jerry's revelation, however, indicated a potentially more significant explanation.

He walked up Pennsylvania Avenue to the White House enjoying the warmth and sunshine of a fine day. After checking the Sit Room hoping to find Hannah, he went back to his desk in the anteroom of Cook's suite. Jerry had been at the White House for more than six months, but still didn't believe that he was truly there. This was his first Washington assignment, after ten years with the Bureau, and it was a real winner. If he didn't screw up, he'd be promoted to a high profile field office like New York.

In the meantime, his wife and infant daughter were making the best of a rented apartment in the Virginia suburbs, the bulk of their belongings in storage. There was no point in looking for a house, if he was going to be transferred in six months or so. Jerry had married his college sweetheart just after completing his FBI training, and had taken her off to his first post in Kansas City. He believed now that FBI special agents should not be allowed to marry until they had completed at least two postings, so that they and their intendeds could become acquainted with the kind of life they were choosing.

After six years of humdrum postings in the mid-west, he had taken a language aptitude test and scored unexpectedly high. The FBI was chronically short of agents with language skills. So, Jerry was sent off to the Defense Language Institute in California to study Spanish, at which he did extraordinarily well, a surprise to a young son of middle America. This led to five years of special assignments at field offices in southwestern states from which he deployed under cover to a range of South and Central American countries, sometimes operating from an embassy or consulate, other times from a seedy hotel room.

At first, Jerry's cases involved narcotics trafficking and related money laundering. He was remarkably successful, particularly for a relatively inexperienced agent, in getting to his targets, finding out what was needed, and getting out without getting himself killed. His personal cover was a stroke of genius. Since he looked exactly like what he was, a clean-cut, white Anglo-Saxon Protestant, there was no way that Jerry was going to pass for Latino, the fluent Spanish notwithstanding. So, he posed as the representative of a well-placed Chicago banker willing and able to facilitate large two-way monetary transactions between the United States and whatever overseas points the client wished to use. He convinced his contacts of his ability by arranging, seemingly with a phone call or an EMail message, the electronic transfer of large amounts of cash among international accounts, from which his "boss" took a percentage fee for services rendered, all duly recorded and facilitated by the Bureau, working with the Federal Reserve.

Only once did Jerry's act fail to convince, and that was not his fault. Someone in the office that was supposed to guide his bogus transactions through the electronic funds transfer system screwed up and a large transaction was lost, seemingly confiscated by U.S. authorities. At the time, Jerry was in Bogota, Columbia being entertained by the man who was awaiting the funds transfer. When it appeared to have been lost, the man accused Jerry of stealing from him, and he was forced to shoot his way out, killing two of the man's bodyguards in the process. His enraged call to the embassy while attempting to lose himself in the city got the wire transfer released, marked "transmission error," and the next day there was a note of apology left at the front desk of his hotel hoping that the stupidity of the bodyguards had not upset a very successful business relationship.

Nevertheless, the Bureau pulled Jerry and sent him to the Chicago field office to cool off. It was only then that he realized how lucky he had been. One day, Assistant Director Detwiler appeared at the field office and, in a small ceremony, bestowed upon him a Director's Award for bravery and an early promotion. After helping the field office close some of the cases he had been associated with, he was ordered to his present assignment in Washingon. He assumed that this was Detwiler's doing, but was unaware of the reason behind it.

The FBI has always considered itself to be a domestic law enforcement agency, and had largely left the area of foreign counterintelligence to the greater overseas resources of the CIA, guarded its leadership prerogative jealously. FCI, as it was called, was not considered a desirable career track for special agents. However, this view was already changing slowly when the World Trade Center catastrophe made it dramatically clear, particularly to the FBI's critics, that foreign-inspired and executed terrorism in the United States was a real and underappreciated domestic law enforcement target. Narrowly escaping the clutches of the newly formed Department of Homeland Security gave additional impetus to the Bureau's need to change. Jerry's assignment was an example of that recognition. When his current assignment was over, assuming he survived bureaucratically, Detwiler intended to assign him to a key position in the FBI's new counterterrorism division.

Sitting at his desk in the White House, Jerry reflected on his experiences in Latin America and wondered for the thousandth time what had allowed him to so blithely cope with such danger and risk when there was nothing in his previous life and upbringing to indicate that he was capable of, for example, beating two thugs with automatic weapons to the draw and shooting them dead in the blink of an eye. He had read the accounts of others who accomplished extraordinary deeds at great risk to themselves, and virtually all of them said that they had acted instinctively, without thinking of either the risks or the implications of what they were doing. That also applied to him, he decided, but did not explain where the instinct had come from in the first place. Surely, he had not been born with a reflexive ability to shoot first and ask questions later.

He had just reached his usual philosophical dead end when Hannah stuck her head in the doorway, and they went down to the White House Mess for a sandwich. She had been out to the lab at CIA Headquarters where the technicians had recovered the stored speed dial numbers from Knee Scar's satellite telephone.

"Six of the numbers," she told Jerry, "are from the same block, and are located in Damascus, Syria. That tends to confirm our speculation that there is a relay switch being used to prevent us from tracing calls to and from Knee Scar's number."

"How does that work?" he asked.

"Each of the six numbers equates to a different destination phone number, so that when Knee Scar speed-dials number 1, the switch directs the call, via landline or microwave, to that destination. Coming the other way, the caller simply dials a number at the relay assigned to Knee Scar, and the switch patches it through to his telephone."

"That's pretty clever," Jerry observed. "Who do we know that has the capacity and resources to install such a thing?"

"Al-Ghabrizi does, but he would have had to use a surrogate with the required technical smarts and unfettered access to the Syrian telecommunications infrastructure. We don't know who that could be."

"Would the relay's existence tend to indicate that Knee Scar is al-Ghabrizi?

"Not necessarily," Hannah responded. Our monitoring indicates that the relay is being used by others as well, and Knee Scar's telephone has been called from numbers all over the Middle East that are not associated with the relay. Since we can't answer the calls, there is no telling who was calling and what it was about."

"So, what do we do?"

Hannah looked quickly around the crowded dining room, then lowered her voice.

"Damascus Station thinks it may have isolated the location of the relay switch, and is planning to go take a look."

Jerry feigned astonishment. "Would that be what the spy novels call a black bag job?"

"The local police will call it breaking and entering," she replied dryly.

Balthazar had one more thing to do before leaving Paris. Unexpectedly, his employers had called to say they wanted to talk with him before he left for New York. This was unusual, since they normally confined their communications to approving or disapproving his proposed targets and timing. Thus far, they had never disapproved one of his proposed operations, only making occasional suggestions designed to increase its psychological impact, sustained casualties or both. In fact, he had never met his employers in person. The benefactors, with whom he had met at dinner the other night, carefully avoided any hint of association with the jihadis, which would have compromised their public stand, and that of their governments, against Islamic extremism. Balthazar could not determine whether they supported him so munificently as a hedge against an Iranian-type revolution in their countries, or because they really believed in the extremist cause. In actuality, he didn't much care, so long as the money kept coming.

Most of Balthazar's communications with the jihadist leadership were telephonic, but occasionally he would meet in Paris with a go-between with the convenience name of Mohammed. This day, he met him at their usual rendezvous point, the pedestrian walkway at the center of the Pont Neuf.

"You are looking as elegant as ever, Mr. Balthazar," Mohammed observed. "And the lady you are staying with is most beautiful."

"Thank you, Mohammed. Your kind observations are most flattering." He didn't know whether he was simply being told that he was under surveillance or that, more ominously, Elodie's well-being was being held hostage to insure his compliance or performance in connection with something of which he was not yet aware. He decided to hedge on Elodie's behalf by adding: "But, if you continue to watch me, you will discover many more like her."

The two walked together toward the Ile de la Cité end of the bridge.

'What is it your masters wish to tell me or ask of me?" Balthazar inquired.

Mohammed hesitated momentarily, deciding how to begin.

"We are very happy with your work. The London operation was very well executed, and has had the desired impact around the world. We are concerned, however, that al-Ghabrizi has not yet come forward, as arranged, to claim responsibility. You were to have arranged this. It is critical that all believe that there is but a single jihad, and that it is worldwide."

Balthazar smiled reassuringly. "I am investigating. There has been some sort of disruption, but I assure you that it will be straightened out shortly."

Mohammed was clearly not convinced. "Be certain," he said slowly for emphasis, "that you understand that your success, and even your life, depends upon our approval and support. You are able to live your elegant life, fornicate with your many women, and get rich while doing it, because no one is aware of your true business. We can change that in an instant, and will do so the moment you are no longer helpful to us. Remember that!"

He turned abruptly and walked back across the bridge. Balthazar watched him go, wondering whether he had time to stop for a visit with Elodie before heading for the airport.

The Bayonne container facility in the Port of New York is a typical example of the revolution that has taken place in the ocean shipping industry. It is a huge agglomeration of forty-foot steel containers, essentially identical except for their paint, piled one atop the other for efficient storage. Loaded with merchandise of every description, the containers arrive and depart on specially configured ships that carry them piled on deck. In port, the ships are unloaded by specialized overhead cranes that deposit the containers one by one on truck trailers or railroad flatcars that are pulled out onto the piers, from whence they are distributed all over the area served by the port. Every container has an identification number and barcode painted on its sides and roof that identifies its owner and can be linked to a bill of lading that describes its contents. The container is sealed after loading, and is not opened until it reaches its consignee, except if the U.S. Customs and Border Protection Service decides to inspect it.

There are, however, many millions of loaded shipping containers arriving at U.S. ports annually, and resources sufficient to inspect less than ten percent of them. So, unless there is intelligence that brings suspicion upon a specific container, say a rigged bill of lading or a shipper or consignee who is being watched, it is likely that a container will enter the United States and be conveyed to its destination unchallenged. That is what happened to container number 38XT7-32869, which was lowered onto a tractor trailer operated by a local trucking company, carried over the George Washington Bridge into the Bronx, and ultimately deposited in the yard of the Tremont Grocery Supply Company.

His small staff having gone for the day, Omar Khalid secured the gate to the yard, then double checked to make sure that no one but himself was still there. He then went to the shipping container and tapped three times, then twice on its side. In a moment, he was rewarded by the same signal coming from inside. Moving a forklift and some wooden pallets to the front of the container, Khalid broke its seal and swung open its two heavy doors. He was faced with an unbroken wall of cardboard cartons, some marked canned fruit, others sardines. He began unloading the cartons onto the forklift, pausing when a pallet had been loaded to move it into the yard's storage building. He did not work as quickly as he could have because it was not yet totally dark, and he wished to take every possible precaution against being observed.

Eventually, Khalid reached the center of the container, by which time night had fallen. Since first contact, he had heard nothing from its interior, and thought admiringly of the patience shown by those within, so close to freedom after almost three weeks of being buried alive. He spoke, in Arabic, a message of welcome, and voices from the other side of the last row of cartons echoed it. The wall was quickly breached, releasing an overpowering stench that almost knocked Khalid down. Behind it was a small chamber, within the stacks of cartons, that had been home to the four bearded, foul-smelling men who now emerged. Their living space was littered with debris from packaged food, plastic water jugs and a chemical toilet. They had several flashlights, but had used all of their available batteries. Even in the darkness, they blinked in the yard's dim illumination and the glare of the street lights outside.

Khalid wanted very badly to squeeze his nostrils shut.

"There is a shower in the office, and I have fresh clothes for you. After you've cleaned up, we will eat and then move the materials into the warehouse," he told the new arrivals. They thanked him, but for the moment made no move toward the door to which he had pointed. Instead, they just stood looking up at the starlit sky and breathing deeply as though they had just learned how. "It is really strange," one told Khalid, "that even after they have surrounded you completely with boxes, and then locked and sealed the container doors so that you could not possibly get out, the most devastating terror comes when they lift the container on to the ship and then pile other containers on top of it. Massoud here wanted to scream, and we had to stuff his mouth until he calmed down."

Later, after they had cleaned up and eaten, Khalid made the men carry the remaining cartons from the shipping container into the warehouse, after which they hosed down the container's interior, adding a liberal application of industrial-strength detergent. Of the container's contents, thirty boxes marked by small tears in their labels contained plastic explosives, another contained fusing material, detonators, and weapons.

Resting afterward, he watched the four laughing and enjoying themselves after their claustrophobic ordeal. The room was filled with smoke, as they quickly ran through the carton of cigarettes he had purchased for each of them. None of them was more than twenty-three or twenty-four years old (Khalid was forty-five), and they were acting as though away from home for the first time, perhaps on a jaunt with friends. Although they knew little of the operation in which they were to take part, all of them were aware that it would cost them their lives. But, not only did that not bother them, but they claimed to be eagerly awaiting the moment when they would enter heaven as martyrs to the jihad. They pressed him for news, and he told them that he was awaiting the arrival of Sheik al-Ghabrizi's personal representative and two more men, who were coming by more conventional means. All preparations were proceeding normally, and they would not have to wait long for their wish to be fulfilled. At the mention of al-Ghabrizi's name, the mens' faces lit up and their smiles grew even larger.

Khalid remembered when he had been that enthusiastic and heedless of his own safety, and wondered why he was no longer that way. Was it because he was so much older now and more skeptical of the prospect of victory? Or was it because his faith was waning and he no longer believed that the jihad was worth the lives of these men and all those they would kill in the course of reaching heaven. These thoughts made him feel guilty and unfaithful to God and the jihad. It was, perhaps, to atone that he had conceived and put forward the idea for the operation in which these bearded men were to participate.

For several months after submitting his idea, through the Imam of a Brooklyn mosque, he had heard nothing and admitted to himself that he was relieved. But, one day he had received a call on the private line that connected Tremont's parent company, Caspian Sea Trading Corporation, with its Paris office. The caller would not give his name, but claimed to represent the Grand Sheik, who could only be al-Ghabrizi. He congratulated Khalid on the brilliance of his proposal and asked whether he was prepared to help carry it out. That would have been the moment to escape, but Khalid was flattered and did not want to appear weak. So, he agreed and, in subsequent weeks, provided his new contact with a plan for executing the operation and an estimate of the people and materiel needed. He was assured that his brilliant planning and management made him too valuable to be sacrificed, and that he would be provided the means for escaping the country so that he could join the leadership of the international jihad. Indeed, he had received separately a week or so earlier three international money orders totaling five thousand dollars, the proceeds from which were now in the office safe. Still, he felt increasingly ashamed of his inability to walk away when he should have.

"You have been very kind to us, brother Khalid," the leader of the four said to him. "But, now that we have washed, eaten, and smoked, we need to have women. We must practice for the five hundred virgins we have been promised. That is, five hundred each."

CHAPTER SEVEN

Hannah and Jerry Ogden were in the Situation Room reviewing message traffic when one of the duty officers caught their attention and pointed to one of the large television monitors that were always tuned to the all-news channels. They looked up to see the banner "BREAKING NEWS" spread across the screen and a news reader talking animatedly in front of a photograph of Anwar al-Ghabrizi. The duty officer turned up the sound, and they heard the reader say what they had already begun to anticipate: that there was an unconfirmed rumor that the archterrorist Anwar al-Ghabrizi had been captured and was in American custody.

"That son-of-a-bitch Norton just couldn't wait," Jerry exploded.

"I wonder if he really knows something or is just making an assumption," Hannah mused. She went to a secure telephone, coming back a short time later. "The Director is on his way down to see the President. He should be here momentarily. Let's go up to hear the fireworks."

Admiral Bergen arrived a few minutes later, accompanied by DNI Bierschmidt. They stalked past Hannah and Jerry without noticing them and rushed into the Oval Office, the Secret Service guard closing the door even more quickly than usual.

"I understand that there is good news," the President noted with a happy smile.

Bergen looked to Bierschmidt, his senior, who barely controlled the anger and frustration in his voice. "Yes, sir. DNA analysis confirms that it is him."

Roger Norton, standing behind the President as if to keep him and his huge desk between himself and the two intelligence officers, threw his arms up signaling touchdown.

'Mr. President," Bierschmidt continued, " Director Bergen and I wish to strongly protest Mr. Norton's action in leaking that information. It has quite possibly placed the United States Government and yourself in a very awkward position."

The President did not appear bothered, which Norton observed with relief. He had sent one of his clean-cut assistants, armed with White House credentials, to the civilian laboratory that was performing the DNA analysis. His appearance there was unexpected, and contrary to the CIA-imposed strictures under which they were operating. But, White House credentials are persuasive, and the man was seeking only a Yes or No answer.

"As long as it is true, what difference does it make?" he asked.

"First of all, Mr. President," Admiral Bergen interjected, "when the people we deal with abroad see that we cannot keep a secret, even at the highest levels of government, they stop telling us things we need to know. Secondly, and more important, we still haven't figured out what al-Ghabrizi was doing in Karachi, and at that meeting. Thirdly, we have told him that we know definitively who he is, but he still refuses to talk, which makes no sense, if what he was concerned about was that we would identify him from his voice print. He had to have been aware of the DNA identification."

"I'm sure that the leak will be of no consequence and that Roger will not do it again," the President responded, looking meaningfully at Norton. In fact, he had approved the leak after Norton's man had returned with the good news. To obtain maximum impact and broadest dissemination of the news, Norton needed to capture the audience's attention before the President's planned press conference, so that everyone would be eagerly anticipating it and paying attention, rather than caught by surprise and unprepared to absorb the all-important message that would come with the good news. In addition, it was already Thursday and the weekend was looming. It is standard practice in the news management business to release bad news, by announcement or leak, on Friday afternoons, after the close of business, because both media and public are focusing on the weekend and paying less attention to what's going on in the world. If the news to be released is good, on the other hand, a capable spinmeister will never let it go during the weekend, if at all possible.

Bierschmidt and Bergen came out of the Oval Office wearing looks of terminal frustration, followed by John Cook who had said nothing during the brief meeting. In the Chief of Staff's office, they paused to regroup, Hannah and Jerry staying discreetly out of the way.

"I didn't find out about it till just before you did," Cook apologized. "The President is totally convinced that this will rescue his reelection bid from the dumpster, and was willing to let Norton do anything short of going to war. They're setting up a press conference for prime time tonight, so that the news can be officially announced to the maximum audience."

Bergen threw up his hands. "We serve at the pleasure of the President, and he's the President. I guess we should be happy that asshole Norton waited until confirmation was in before he leaked it."

The SUV cruised slowly through a poorly lit industrial section of the Syrian capital Damascus, its passengers scanning the rooftops of the small buildings along both sides of the street. There was no activity on the sidewalks and few other cars passed by, their drivers and passengers averting their gaze. The SUV was of the type and color known to be used by the security police, and no one wished to run afoul of the vaguely written, but vigorously enforced law. Eventually, the searchers spotted what they were looking for, and parked the truck in a nearby alley. It was a satellite dish antenna not much different from those sprouting like toadstools on the roofs and balconies of buildings all over the world. If this had been a residential neighborhood, it would never have been spotted among its clones.

The four men in the vehicle pulled on ski masks and made their way to a rear entrance of the building on which the dish antenna was mounted. The only problem they had with the door locks was making sure it would not be apparent later that they had been opened. Soon, the team found itself in the office suite directly below the antenna. It was fully furnished, with papers on the desks and in the out baskets and notices tacked to the bulletin board. Even the wastebaskets and ashtrays held trash and cigarette butts. However, the rooms smelled too clean. There was no ingrained smell of tobacco smoke and strong Turkish coffee, inevitable artifacts of any place in the Middle East where people gather.

"A dummy," the team leader observed. "Look for the switch."

They soon found it in a locked cabinet from which an armored cable extended up through the ceiling. The electronic device they found within, beeping away contentedly, was a fairly unsophisticated computer that did its specialized job exceedingly well. The antenna on the roof was equivalent to as many as fifty separate satellite telephone terminals. When a call was directed to one of these phones, the antenna intercepted it and the computer in the closet checked its memory to determine the number really being called. It then redirected the call out through the Syrian domestic telecommunications system to that number, all without apparent delay to the calling parties. The effect of the switch was to prevent someone tracking satellite calls from determining to whom the calls it received were really directed. It also worked in the opposite direction, so that someone calling al-Ghabrizi's satellite phone via the switch could be anywhere in the world without that fact becoming apparent.

"Do we bust it up?" one of the penetration team asked.

"We leave it exactly as is," was the response. "No one should know we were here. Headquarters wants a copy of the call transfer table in memory, that's all."

As the Air France jetliner squared away on its westerly course, still gaining altitude, Balthazar stretched comfortably in his deluxe class seat and anticipated the champagne that was now being served. The flight's departure and flying times were calculated to get passengers to U.S. east coast cities early in the day, so that appointments could be kept and meetings attended. After a late supper, Balthazar would extend his seat into a full length lounge and sleep for several hours before arrival. He was extremely content with himself for having acted on a brilliant thought that came to him shortly after his meeting with Mohammed. Calling Air France, he had changed his reservation from their overnight flight to New York to one going to Dulles International Airport that served Washington, D.C.

For all his travel, Balthazar had never been to the American capital, and now seemed an appropriate time to visit, particularly since he didn't have to be in New York until Monday or Tuesday, and tomorrow was only Friday. He would wander around like any tourist, taking in the sights and visiting the museums. But, his principal incentive was the possibility of seeing Hannah Crossman again. They had met at an embassy cocktail party in Geneva almost a year ago, and he still recalled every detail of how she looked and what she was wearing.The idea of detouring via Washington had occurred to him while in bed with Elodie, and the thought had informed their lovemaking.

The flight attendant serving champagne greeted him warmly, extending her tray of flutes, while a companion served him caviar and smoked salmon with capers. Balthazar was well known to them and the airline, and their instructions were that he was to be given anything he wished, short of control of the aircraft.

"The pilot told us that there is word on the radio that the Americans have captured Anwar al-Ghabrizi," she whispered. "Isn't that marvelous!"

Balthazar managed to suppress his shock and surprise. "Indeed, it is," he replied.

An announcement that the President would hold a press conference at 8 PM was anticipated by the media, which had been going full bore since the first rumor about al-Ghabrizi had been leaked by Norton that morning. The White House briefing theater was full three hours before the scheduled start time, every broadcast network, news channel, and significant newspaper positioning its chief correspondent in the front rows where they would be seen by the cameras and by the President's press secretary who selected the questioners. The event was to be televised live worldwide, even in those regions where it was the middle of the night. When the TV lights came up, the room became instantly quiet.

Marjorie Wilkes, the President's Press Secretary, appeared at the podium first to welcome attendees and the TV and radio audiences and to announce, to no one's surprise, that the President would make an opening statement before taking questions. She then introduced President Tucker.

"My fellow Americans," he began and then stopped with a smile. "Or should I say: My fellow citizens of the World, because my announcement today will be of importance to all of you, and a source of great joy and relief. The rumors you have been hearing all day are true: the forces of freedom have captured the notorious murderer and arch-terrorist Anwar al-Ghabrizi and placed him in jail in this country. The arrest was actually made several days ago, but we wanted, through DNA analysis, to be absolutely sure of his identity. This is a great day for all of us."

He went on to recount al-Ghabrizi's crimes against humanity, including the London bombings of a few days earlier, and thanked the governments of allied nations (without naming them) for their participation in this great achievement.

"While there will be more terrorists, and our battle is by no means over," he concluded, "we have clearly passed a major milestone in the war on terror and served notice to people who would harm our country and citizens, and those of our friends and allies, that they will be brought to justice. May God bless America, its citizens, and its friends. This is a great victory!"

He threw his arms up, making the V sign, as the room erupted and hands waved seeking recognition by Marjorie Wilkes, who moved to the front of the stage. As customary, she recognized first Dennis Crocker, dean of the White House press corps.

"Mr. President," he asked, "is al-Ghabrizi telling us anything useful?"

"At the moment, Dennis, he's not telling us much of anything, and we are being very scrupulous in according him his rights."

"What will be done with him?" another reporter asked.

"Eventually, he'll be put on trial before the world in an international court, so that the evil he has done will be plain to everyone," the President responded.

Bierschmidt, Bergen, and Cook watched the press conference in the latter's office, Hannah and Jerry lurking in the background. President Tucker, who normally hated meeting with the media, was thoroughly enjoying himself, and the TV cameras occasionally caught a glimpse of Roger Norton standing on the side with a look of extreme ecstasy on his face.

"Well, at least it's out," Bierschmidt said with a shrug.

"Just in time for the weekend", Bergen observed dryly. He turned to Hannah.

"You guys don't have to lurk around the White House anymore," he told them. "But, we still need to stay current on the al-Ghabrizi business. There's a stink to it that I don't like, and I would like to keep Norton from getting us into more trouble than he already has, although that's probably impossible."

With the press conference over, they were getting ready to leave when Roger Norton stuck his head in, the same ecstatic look on his face.

"We just got the flash poll results. We're up 20 points and rising!!"

CHAPTER EIGHT

"Hannah, it's John Balthazar. I hope you will recall our meeting in Geneva. I'm here in Washington at the Willard, and thought I'd surprise you. I would like to see you this weekend, if you can break free of all those visas and passports. I'm in Room 903 here, and look forward to hearing from you."

Hannah had not reached her apartment until past 11PM. After leaving the White House, she had stopped off at Headquarters to check in at the AGWOG to see whether anything had come in regarding a claim of responsibility for the bombing in London earlier in the week. There was nothing, except for the people on duty speculating to one another about what was going to happen to the AGWOG now that al-Ghabrizi was no longer on the loose. So, she went on home, reflexively hitting the button on the answering machine upon entering her apartment.

She had recognized Balthazar's voice instantly, although they had met only once. Hannah was in Geneva for a covert meeting with an Arab petroleum mogul, and was using her standard State Department cover, the nice part of which was that it had to appear as no cover at all. There was no ostensible reason why a passports and visas administrator should have to skulk around looking over her shoulder, so Hannah did not. The cocktail party was a reward for her close attention to keeping her cover plausible.

After it became apparent that neither of them was interested in what the other did for a living, they had discussed art, music, and public affairs in English, French, and in Arabic when the conversation's focus had shifted to the Middle East. Balthazar was impressed by her facility with the language, for an American, which led to the discovery that both were of Lebanese extraction. They laughed about how Lebanese mothers were pretty much alike whether they lived in California or France. Hannah noted that Balthazar was well informed on international affairs, he replying that his business required it. He was dependent on countries caught up in the jihad, to one extent or another, for supplies of the specialty foods, like caviar and pistachios, that he sold to importers in the West. Since he often visited these countries, it was also important that he be aware of the state of political play between them and the West, so that he did not find himself suddenly rousted from his hotel room at 3AM by an overzealous political policeman trying to make a point. Balthazar professed to be extremely happy that he traveled under a French and not an American passport.

When they realized that almost all the other party guests had gone, Hannah and Balthazar continued their conversation at a small restaurant that served north African food, where they ate, drank, and talked until both realized that they needed to go get ready for morning flights. They exchanged business cards, and Hannah gave him her home telephone number as well, something she later thought about many times before forgetting about it. Generally, the rules of covert operations require that the operative keep a cover identity strictly separate from his or her personal life, since crossover could cause confusion, if not exposure. Balthazar was the first person to whom she had given more than the dummy State Department office phone number that supported her cover.

She had believed that she would never see him again, and was now surprised to find herself warming to the prospect. She told herself that she would not return his call, that it would make things too complicated, particularly with everything she had going on at the Agency. Then, as she stared into her mirror before getting into bed, she knew that she would call him.

When Anna Mingkovsky arrived at the Tremont yard at 9 AM on Friday, she found four strange men puttering around, moving boxes and cartons from one pile to another. After staring at them long enough to make them uncomfortable, she went into the office to find Khalid. Anna was Tremont's clerk and book-keeper, actually the only staff other than the truck crews that had already left on their delivery rounds. She found the Manager watching the small office television set, which was tuned to a news channel.

"Khalid, who are those terrible-looking men out there, and what are they doing here?" she demanded.

The Manager was intent on a program recapping the President's press conference of the night before, and did not welcome the interruption. He also realized suddenly that he had failed to anticipate Anna's presence while the men were around. Hiding his confusion behind anger, Khalid turned on the elderly woman:

"Why would you say they are terrible-looking? They are poor refugees from torture by religious fanatics. Mr. Ghoravi is helping to find a place where they can settle down in peace. They will be gone in a week," he chastised.

Invoking Ghoravi's name was sure to work, Khalid believed, correctly. Anna had never met or even seen the big boss.

But, if he was behind the men being there, it had to be all right. In any event, a week was not very long. Still, they made her feel very uncomfortable, although she didn't really know why. Perhaps, it was because they looked like the people she saw on the evening news every night, the ones milling about the streets of the Middle East shouting in anger and waving rifles.

The men, in turn, were not happy with Anna, particularly when they discovered she was Jewish. Khalid had to perform damage control with them as well, finally having to tell them to shut up and do as they were told. Despite his years with Hamas and involvement in operations in which many people on both sides had been killed, it always shocked him how those who had decided or been convinced to become martyrs cared nothing about the rights or well-being of anyone else outside the gates of heaven.

"What do you think of the al-Ghabrizi business," Anna asked. "Isn't it wonderful that they finally caught the murdering son-of-a-bitch?"

Khalid was once again engrossed in his thoughts, and just nodded perfunctorily. If al-Ghabrizi was captured, what did that mean for the operation? The men and materials just arrived had been en route for weeks, but what about the two additional men still missing and the person who had contacted him, who was supposed to arrive in New York the next week? If the operation is off, he worried, what was he going to do with the four men and all the explosives? It also occurred to him that the Americans surely hadn't just caught al-Ghabrizi. They probably had him in custody for a while, perhaps before Khalid had been called and told that the operation would proceed. If that was the case, what the hell was going on?

It was fortunate that the new arrivals understood little English. Khalid had decided immediately that he would not tell them about al-Ghabrizi's capture, particularly since he himself had no idea what impact it would have on the operation.

Khalid looked over to Anna, who was busily making herself a cup of tea. It was lucky, he told himself, that she never went into the warehouse.

Jerry arrived in the conference room at CIA Headquarters just as the meeting was getting underway. He had been called at the White House by Hannah and was glad to get away, since nothing was happening. Everyone in the West Wing was still euphoric over the public reaction to the President's news about al-Ghabrizi, the poll numbers having risen virtually straight up. Only John Cook, the Chief of Staff, seemed concerned about something, and he wasn't talking. Jerry knew that Hannah would not be dragging him out to Langley for nothing, and he needed something of interest to tell Detwiler at their next meeting.

The meeting was being chaired by the AGWOG's technical advisor, who was in charge of exploiting the satellite telephone that had been taken from al-Ghabrizi. On the wall behind him was a screen, and there was a projector on the table. As Jerry and another recent entrant sat down, he pressed a button on the remote control in his hand and an elaborate hub and spoke diagram appeared on the screen.

"Our people in Damascus," he began, "have secured a copy of the call transfer table from the computer relay switch that al-Ghabrizi was using. It allows us to determine the real phone numbers involved in his incoming and outgoing calls."

The table contained more than fifty number pairs, almost all of which had been active in the relatively short period that U.S. intelligence agencies had been closely monitoring traffic to and from the relay. While it had to be assumed that all usage was somehow terrorist-related, it was not yet known who established and maintained the relay facility, and how the phone numbers contained in its transfer table were chosen.

"What do we know about the activity associated with al-Ghabrizi's phone?" Hannah asked.

"Well, for one thing, he never seemed to use it," came the answer. "As best we can determine, he did not make a single call in the week prior to his capture."

"How about incoming calls?"

"That's a bit strange. He apparently received no calls either during that period, but there were a number of attempts to reach him after he was captured. Several were direct from other satellite numbers in the region, but there was one a day for the next five days via the relay, all originating from the same number."

Everyone in the room leaned forward in their seats.

"We have been unable, thus far, to find out who the number belongs to, except that the subscriber is registered through the Syrian telecom company. If I had to guess, I'd say that whoever owns that telephone also owns the relay. The good news is that we've been able to backtrack the telephone's location up until the last time it was used to try to reach al-Ghabrizi. Operating company records indicate the phone was placed in use about three weeks previous and was used a number of times in London and Paris, as well as elsewhere in France."

"Do we have any idea what the parties were talking about?" Jerry asked.

"No," was the response. "The phone company records times, locations, length of contact, etcetera for billing and network management purposes. But, they do not record the content of conversations. It takes NSA to do that, and NSA was not on the case at that time. There's too much traffic out there to suck up everything."

"So," Hannah wondered, "where does this leave us? This number looks like our only lead, because it's the only one directly associated with al-Ghabrizi. But, we don't know whether or not the phone is still in service and, if it is, where it's located. The whole thing could very well be just a big puff of smoke."

"You're right, Hannah," the briefer replied. "But, we're going to run a test to see if we can get some later info. On Monday, we're going to call the number to see whether anyone answers. If someone does, we'll know that the number is still live and where the phone is. We're going to wait until Monday so that, if the phone turns out to be owned by some business, it is more likely to be answered during the work week than on the weekend."

He shrugged. "We have nothing to lose."

Hannah looked around the room seeking volunteers of additional information or insights. There were none.

"Okay," she said, "thank you very much. I'll report all of this upstairs, and we'll hope for the best on Monday. We need to stay hot on this. Both Admiral Bergen and the DNI believe there are unanswered questions here."

The briefer intervened. "There is one more item. Whoever's got our phone made two phone calls from London, a couple of weeks ago, that did not go through the relay switch. They went to Paris, to the switchboard of a Caspian Sea Trading Company. The phone company recorded that because that switchboard is considered, for billing purposes, an extension of the main office switchboard, which is in New York City.

Amid the continuing good cheer and high-fives that characterized a White House suddenly freed from a seemingly endless siege of bad news and declining poll ratings, John Cook seemed concerned and unhappy. He arranged an unscheduled meeting of senior policy staff members concerned with international terrorism and homeland security, inviting also Director of National Intelligence Bierschmidt and senior Defense Department officials with the same portfolio. Finally, he dragooned a reluctant Roger Norton, who had taken to hanging out in the press quarters, now that he no longer needed to avoid embarrassing questions.

Cook saw that he was going to have a hard time keeping his audience's attention, its members being more interested in telling one another how wonderful it was to be respected once again. So, he began with a bit of flattery, not totally undeserved.

"All of you know that this White House prides itself on being prepared for all eventualities, whether they be good or bad. The reason we were able to hang in there for the past year while getting beat to shit on almost every front was that we were never caught by surprise. We were always able to limit the damage by preemptive action of our own to take the sting out of bad news or to divert attention away from it."

He was not going to get an argument from this audience, which was now waiting for him to come to the point.

"The al-Ghabrizi business hit us out of the blue, but was fortunately a good surprise. But, now we've got to get back to reality and to what we've become good at: planning ahead."

The look on his listeners' faces became no more knowing.

"Let me ask you a couple of questions," Cook said.

"How many of you believe that, now that al-Ghabrizi is out of the game, terrorist attacks are going to cease?

They looked at one another. Was this a trick question? No one raised his hand.

"Okay. If the attacks continue, who are we going to say is responsible for them? Are we going to let ourselves be jerked around by every pisswilly splinter group that comes up on the Internet to say that they did whatever it was in the name of God?"

Cook could see that his point was beginning to register, particularly on Norton, whose instinct for pitfalls was highly developed. Al-Ghabrizi had been the symbolic focal point of the terrorist threat. Rightly or wrongly, virtually every Islamic terrorist event that occurred, anywhere in the world, was blamed directly on him and his organization. In recent years, he had reinforced this judgment by immediately claiming credit for every significant incident. But, until his recent capture, no one in the West had actually seen al-Ghabrizi for almost five years.

"We need to plan for the probability that this war will continue," Cook insisted, speaking slowly for emphasis. "The public needs to have a very specific image of what the enemy looks like, so it knows whom we're fighting against on the level of us against them. In World War II, we had Hitler, Mussolini, and Tojo. In the Korean War, Kim Il-Sung. But, in Viet Nam, we fought the faceless Viet Cong, and our political leaders were never able to provide the people a realistic definition of what winning meant, let alone how it was to be achieved. This is the very real danger in the war on terrorism. If we cannot define, beyond vague ideological labels, who the enemy is, we will not be able to convince our people that the right strategy is being pursued and that we shall ultimately win."

He now had their attention. "So, what do we do?" Norton asked.

"In the sense that he provided a focal point for our anti-terror campaign, al-Ghabrizi was helpful. It took us a long time to get him, but we did. This has raised the President's credibility a great deal, but we've also seen the end of al-Ghabrizi working for us. So, we've got to do two things: first, we need to find a replacement for him and, second, we need to keep things from blowing up before we do.

"What do you mean by a replacement?" Cook was asked.

"Someone in the international terrorist movement has got to become the new al-Ghabrizi, at least in the minds of the American public. If there turns out to be more than one guy, that's okay, so long as everyone believes we are able to handle it. We need to be perceived as having recognized that al-Ghabrizi's capture was not the end of the battle and refocused smartly on the next generation of bad guys. We absolutely cannot be seen to be flailing about trying to figure out who's in charge, even if there really is no one in charge. But, the really worst-case scenario would be if the terrorists pull a big operation somewhere in a way that shows we had no idea of what was going on or who was behind it. If that should happen, I'm afraid the President's prospects go down the toilet once again."

The last brought everyone up short. Most shaken was Norton to whom the prospect was tantamount to his own death.

"That can't happen," he replied forcefully. "What do we need to do?"

Cook addressed the group.

"At the moment, we are operating largely in the dark. The al-Ghabrizi business still has some important question marks (he looked meaningfully at Norton), and we need to get some idea of what's going on in the world he came from. I want all of you to immediately get with the departments and agencies you deal with, not just the intelligence outfits, but also law enforcement, international trade, the State Department, anybody who could conceivably obtain relevant information. Make the bastards talk with one another. Tell them the President demands it and that, if there is another 9/11, we will turn their asses into charcoal."

A young NSC staffer raised his hand. "Can you give us an idea of what we should tell them to look for?"

"Shit, I don't know," Cook replied, throwing up his arms. "That's the thing about intelligence: it's bits and pieces, any one of which may be meaningless without the others. We need our people to find the dots and connect them, as they say, and to be willing and able to take action on the basis of the indicators, even if they are uncertain. If we can't do that, God help us."

Hannah met with the Director and the Clandestine Service chief Glover to relay the findings of the meeting she had attended earlier. Bergen approved waiting until Monday to ring the suspect satellite phone. He and Glover agreed that it was unlikely that it would be answered, but warned Hannah to make sure that everyone was prepared to exploit what could be a fleeting opportunity. This was particularly true of the technicians who would attempt to fix the location of the handset, should it respond to the call.

Afterward, Hannah didn't go back to her office and the risk of being waylaid by another urgent message or endless visit. Instead, she deposited her classified papers in an AGWOG safe and left the building for her car in a growing state of excitement. Not only was sneaking out unusually early, even for a Friday, but she was doing so to go downtown to meet John Balthazar. As she looked at herself in the dressing room mirror before putting on her clothes, she was not thinking of the AGWOG.

CHAPTER NINE

Balthazar was engrossed in a news channel report playing on a TV set over the bar, and did not see Hannah enter the room. When she appeared next to him, he greeted her as though they had last seen one another the day before. He remembered what she had been drinking at the party at which they met, and ordered one for her.

"You look marvelous," he said, squeezing her elbow.

She thanked him, feeling herself blush. He, in fact, looked better than she had remembered. They toasted their reunion, and Balthazar pointed to the television screen.

"Your government has had a major victory. Congratulations are in order. The pilot on my flight from France announced it over the intercom and brought forth loud cheering, followed by another round of champagne, at least in first class."

Hannah smiled. "We've been trying to get al-Ghabrizi for a very long time, and managed to succeed at a critical moment. Our President was getting pretty beat up about our inability to keep him from pulling off that string of spectacular operations that he's taken credit for."

"But, none have been in the United States since 9/11," Balthazar observed.

"True," Hannah replied. "But, if we didn't know where al-Ghrabizi was and what he was up to, how could we be certain that the U.S. is not the next target and that it will not happen the day after tomorrow."

Balthazar shrugged. "Surely, you don't think that he did all of this personally from a cave in the mountains?"

"Of course not. He obviously had people on the scene who did the direct planning and management. It's probably them we should be worried about," Hannah responded.

"I would think so," Balthazar agreed.

Looking up at the television screen, where a discussion of the al-Ghabrizi affair was still going on, Hannah sighed.

"If only we could quit while we're ahead. There's no more news about al-Ghabrizi, so we add interpretation and speculation, and plain old wishful thinking to what we've got. Anyone with any sense knows that others will turn up claiming leadership of the jihad, and we'll be off to the races again. Maybe the jihad doesn't need another al-Ghabrizi."

"There, I disagree," Balthazar quickly interjected. "There needs to be an overall leader and a central organization to demonstrate that the jihad is universal and not just gangs of local insurgents who can be cleaned out one at a time. If the jihad is to come to terms with the big governments of the West, it will have to be represented by someone of power and authority."

"The thought of that makes me shiver," Hannah responded bitterly. "I would give my life to keep it from happening."

"Well, we need not be concerned about it happening tonight," Balthazar quickly observed. "I would like to start my tour of your capital city right now, while there is some light left. Let's walk for a while before dinner."

The Willard is one of the best situated hotel in Washington, located on Pennsylvania Avenue three blocks from the White House and within walking distance of the headquarters of many departments of the U.S. Government. A leisurely walk brought Hannah and Balthazar to a point from which, looking left, they could see the Capitol at the far end of the National Mall and, looking right, the Washington Monument, beyond which lay the World War II Memorial, the Reflecting Pool, and the Lincoln Memorial.

"This is quite impressive," he said. "We must come back tomorrow for a longer look."

"The tour companies can do a lot better than I can," she responded.

"I didn't come to Washington to ride a bus. I came to see you. Surely, your Government's passports and visas will be safe enough, if you take the weekend off." He feigned anger well.

"How do you know that I don't have a husband or a boy friend?"

"I hope you do," he responded quickly. "I become suspicious when a beautiful woman is without a man. I don't care whether you have a husband, a boy friend or five of each, the choice of spending time with me is yours. I am prepared to fight them for you!"

She laughed. "I'll reserve my decision until I see what kind of dinner you buy me." They turned to retrace their steps.

At 10 PM, Richard Caplin took a last look around his New York City operations center before leaving for the day, hopefully for the weekend. The ships participating in Fleet Week had begun arriving at their designated piers and anchorages, signal flags streaming, their crews already beginning to hang bunting over every available rail and stanchion. From now on, the manning level at the ops center would not shrink at night, nor would the number of Coast Guard and NYPD patrol craft scurrying about the lower and upper bays peeking into every inlet and port facility. Caplin lived on the Upper East Side of Manhattan and had a direct video/teleconference line with the ops center. He secretly enjoyed the times when some emergency required his presence downtown and a police radio car picked him at home and drove him, siren screaming and lights flashing, down Broadway at what seemed like seventy miles per hour. At the moment, however, nothing appeared amiss, and the Mayor's point man on terrorism hoped to be able to rest up for what was unquestionably going to be a very busy week.

At the end-of-the-week review meeting he had held earlier in the day, the one attended by the principal representatives of all the metropolitan area organizations represented on the Mayor's anti-terrorism task force, Caplin had found no one with any indication or even suspicion that the City was going to be a terrorist target during Fleet Week. Even the FBI and Homeland Security liaison officers who attended these meetings reported they had received nothing from Washington to that effect. But, of course, they all acknowledged that Fleet Week was an extremely juicy target, in terms of both damage and symbolic potential. The worst-case scenario was that something was, in fact, going on, and they were not aware of it.

The significance, if any, of al-Ghabrizi's capture was discussed at length. It was agreed that, if there were some sort of plan to attack during Fleet Week, he would be behind it. But, it would have gotten underway before the arrest, and they could not safely assume that al-Ghabrizi's capture would have caused it to be cancelled. On the contrary, there would be a strong incentive to demonstrate that the jihad was not dependent on a single man. So, in New York City, there would be a need to be even more vigilant, to take greater precautions, and to worry more. Caplin knew that he would become a nervous wreck, as Fleet Week progressed, and intended to make sure his colleagues joined him.

After Anna left for the day, the men came in from the yard to join Khalid in the office. She had been on him all day about them, constantly peeking out the windows to see what they were doing. She asked whether Mr. Ghoravi had actually seen them and, when Khalid made the mistake of admitting that he had not, she proposed calling to warn him. It was all Khalid could do to reassure her that Ghoravi knew everything about them, and that she need not be concerned because they would be gone in a week. Then she proposed calling the FBI.

"They tell us to report suspicious activity," she urged.

Anna was a large-scale pain in the ass. "They are not suspicious," Khalid maintained. "They are merely homeless."

"But, they look just like those people you see on the news dancing around streets in the Middle East waving guns over their heads," she complained.

"Everyone there looks like that. They are Iranians," Khalid maintained.

"What is to be done with them?" she asked.

"They are going to be sent home," Khalid replied.

Now, the men were sitting around his office watching television and eating pizza. On the night they emerged from the shipping container, they had run through the food Khalid had brought for them in a few minutes and demanded more. The only thing filling he could find for them at that hour, that he was certain did not contain meat, was tomato and cheese pizza from an all-night carry-out in the neighborhood. The men had, of course, loved it, and now insisted upon pizza at every meal.

Follow-ups on the al-Ghabrizi capture were still filling many TV time slots, and the men reacted to the appearance of al-Ghabrizi's photograph and film clips of street scenes in the Middle East. Their English was poor, and they peppered Khalid with questions.

"If Sheik al-Ghabrizi has fallen, does this mean we will not get the opportunity to enter heaven, as we were promised?" one asked plaintively.

"And the virgins. Do not forget the virgins," another reminded, laughing nervously.

"On Monday I will know," Khalid responded. "But, one way or another, I think you will get your opportunity to enter heaven."

"Do you know what we are to do? I hope it is something bold and spectacular so that the entire world will praise our sacrifice in the name of jihad."

"Yes, I do know what it is. And I believe that all of your people will be proud to have known you, and will honor your memory in their daily prayers."

The men were happy, and tore into another extra large, extra cheese.

President Tucker was also eating pizza, a late evening treat delivered to a rear gate of the White House and hustled up to the family quarters by the Secret Service. With him were John Cook and Roger Norton, both enjoying the informality and extra calories.

"Gentlemen," the President exulted, biting off the drooping point of a fresh slice, "we are back in business. The polls numbers haven't stop climbing, and the attaboys have been coming in from overseas, some from leaders who haven't been exactly friendly."

"Congratulations, Mr. President," they responded, almost in unison.

"John, Roger tells me that you're concerned about where we go from here in the war on terror, now that al-Ghabrizi is gone."

"That's right, Mr. President. The people know that the war isn't going to end just because we've caught al-Ghabrizi, but the focus has been on him for so long as the man behind almost all the major attacks around the world that they are expecting some significant improvement in security, now that he's out of it."

"Don't you think that's justified?" Tucker asked.

"I don't know," Cook replied. "I don't think any of us does. Director Bierschmidt and Admiral Bergen are antsy about the whole thing. We never had a helluva lot of good information about al-Ghabrizi and his organization."

"Which is why it took a lucky accident to catch him," Norton scoffed. "The Intelligence Community people are a bunch of old ladies who never saw a weasel word they didn't like."

"So, what do you think we should do?" the President asked.

"I've tasked the National Security Council staff to jack up the intelligence and law enforcement agencies to prevent a post-al-Ghabrizi let down," Cook replied. "If some threat is going to develop, sir, you absolutely need to get out in front of it early."

Norton stopped chewing long enough to nod emphatically. "Amen to that," he said.

CHAPTER TEN

Hannah and Balthazar walked back to the Willard in the evening air now growing cool. She felt the pager in her jacket pocket vibrate, as it had several times during dinner, but again ignored it. They had talked all through dinner, and were amazed to be still talking three hours later. The range of subjects they had touched on was so broad, and the transition from one to another so rapid, that, at one point, Hannah had become panicked that she would inadvertently blow her cover by talking about something or someplace not in keeping with the Hannah Crossman whom Balthazar thought he was getting to know.

He, in turn, had filled in the gaps left from their first meeting in Geneva. His parents had left their small farm in southern Lebanon after their house had been destroyed by Israeli forces trying to root out guerillas who had taken refuge there. The family arrived in the south of France just in time for John to be born, and settled in the Muslim ghetto of Marseille populated largely by North Africans. They were very poor, and it took two years for John's father to begin earning enough money at three jobs to support the family. In the interim, they were dependent on charity, some of which came from French authorities and international refugee aid organizations. Most, however, came through the neighborhood mosque that was the center of the immigrant community.

Balthazar recounted how his parents, who had not been particularly religious to begin with, became gradually more devout as their gratitude increased along with their anger at those they believed responsible for their poverty and anomie, as explained to them over and over again by the Imam of the mosque. By the time John was ten, and had begun to understand what was happening beyond the few city blocks of his childhood range, they were dedicated to what they called the jihad. But, they had little to commit to it, except for their son, the two other children born since their arrival in France having turned out to be female. So, John was enrolled in a madrassa, a religious school attached to the mosque in which boys of his age, and even younger if they could read, spent their days memorizing the Koran. Their understanding and appreciation of what they were reading were enhanced by lectures from the mosque's clergy that demanded the faithful revenge their perceived oppression through a just holy war. The parents of every student, always needy, received a small stipend.

"I can still recite large portions of the Koran from memory," Balthazar mused. "I graduated at the top of my class, and there was talk of sending me to Pakistan for advanced religious training."

"What happened?" Hannah asked.

"I was bored. By then, I was twelve years old and would much rather be playing football than sitting in that stifling classroom rocking back and forth. More important, though, was that my father had gotten a job as deliveryman for a large French food chain, like Fortnum & Mason, and he let me go with him on his rounds. I got to see how the people who owned the world lived, and noticed quickly that they didn't spend their waking hours plotting attacks on Muslims, as we were told they did. At that time, Israel was still an abstraction to me, although the name was mentioned, as a part of a curse, a hundred times a day in the mosque. I felt that, if God really needed me to dedicate my life to the jihad, he would tell me himself and not pass the word through a bunch of smelly mullahs. When I told that to my parents, my father laughed and my mother began to worry that I would burn in hell long before my time."

Balthazar took Hannah's hand as they walked, and she clasped his. She smiled to herself as she tried and couldn't remember the last time she had been on date with a man who had taken her hand.

"When I was fifteen," he continued, "my father lied about my age and got me a job as a stock boy at the store for which he worked. That was where I learned the business I'm in today. I also learned about what you Americans call upward mobility. By watching the people who ran the store and the big company it belonged to, and the regular customers for whom I would prepare and deliver special orders, I saw that being poor, a foreigner, and a Muslim would not necessarily prevent me from making my way in the world. At about the same time, I discovered that I was attractive to women, and began screwing my way around the business community of Marseille."

He looked at Hannah to see if he had shocked her, and she felt it necessary to pretend that he had.

"Having been born after my parents arrived in Marseille, I was a French citizen and, with the patronage of friends I had made, I went to university and acquired the qualities I needed to be successful in business and elsewhere. Upon graduation, I changed my name because, I'm not ashamed to say, I wanted people to think I am European and not a displaced Lebanese."

"What about your name?" Balthazar asked. "It's not exactly a common Lebanese name."

"They changed our name when they got to California and discovered that no one could pronounce it," Hannah explained. "They didn't know what name to adopt, so they took the name of a small town near where they had settled because it sounded American. Hannah was their idea of a nice American girl's name."

"I like it," Balthazar said.

"Actually," she admitted, "so do I."

Back at the Willard, they went again to the bar for a nightcap. It was not very crowded, but everyone in the room, including the serving staff, was gathered in a knot looking up at the television set, which was still tuned to a news channel. As, Hannah and Balthazar approached, they noted a "Breaking News" banner across the bottom of the screen and, as they got closer, a headline in smaller type reading "Al-Ghabrizi Claims London Attack." They could not hear what the reporter on the screen was saying because all of the viewers were talking loudly to one another.

"Is this a surprise?" Balthazar asked Hannah. "I thought everyone assumed he did it."

"I certainly did," she replied. "I wonder why everyone is so excited."

They approached the group and asked the one man who was not busy shouting at someone else what was going on. He told them that Al-Jazeera, the satellite television news service operating out of Qatar, had played an audio tape, allegedly of al-Ghabrizi's voice, on which he claimed credit for the recent attack in London and spoke of other attacks to come soon. Hannah asked what the great excitement was about, since it was likely that the tape had been prepared in advance of the operation, before al-Ghabrizi had been captured. The response was that the voice, in addition to talking about London, had also talked about other events, the arrests of several low ranking jihadis in Africa, that had occurred only two days earlier. The tape could not have been prepared before the London event, so either the man speaking or the one in American custody was not al-Ghabrizi. It was even possible that neither was him.

Hannah looked at Balthazar who smiled sympathetically.

"As Durante would say: 'What a revoltin' development!'"

"I didn't think you were that old, John," she responded defensively, as the pager in her pocket started vibrating again. This time, she pulled it out and looked at the tiny screen, knowing already what the message was about. The problem was how to break free of Balthazar without discouraging future contact and, at the same time, keeping him from becoming aware that she was involved in the al-Ghabrizi business. It was not usual for State Department passport and visa administrators to be urgently paged late on a Friday evening.

"Don't tell me you've arranged to be called away just as I was about to ask you to share a bottle of wine with me upstairs," Balthazar complained, only half-humorously. "I have been repeatedly warned against personal relationships with Americans, particularly with American women. I should take these warnings more seriously."

"I'm sorry, John," Hannah replied, inserting unhappiness into her voice without difficulty, "but my office is running an exercise with the customs and immigration people to see if we can help them catch more people trying to sneak into the country with false papers. Something's gotten screwed up, and I'm on call."

She got off the bar stool and kissed him lightly on the cheek. "I'm very sorry, John. I didn't intend to run out on you. I'll call you tomorrow, and we'll see what we can do with the weekend."

Hannah left before he could reply and, once out of the room, pulled out her secure cell phone and dialed the AGWOG. The duty officer, whom she knew, said he had been trying to reach her for several hours. When she told him that she was out on a date, there was an incredulous pause (which Hannah thought impertinent) before he gave her the message. The Director was looking for her. He's on his way to the White House, and wants Hannah to meet him there. She stowed her phone with a sigh of relief, and dashed out of the hotel to cover the three blocks at warp speed.

Admiral Bergen waited in John Cook's office for his senior, Director of National Intelligence Bierschmidt, to arrive. They were then ushered into the Oval Office together. For once, Bergen was glad to be playing second fiddle to the DNI, to let him take some of the heat. The President, in sports clothes, was agitatedly pacing the room, shadowed by Roger Norton. As the two intelligence directors entered the room, he did not wait for the door to close behind them before lashing out. Hannah, waiting in the anteroom outside, heard him almost shout:

"Gentlemen, can you tell me what the fuck is going on here?"

"We are still analyzing the tape, sir," Bergen responded, "but there is no doubt that the man we hold is al-Ghabrizi. We don't know who the voice on the tape belongs to, but it appears to be the same one that has made all of his post-attack claims for at least the past couple of years. We believed that it belonged to al-Ghabrizi himself, but obviously we have been wrong. But, it's not clear that the man's identity is significant: he could very well be just a spokesman chosen because he has a good voice."

"That's not the big issue, Admiral," Norton irately interjected. "Isn't it possible that, because we were deceived about the identity of the person making the claims, al-Ghabrizi may not have been involved at all, that someone else is running the show and has been using al-Ghabrizi for cover."

Bergen and Bierschmidt looked at one another.

"Should that turn out to be the case," John Cook added, "we are in truly deep shit because, one, the President has just told the world what a truly great victory capturing al-Ghabrizi was, two, it makes us look fucking incompetent and, three, we're going to have to deal with a big rise in public apprehension and lack of confidence in our ability to keep the terrorists away from our shores."

The President pointed at Bergen and Bierschmidt. "I want you two, and those who work for you, to get out there and find out immediately what the true story is. If it turns out to be as Roger and John fear, you need to work with the law enforcement agencies and the Defense Department to cover every possible point of vulnerability. The thought that there is someone we don't know of wandering around the world masterminding these attacks is intolerable. I will speak with the SecDef, Attorney General, and Secretary of Homeland Security. If you two are not up to this, I will find people who are...and soon."

He turned away, signaling that the meeting was over. Hannah was surprised when Bierschmidt and Bergen came out so soon, and followed their grim faces to John Cook's office. Bergen turned immediately to Hannah:

"I want you to go back over everything we know about al-Ghabrizi, in particular the last couple of years. Look for anything that could be interpreted to indicate that he was not actually in charge out there. Of course, if you find such an indication, I would also like to know who really is in charge."

Jerry appeared in the doorway, relieved at finding Hannah in the room. "I took a call for you from the AGWOG. Al-Ghabrizi is talking again.'

Biershmidt looked at the others. "Now we know why he refused to talk. He knew that we'd recognize immediately that his voice is not the one we've been hearing on TV."

"But, why should he be that concerned about it, if the voice is just a spokesman. Unless, of course, it is really that of the real leader," Cook offered.

"Well, at least now we can go ask him," Bergen pointed out. "Hannah, go down and talk with him. Maybe he'll tell us something useful."

Jerry didn't look hopeful. "The first thing the son-of-a-bitch did was complain about the food."

Leaving the White House, Hannah walked back to the Willard to retrieve her car from the hotel garage. She was tempted to call Balthazar, but realized reluctantly that she would not get away before morning. So, she drove out to CIA Headquarters, which was on her way home. Something had occurred to her that she needed to follow-up on before seeing al-Ghabrizi the next day. From the AGWOG, she sent a message to Jed at

Bagram asking him to find out how the Pakistani police knew to raid the hotel room where they found al-Ghabrizi. She also wanted to know whether the Pakistanis had recognized al-Ghabrizi in the hotel room or later when they had him custody. After sending the message, she drove home to find a message from Balthazar on her machine saying how much he looked forward to seeing her the next day. With a bit of luck, she could go down to the stockade in southern Virginia, interview al-Ghabrizi, and be back in time for dinner with Balthazar. Hannah smiled as she slipped between the sheets for a few hours of sleep.

Almost all of the visiting ships participating in Fleet Week had arrived at their assigned locations, their crews preparing for the opening ceremonies and beginning of visiting the next day. A very large aircraft carrier had been pushed into the berth normally used by transatlantic liners and cruise ships, and two tall-masted training ships belonging to foreign navies occupied the adjacent pier, their yards and braces already strung with bunting and pennants. At the entrances to the piers, NYPD Emergency Services was completing the installation of long rows of metal detectors and barriers designed to enable police to keep the crowds orderly and assure that no one slipped by the inspection points.

Richard Caplin had been waylayed on the way to his car by Jon Menna, the Mayor's Fleet Week Coordinator, and dragooned into making a quick tour of the visiting sites along the Hudson and East River waterfronts. Afterward they met with the Deputy Police Commissioner and Chief of the Transit Authority Police, whose special charge it was to safeguard the subway system and its riders. The vast majority of visitors would be arriving by subway and by ferry from Staten Island and New Jersey on the other side of the Hudson River and New York Bay. All of the trains and boats would be packed, and loss of life would be extreme, if terrorists succeeded in smuggling bombs aboard, as they had done in other cities.

Ultimately, the measures that could be taken to preclude such a catastrophe could not guarantee public safety. The advent of the suicide bomber had made execution of a terrorist operation significantly easier by eliminating the need to provide for the perpetrator's survival and escape. As a practical matter, the only real way to protect public transportation was to prevent bombers from getting into subway cars, busses, and ferries to find the maximum number of targets. New York City's subway system is, however, enormous, with most lines interconnecting. People headed for Fleet Week festivities at the tip of Manhattan would be packing subway cars in the far reaches of Queens, Brooklyn and the Bronx, not to mention those coming in to Grand Central Terminal and Penn Station on commuter trains from bordering Connecticut and New Jersey. Caplin and Menna accepted the plans that were outlined to them, because they knew that all available resources were being devoted to the effort. However, they were neither happy nor confident.

CHAPTER ELEVEN

Hannah used her position as an assistant to the Director to ar-range for a plane to fly her down to Langley Air Force Base and back. The Agency owned a fleet of small passenger aircraft, some with intercontinental capability, that it used for sundry purposes around the world. Their paint and markings were inconspicuous and different, one from another, and not dissimilar from those of corporate aircraft. In the Washington area, they operated from a hangar in a secluded section of Dulles International Airport, which facilitated handling the occasional blindfolded passenger without public notice.

It was a Saturday morning, traffic was light, and Hannah was at the hangar by 7 AM. Airport traffic was also light, and they were airborne shortly thereafter on the half hour flight. En route, Hannah received an EMail from Jed, forwarded by the AGWOG, telling her that his police contact told him that they had received a tip about the hotel room meeting from a source who almost always gave them reliable information. Al-Ghabrizi's name was never mentioned, but Jed's informant believed that the terrorist leader was recognized by the more senior officers at the police station, and that the decision to turn him over to us solved a dilemma for them: they couldn't let him go, but neither could they prosecute him without touching off endless riots throughout the country. They greatly appreciated our taking full credit for his capture.

So, he was ratted out, Hannah mused. But, who would have done it? Internal rivalries within political movements were not unusual, even ones resulting in the assassination of one of the competitors. At the extremes of Islam, the murder of clerical leaders by their rivals was also not unknown, particularly where religious and secular politics were intertwined, a commonplace in Central Asia and the Near East. But, al-Ghabrizi was not known to have a serious challenger, someone who would obviously benefit from his disappearance from the scene. And, if there is such a person, she pondered, why didn't he just have al-Ghabrizi killed.

If whoever tipped off the police knew that al-Ghabrizi was going to be in that hotel room, he presumably also knew why he was there, which would imply an insider. Hannah had not heard a single, halfway convincing speculation as to what al-Ghabrizi was doing so far from home meeting with nonentities. It occurred to her, however, that perhaps the snitch had set up the meeting as a convenient pretext for making al-Ghabrizi available to the security police. If that was the case, why was it done at that particular time? Presumably, an insider aware of al-Ghabrizi's activities who wanted to get rid of him would have some choice of time and place. Why then?

Khalid opened the gates, then drove the empty truck into the yard and parked it next to the others. He was happy that it was Saturday, and Anna would not be in. Tremont was normally closed on weekends, but since Ghoravi had gotten the tour boat provisioning contract, one truck had to make a trip to the dock on Saturday and Sunday. Normally, it was done by one of the regular truck crews, but this weekend Khalid had allowed his regular employees to take the days off, while he drove the truck and took   two of the new arrivals along on each trip as helpers. It was a good way to show them where they would be going when the time came.

When Khalid came back to the office, the other two were watching the television set, again tuned to a news channel. One of them waved a copy of a tabloid newspaper at him, the front page of which was taken up mostly by the familiar photograph of al-Ghabrizi over which blared the headline "AL-G A FAKE?"

"What means this fake?" he asked.

Khalid grabbed the newspaper and began to open it, but noticed that the television set was showing almost the same headline. He listened to the accompanying story, then explained to the men, in Arabic, that the Americans suspected that al-Ghabrizi was not really the grand leader of the jihad, but just a puppet being manipulated by someone else. The men were bewildered. They had come thousands of miles, under unspeakable conditions, to sacrifice their lives at the urging of al-Ghabrizi, now to be told that he was not worthy of their gift.

"Is this true?" they asked Khalid.

He himself wanted to know. But, he couldn't very well let the operation disintegrate, at least not before he talked with the contact who was supposed to reach him next week. So, he told the men that it was a lie made up by the Americans to make the soldiers of the jihad lose faith. Do not listen to the lies, he told them, and they cheered.

Hannah was met upon landing by the young man who was the Agency's liaison officer at the stockade. While driving there, he briefed her on al-Ghabrizi's condition and activities. When the terrorist attack in London occurred at the beginning of the week, Hannah had called down and asked that al-Ghabrizi be placed in a cell with a television set tuned to one of the Arab satellite news channels. The set was to be situated high enough on a wall that the prisoner could not reach it, and was to be left on at all times at moderate volume. It was to have a covert video camera built in, with associated recorder, so that a time-synchronized tape of the program playing at any given time and al-Ghabrizi's facial reaction to it was created. Hannah decided to review the tapes before interviewing al-Ghabrizi.

What she discovered surprised her. When first exposed to news of the attack, al-Ghabrizi had shown no surprise, as expected, but also little interest. More significant, as video clips of the chaos and damage were shown, he paid little attention and showed no gratification or exultation. At other times, when news or analysis sequences addressed his capture and surrounding events, he did not watch at all, preferring to lie on his bunk with eyes closed. There, of course, was no way of telling whether or not he was listening.

Even the ultimate claim of responsibility in his name did not appear to merit more than mild attention. He obviously knew that it was not him speaking. But, his reaction to the subsequent speculation in the West that he was merely a front for someone else was surprisingly strong. Again, he must have known what his true status was, so why was he disturbed? Hannah talked with the CIA psychologist who had analyzed the tapes. His conclusion was that al-Ghabrizi's reaction was embarrassment.

The holding cell in which the terrorist leader was living was long and narrow, furnished only with a bed and a single chair, both fastened to the floor, a sink and a commode. The television set was on a shelf above the door where it could be watched from the bed and the chair, and where the installed video camera could image the occupant doing so. The camera operated through one of the ostensible controls on the front of the set, and had a built-in zoom capability that yielded sharp close-ups of the viewer.

Al-Ghabrizi was seated on the bed looking down at the floor, and did not react when Hannah entered the cell. When he realized that she was not a guard come to check on him, he stood up and stared at her, his eyes widening when she addressed him in native Arabic.

"Good day, Sheik al-Ghabrizi. I hope you are well, considering the circumstances."

Hannah had to look closely to recognize the man whose framed photograph sat on her desk in the AGWOG for three years. He looked older certainly, but he did not have the gaunt, haunted look of the iconic photograph with his principal deputies and AK-47s in their mountain hideout five years earlier. He spoke in a weak voice, as though his throat was parched, although there were several plastic bottles of water near his bed. Hannah reflexively compared his voice with the recorded one they had been accustomed to hearing after every bold attack. It was obviously not the same, but she was struck most by the absence of the zeal and authoritative tone that characterized the latter.

"How should I be well," he replied sadly. "I have been forcibly kidnapped from my home, dragged across the ocean to an American prison and, now, the great CIA has sent a woman to interrogate me."

"It is true that I'm from the CIA, but I am not here to interrogate you." Hannah was speaking in a low, respectful tone.

"I have spent the better part of ten years following your activities and trying to understand you. I could not forego the opportunity to actually meet you."

Al-Ghabrizi made a brief, unconscious attempt to rear-range his clothing, a bright orange jumpsuit, and Hannah thought she detected a flicker of vanity.

"Unfortunately, you do not find me at my best. Not only have I been roughly handled, as you know, but now they are call-ing me a fake." He glanced in the direction of the television set.

Hannah allowed as how she was shocked as well. "But, I am not sure that they can be blamed, if it is true that you were not really the mastermind behind these great operations," she told him, hoping that he would rise to the bait.

He paused, drinking from one of the water bottles, and increasing Hannah's suspense. He appeared to be reviewing in his mind the long chain events that had brought him this mo-ment. Finally, he began to speak:

"When the Americans first came to Afghanistan, we be-lieved they would rush around making a lot of noise and then go home. But, they stayed and brought with them helicopters and spy satellites and little planes with television cameras. When we went out to go from place to place, they would see us, and soon planes would come to drop bombs and rockets. We couldn't have fires to warm us in winter because the rockets homed in on the heat they gave."

He paused again to drink from the bottle.

"As we moved deeper into the mountains, it became more and more difficult to communicate with the outside. We had satellite telephones and radios, but we could not use them very much because the enemy would listen and locate us by the signal. Eventually, I could communicate only by sending messengers to towns and villages where there were normal communications. I could see and hear what was happening in the world through the television satellite, but I had to rely on others to relay my orders and deal with organizational matters."

He turned away from Hannah and stared at the blank wall of his cell.

"It was not long before people began acting in my name, people I had never heard of. They began organizing operations, and stopped coming to me for funds, which was good because the enemy had cut off virtually all of my sources. Many times, I found out about the operations you speak of at the same time you did."

"Were you able to find out who these people are?" Hannah asked.

"They were just messages sent to me or, occasionally, voices on the telephone," he replied. "I believe they were in the West, but one cannot be sure. Our movement exists all over the world, but in most places our people cannot live in the open or communicate directly with one another. So, it is often not clear where a person who is sending you a message actually is."

"What were you doing in Karachi on the day you were taken by the police?" Hannah asked.

"I live there," was the unexpected reply.

"You live in Karachi?" Hannah was floored. "We believed that you were living in the Pakistan-Afghanistan border area. When did you move to Karachi?"

"About two years ago, I was not well and needed medical treatment. As I have said, I was isolated in the mountains, no longer leading the jihad, and dependent on subsidies from people I did not know."

His voice was bitter now.

"They were paying me for the use of my name, like a kept whore. So, I decided that a well-kept whore should have a house of her own, not a cave in the middle of nowhere. When I came to Karachi to see the doctor, I stayed. My patrons found a small house for me in the suburbs, I cut my beard as you see it, and began to dress as everyone in the city does. Who would suspect that the man tending his garden in the bungalow down the street is the great Anwar al-Ghabrizi."

Hannah had still not recovered from al-Ghabrizi's revelation.

"What about the meeting you were at when the police found you?" Hannah prompted.

"They told me that the men I was to meet with were going on a very important mission, and that I was to encourage them by revealing to them my identity, as well as providing them money for their expenses. I did not get the opportunity to do either."

Hannah pressed. "Did you know where they were going or what they were supposed to do?"

Al-Ghabrizi bristled. "You said that you weren't here to interrogate me. I would not answer that question, but it happens that I do not know. The meeting was interrupted almost as soon as it had started. I did not even know their names."

"Our sources in Pakistan tell us that you were betrayed, that the police were informed of your meeting." Hannah watched closely to see his reaction. There was a sharp intake of breath, and al-Ghabrizi stared at her for a long moment, perhaps to determine whether she was telling the truth.

"I wondered how they knew about the meeting. It also explains why the Pakistani police turned me over to your people so quickly. They must have recognized me."

"Do you know who might have done this?"

Al-Ghabrizi shook his head. "I have thoughts, but I will not say."

Hannah pressed further. "It obviously must have been one of your patrons. Who else knew you would be there? It suggests that they considered you expendable."

Al-Ghabrizi sighed and sat down on the bed. He did not respond immediately, and Hannah could not tell whether he was pondering the question or considering its implications. Finally, he looked up at her and spoke in a voice that was far more tired than when they had begun their conversation.

"What you say is, perhaps, true. But, what difference does it make now. There is nothing I can do to save myself or to obtain revenge for what they have done to me. If I knew who they were, I could tell you, and you would hunt them down. But, I don't know, and I would not tell you, in any event. The jihad they are fighting is different from mine, but it is the only one we have at the moment."

"How is it different?" Hannah asked.

"When we started, our primary goal was to call attention to our grievances, and to force the West, in particular the United States, to do something to help the Palestinians. As years passed and nothing significant was done, we adopted more spectacular and destructive measures. But, we were always operating within the existing economic and political power relationships. We had no territory, no government, and no armies that we directly controlled. We could not participate in negotiations, or even send representatives, because we would all have been arrested. So, while our operations in the infidel states were becoming more frequent and more sophisticated, we were not making real progress toward achieving our goals. To the contrary, the enemy sent forces to Afghanistan and Iraq, and subverted the government of Pakistan, making it difficult for us to function even in our home countries.

My impression is that the people who have taken over leadership of the jihad are seeking to achieve a place of equality, if not superiority, in an eventual negotiation that will divide the world between Muslims and non-Muslims. They recognize that the jihad, as it has been conducted, could never by itself lead to such a fundamental change. So, they have become better organized and more focused on longer term goals. I don't know by when they expect to achieve them, but they won't give up trying."

Hannah was going to ask another question, but al-Ghabrizi put up his hand to stop her.

"You are going to ask how they intend to pursue these goals, and I have already told you that I do not know. Also, I am tired, and don't wish to continue. You speak our tongue very well, and I've enjoyed talking with you."

"If you will, please, Sheik al-Ghabrizi, one final question," Hannah begged. "After you were arrested, you refused to speak until after we discovered that the voice identified as yours on television was not really you. Why did you do that? It wasn't something you could maintain for very long."

Al-Ghabrizi smiled ruefully.

"I was asked to do that by my patrons, and it appeared strange to me at the time. But, the request came as I was moving to Karachi, and I thought it had something to do with that, so I agreed. I was told that, if I fell into the enemy's hands, I should prevent them from learning, for as long as possible, that mine was not the voice speaking for the jihad.

"Why would they do that?" Hannah asked, although she had a pretty good idea.

"The purpose would be to show the infidels that they have no idea what we are doing and where we are going to strike next," he replied. "I thought it was a pointless promise. But, if what you have told me is true, they may have been planning, already back then, to betray me."

At the end of their conversation, which had consumed no more than fifteen or twenty minutes, al-Ghabrizi looked to Hannah to have aged twenty years. He turned away from her and began to chant a prayer in a low voice. She rapped lightly on the door, and was let out of the cell.

On the plane back to Washington, Hannah called the Director's Office Duty Officer and was, after a moment, put through to Admiral Bergen. She briefed him on her interview with al-Ghabrizi, confirming the conclusion that the media had leaped to earlier. He was just as surprised as Hannah had been regarding the news of al-Ghabrizi's emigration to Karachi, and directed that no one be told of it until he was able to brief the President's handlers. Added to the embarrassment with which the White House was already struggling, the word that the feared international terrorist leader had become a homesteading suburbanite, and we didn't know it, would be devastating. Bergen told

Hannah that he was at home and planned to stay there for the remainder of the weekend, barring some emergency. Everything they knew to do was being done, and next week could turn out to be a black hole. So, she was directed to get some rest and be ready on Monday.

Hannah tried to call Jerry, but was unsuccessful. Remembering the Admiral's order, she decided to wait until Monday to try again. Then she dialed her home answering machine on an non-secure phone circuit and heard the usual message from her mother and one from Balthazar. He reported that he had just returned from a four hour guided tour and now knew more about Washington than he really cared to know, including where the State Department is. If Hannah didn't call him soon, he promised, he was going to go down there and root her out himself.

CHAPTER TWELVE

"I am amazed at how tranquil this city is, when you consider all that is going on," Balthazar observed, as he and Hannah strolled in front of the White House after dinner. "If this was Islamabad or Ankara, there would be a mob in the street raising hell about something. Even in Paris and Rome, somebody is always on strike or protesting something the government did or did not do. But here, just peace and quiet."

Hannah laughed. "We have our share of protests, but fortunately they rarely become violent and destructive. I think that it's not that Americans are incapable of it as much as it is that they have no reason for doing it. But, I'm told that, during the Vietnam War, things sometimes got pretty hot around here."

"Do you think there will be a strong public reaction to this new al-Ghabrizi business?" Balthazar asked. "If what the television and newspapers are saying is true, your government is going to look very incompetent."

Hannah had been wondering the same thing herself, particularly since the public did not know about the terrorist kingpin's bungalow in Karachi, and hopefully never would. She was impressed by how well keeping al-Ghabrizi mute had worked for his unknown patrons. If he had talked from the moment of his capture, it would have been immediately apparent that he was not the person making the claims of responsibility for a string of terrorist attacks around the world. Consequently, the President would never have boasted to the world of the great progress in the war on terror that al-Ghabrizi's capture represented. What impressed Hannah even more was that this ploy was not a spur-of- the-moment trick, but had apparently been arranged some time earlier.

"I doubt there will be riots," she responded, "but, there is an election coming up next year, and I assume that the President would like to be reelected."

"What will he do, then?" Balthazar persisted.

"Well, he hasn't confided in me," she joked. "But, I suspect he'll do and say things to reassure the American people that he and his administration are doing everything possible to keep us safe."

"Do the people believe him?"

Hannah thought about it for a moment, before responding. "It's really hard to tell. Many feel that they have no other option, since there isn't very much they can do for themselves. Fortunately, we've been able to, for the most part, prevent attacks on Muslims, and people have been largely going about their daily lives without fear."

"How much of that is because there have been no terrorist attacks in America since the World Trade Center?" Balthazar asked.

"Probably a lot," Hannah answered quickly. "Another major attack in the United States, particularly soon, could have a very serious impact."

Balthazar smiled at her. "I shall have to be very watchful, then, when I go up to New York on Monday."

They walked along in silence for a while, enjoying the soft spring air which was only beginning to show the humidity for which Washington in late Spring and Summer is famous. Balthazar took her hand, and Hannah looked up at him. He was obviously enjoying himself, and she was happy.

"You travel all over the world for your business," she continued. "How do people in cities outside the United States deal with the threat of bombs in their crowded public places?"

He shrugged. "That depends," he replied, "upon how real the threat is to them. In places like Israel, Iraq, and even Lebanon, such attacks occur with some frequency. Their people factor the risk into their lives. It is certainly not easy for them, but it is even harder to live paralyzed by fear of something you can't detect and fight against. Terrorism is most effective when it causes the people who are affected by it to feel that their leaders and institutions can't protect them, and the leaders themselves to doubt their abilities. The first attack in a country or against an unsuspecting target is always the most effective because it suddenly transforms nameless fears and doubts into terrible realities."

Hannah was impressed. Balthazar had obviously thought about the subject, which was not surprising given his constant exposure, as a traveler, to security measures taken around the world to prevent the state-to-state movement of terrorists and the funding and materiel they require. She knew from her own travels that going from country to country involved long and tedious waiting lines, document reviews, and surly, overworked immigration officials, even when one was traveling with an official passport. Of course, Balthazar, with his handsomely tailored suits, fine luggage, and first class ticket probably escaped much of what the average coach passenger endured.

"Do you find that, as a Muslim, you are subjected to extra scrutiny when you enter the United States or another western country?" she asked.

"I don't travel as a Muslim," he scoffed. "I have a French passport and a special document signed by the Minister of Trade identifying me as an important citizen. The major airlines consider me a national treasure, and immigration inspectors at the major ports of entry around the world recognize me, or at least my name, when I appear in front of them. Travel is more difficult now than it used to be, but can still be pleasant, if one knows how to do it."

He turned to her and began to laugh. "That sounded pretty pompous, didn't it? I'm sorry." He put his arms around her and pulled her close, planting a soft kiss on her forehead.

"Is there some place around here where one can dance? You know, the kind where the man actually holds the woman in his arms."

They found what they were looking for in a small lounge at Balthazar's hotel: dim lighting, a three-piece combo playing old standards, and a girl singer with just enough loneliness in her voice to make the handsomely appointed, well-fed patrons feel lucky. Several hours later, Balthazar led her, not unwillingly, to his room, where a freshly iced bottle of champagne and a tray of hors d'oeuvres were waiting.

"Why do I feel that you knew well in advance that this was going to happen," Hannah teased upon seeing the refreshments.

"In my line of business," he responded while kissing her on the neck and behind the ear, "one must always be prepared for success."

He undid the catch at the back of her dress and opened the zipper. The dress fell away and he ran his tongue down her chest and between her breasts. As she felt herself pleasantly losing control, Hannah remembered that Agency regulations required that she report all contact with foreign nationals outside of established business channels. She decided to think about it in the morning.

The first full day of Fleet Week had passed uneventfully, except for minor incidents that are inevitable whenever large crowds of people gather, especially in big cities. As anticipated, visiting was heavy at the ships tied up at piers along the Hudson River, but was expected to taper off somewhat during the week, then build anew until the fireworks and other big events on closing weekend. The crowds, thus far, had been orderly, and the Harbor Patrol and Coast Guard had reported no signicant incidents of private boats trying to enter the exclusion area around the visiting naval units. Deputy Commissioner Caplin had just concluded his first end-of-day wrap-up meeting in the Ops Center, and the day shift staff was rapidly departing for home before something happened to keep them on duty.

As the Mayor's Fleet Week Coordinator, Jon Menna's job was essentially done. He had organized the event, secured commitments from participating nations, overseen the berthing and visiting arrangements, and worried over security. Now that Fleet Week was actually underway, it was out of his hands, and he felt useless and somewhat embarrassed hanging around the Ops Center like a mother hen. As Caplin passed by on his way out, Menna asked him whether anything new had been heard from Washington relative to security. The Deputy Commissioner stopped and shook his head.

"The short answer is No. But, I think they've gotten themselves so wrapped around the axle by this al-Ghabrizi business that they're not sure whether they're coming or going. We can't depend on them for reliable warning because they have this need to cover their asses. If something does happen, they want to be able to tell the voters that they warned us. Problem is, we get warned many more times than we get attacked and, while zero attacks is the right number, our folks get totally exhausted from chasing their tails. I would rather we not have to pay the price of Tucker's posturing."

"So we do nothing?" Menna asked, anxious to be reassured.

"Until we get some indications on which to act. I've borrowed some additional explosives-sniffing dogs and their handlers from the Boston and Philadelphia PDs to nose around in the crowds. All of them should be in place tomorrow. Now, let's go home!"

For Khalid, the worst part of the waiting was figuring out what to do with his four guests to keep them occupied and out of trouble. It was only Saturday night, a full week yet to go, and they were restless and horny. Being deliriously certain that their lives would shortly be coming to a spectacular and hugely fulfilling end proved extremely liberating for the four. Khalid tried to impress upon them the need to avoid doing anything that might bring them to the attention of the authorities. He kept them busy loading and unloading trucks and shipping containers, and moving stacks of boxes from one part of the warehouse to another. But, boredom ultimately overcame caution and one or two of them would slip off into the neighborhood, mostly to ogle passing women on the main thoroughfares. Fortunately, the people of the neighborhood apparently mistook the men for Hispanic illegals, of which there were many, so the fact that they spoke virtually no English did not surprise anyone. Only Anna appeared to bother them. They could feel her glaring at them through the office blinds as they puttered around the yard.

Khalid had not heard further from his contact and did not know whether he was yet in the City. He had also heard nothing from the two additional men who were to arrive for the operation. That worried him; he hoped that there would soon be good news.

The President was at Camp David, up late watching an action thriller in the compound's theater because he couldn't sleep. He was in a foul mood, and Roger Norton was careful to sit several rows directly behind him, so that his boss could turn around to shout at him only with great difficulty. Tucker was planning to base his reelection campaign on his unblemished record in keeping America safe from terrorism. But now, the public was beginning to get its wind up because it appeared that its leaders had been far more lucky than competent. The President was particularly bothered by Admiral Bergen's call to his Chief of Staff earlier in the evening informing him that al-Ghabrizi had almost certainly been betrayed to the police and the CIA by parties thus far unknown. That, coupled with the terrorist leader's refusal to speak until it became apparent, before the entire world, that he was not the kingpin whose capture the President had proclaimed a great victory, were the causes of Tucker's fury. He felt that someone was orchestrating a great conspiracy, and it was aimed directly at him.

In Paris, Mohammed was lurking in the back of a darkened night club filled with the heavy, pungent smoke of Turkish tobacco and hashish. It was already past dawn, but nubile women in filmy Arabian Nights costumes continued to dance on a small, spotlighted stage. He was waiting for the signal from his employer that he might approach, having been summoned from his bed. Finally, a flick of the finger and he made his way among the recumbent bodies to a low table near the stage covered with bowls of fruit, sweetmeats, and nuts. Also on the table, was a hookah from which flexible tubes extended, through which smokers drew in the pungent fumes of hashish. The man who spoke to Mohammed had been at the table when Balthazar was given the suitcase full of currency several days earlier.

"Today is the day of Balthazar's operation. Have we heard anything yet?"

"It is today a week, Excellency," Mohammed replied with a bit of trepidation.

"Do we know that everything is proceeding well?"

Mohammed hesitated. His employers had a penchant for reacting to unpleasant news by punishing the messenger, who often was him. But, this time he had little choice but to tell it straight.

"I do not know, Excellency. We have heard nothing from Balthazar since I saw him here in Paris several days ago. But, it is not unusual that he would not communicate at such a time. He has never failed us.

"That is true," came the reply. "But, I do not trust him. He does these things for us only for the money and the challenge. He fancies himself an artist."

Actually, Mohammed knew that Balthazar had departed Paris, and that he had gone to Washington and not New York. If the operation did not occur as scheduled, he would tell this to the employers, and Balthazar would be made to explain. Otherwise, only results mattered. He had already prepared the many the wire transfers that would cumulatively deposit ten million dollars in Balthazar's various offshore bank accounts.

Mohammed uttered reassurances, but his employer had already transferred his attention back to the girls.

CHAPTER THIRTEEN

Fresh from the shower, Hannah was sitting at the breakfast table scrunched in a thick terrycloth robe with the hotel's crest on the pocket. She could hear through the open bathroom door Balthazar singing to himself as he shaved. The room service breakfast, served on elegant china with heavy silver utensils and coffee pots, had been delicious, and Hannah was relaxing before getting dressed.

"You certainly sound happy with yourself," she called in to him.

He stuck his head out the door, his face still dotted with shave cream. "I think that I have every right to be happy with myself," he replied, bestowing upon her a big, conspiratorial smile.

"Do you live this well all the time, or is this fancy hotel room in my honor," she teased.

"I travel deluxe all the time," he assured her. My companies are very successful and, of course, my travel expenses are tax deductible. Since, I am on the road most of time, why should I not enjoy myself."

"You said companies. I thought you had only one."

"Actually, there are five: Continental Fine Foods, Levant Trading Ltd, Marseille International Corporation, and so forth," he responded.

Hannah's attention suddenly sharpened. She had heard or read one of those names before, but couldn't think where. When Balthazar went back into the bathroom, she went to her handbag on the dresser and jotted it down on a scrap of paper. It did not sound like a totally uncommon name, so she could be confusing it for another she had come across somewhere. But, it was odd that it should suddenly ring a bell in her mind.

Balthazar came back into the room, smelling of expensive cologne. He came up behind Hannah and wrapped his arms around her, his hands finding their way inside her robe and around her breasts. As he ran the rough palm of his hand back and forth across her left nipple, he asked: "What shall we do today?"

Khalid drove the Tremont supply truck down to the dock on the East River where the Manhattan Island tour boats were serviced and parked when not in use. Both he and the truck were well known to the tour company people who ran the facility from a small building at the foot of the pier. Security precautions put in place after the World Trade Center attack required armed guards on both the pier and the boats themselves. For Fleet Week, the hired guards had been replaced by National Guardsmen in camouflage fatigues carrying automatic rifles. It was considered a choice assignment among the mobilized weekend warriors, some of whom were from the western end of the state and were in New York City for the first time in their lives.

Mornings on the dock were chaotic as the company's staff and contract suppliers, like Tremont, rushed to get four boats ready to go downstream and around the tip of Manhattan to the tour terminal pier to pick up the passengers who had begun lining up at dawn. In addition to the driver, the Tremont truck carried three helpers who assisted in transferring the crates and boxes of foodstuffs and consumable supplies onto the boats, where they were stowed in the snack bar pantry amidships. Tremont also employed the uniformed food service people who manned the snack bar during the boats' passenger runs. Three days earlier, after helping to unload the truck, Khalid had stayed behind when it left and boarded the next boat to leave downriver. He climbed up to the wheelhouse and chatted with the pilot, who knew Khalid and was happy for the company.

The sun had just risen over Brooklyn as the unburdened tour boat picked up speed. The Guardsman outside the wheelhouse put on his sunglasses and Khalid turned away to watch the heavy traffic on the FDR Drive. The Fleet Week sponsors had lucked out again: it was going to be another fine day.

Khalid mused how, despite himself, he had come to love the city. The longer he was away from the Middle East, from the implacable hatred that soured every moment of daily existence, the more difficult he found it to blame the people who filled New York's buildings and streets. It was critical that hatred be embraced, at least tacitly, by all Muslims as a way of concealing the narrow extremism of the jihad's goals. A universal hatred would also permit the jihad's leaders to declare everyone a combatant and so justify terrorist attacks in population centers all over the world. When he was in Lebanon and in Gaza carrying grenades and an AK-47, Khalid waved his arms and shouted slogans with everyone else, louder perhaps. But, away two years, he had felt the fervor and certainty slipping away, subverted by the comforts of a pleasant, peaceful life in New York thanks to Mr. Ghoravi. But, Khalid's enjoyment of his new life had become increasingly disrupted by pangs of guilt as the media brought the jihad into his life every day. He was still dedicated to the cause, although the indiscriminate killing of innocent people appalled him. For the life of him, however, he could not find an alternative path that he could believe would bring victory. So, eventually, he felt compelled to rejoin the battle, although not so strongly as to abandon the streets of the Bronx for those of Ramallah.

As the boat approached the southern end of Manhattan, traffic on the FDR became even heavier as early arrivals rushed to get the relatively few parking spots available in office building garages at outrageous fees. The police had banned street parking throughout Lower Manhattan, during Fleet Week, as a precaution against car bombs and had closed the streets approaching the waterfront to all but foot traffic. Khalid saw a stream of NYPD radio cars, lights flashing but sirens silent, dispersing to their assigned locations for security and traffic control.

Crowds of people were already in line at the tour terminal when Khalid's boat arrived, soon followed by a second. He got off, watched the passenger embarkation process for a while, then walked downtown toward the piers at which visiting vessels were open to touring. By the time he arrived, long lines of people had already formed at the barriers constructed by the police. The authorities had established a ban on knapsacks, coolers, and other containers that had been well publicized in the media. But, there were still families faced with the choice of saving their picnic lunch or seeing the insides of a British destroyer. It being New York, some enterprising street people had set up a bag minding service complete with claim checks, but with no guarantee that all of your tuna sandwiches would be there when you returned.

Khalid stood for a while closely observing the security check process until he realized that he himself was being watched by a mounted patrolman hovering above the crowd. Trying to appear casual, he sauntered off, making his way to a subway station and the long ride home to the Bronx.

Said Ghoravi stood at the window of his office looking down at the Fleet Week panorama spread out some thirty stories below. He was in his late thirties and of striking appearance that he was told, by other Iranian emigres, resembled the late Shah. His father, who had established the company upon fleeing the Iranian revolution, was an almost dead ringer for the lamented Reza Pahlevi, and had enhanced an extraordinarily successful and lucrative military career by standing in for him at particularly dangerous public appearances.

Maintaining the Caspian Sea Trading Corporation's head office in a skyscraper at the foot of Manhattan was a very expensive luxury for which Ghoravi's now-retired father constantly berated him. The firm could operate just as effectively from a much cheaper loft in Brooklyn or the Bronx he was told. It was true, but such mean surroundings offered none of the satisfaction and feeling of accomplishment that did peering down on the city from such great eminence. He had been in an elevator approaching his floor when the first airliner hit the nearby World Trade Center, the shock wave rattling the rising car. Rushing into his office, along with the staff already present, he saw the smoke and flames erupting from the building's pierced metal latticework. Through the telescope his wife had given him as a gift when the company moved into the office suite, he could see people at windows above and below the impact area waving for attention and rescue that for most would not be possible. When the second plane hit, he knew it was not a terrible accident, and stood riveted at the window as the buildings came down and his own vantage point was enveloped in an impenetrable fog of smoke, dust, and swirling bits of paper that, a short time earlier, may have been memos in someone's in-basket.

This experience and the changes that the event wrought on life in the United States had altered Ghoravi's existence forever. His business required that he travel extensively overseas, and the sharpest and most immediate impact of the nation's catastrophe became apparent at airports, particularly those serving international flights. He was a Muslim with an exotic, foreign name and, although an American citizen, suffered repeated delays and indignities virtually every time he sought to reenter his own country. His wife and two young children, while sheltered in a high end suburb of Westchester County, were nevertheless stared at and occasionally subjected to derogatory remarks while at local shopping centers and fast food restaurants. The kids spoke little Farsi because Ghoravi and his wife had decided that they needed to be completely American, and so virtually ceased speaking it at home. They, of course, knew of the 9/11 disaster and its impact, but couldn't understand why anyone would associate it with them.

Despite the difficulties, and the flashes of resentment he still experienced, standing at his office window looking out at the Fleet Week displays, Ghoravi was content and might even be happy again one day. The business was growing and prospering and his father, still a major shareholder, had gone out of his way to praise his son's stewardship of the family's assets. His expansion program was off to a promising start: operating the refreshment facilities aboard Manhattan tour boats was proving very profitable, and Ghoravi was already looking for additional opportunities. Key to his success was the performance of Tremont and its manager, Omar Khalid, whom Ghoravi had been astute enough to hire, even though he suspected that the Lebanese was in the United States illegally. Ghoravi had picked up

Tremont for practically nothing, and had actually visited it only once: a couple of days before he signed the purchase papers. So long as its customers were happy, and their number increasing, he was content to let Khalid run the show, while he checked the bank deposits. America had been good to the Ghoravi family, and he did not propose to turn away from it. Whatever indignities he and his family had to endure were a hell of a lot better than being in Tehran.

CHAPTER FOURTEEN

The golden age of the U.S. Intelligence Community effectively ended with the disintegration of the Soviet Union and its satellite empire. Over the almost fifty years during which a major Communist military and political menace was recognized, the United States and its principal allies had constructed an awesome intelligence collection and surveillance infrastructure designed principally to provide warning of an impending attack sufficient to preclude destruction of the West's retaliatory capacity. The dominant doctrine of the era, called Mutual Assured Destruction, held that the Communists would not attack if they could not prevent us from inflicting unacceptable damage upon them in return. During the entire course of the Cold War, there was never a moment in which the West detected a Soviet approach to the nuclear threshold nor was there ever a real threat of general, nonnuclear conflict. A good measure of the credit for this is arguably attributable to Soviet inability to achieve strategic surprise on a significant scale and their awareness of that limitation. There was also fear that the United States might misinterpret the evidence of its sensors and attack preemptively.

The Cuban Missile Crisis of 1962 marked the closest approach to war of the two superpowers or, at least, so it appeared in press reports at the time. The Soviets had shipped a number of medium-range ballistic missiles to Cuba and were establishing them in launch positions from whence they would menace the continental United States. The shipments had been detected early by the U.S. Navy and identified, because the size of the missiles required they be shipped as deck cargo, which was seen and photographed by reconnaissance aircraft. The preparation of launch sites in Cuba was detected by low altitude Air Force reconnaissance aircraft and U-2s. When President Kennedy declared a blockade of Cuba, ordered Soviet ships in the Western Atlantic placed under close surveillance, and began to mobilize forces elsewhere, what the world perceived to be a highly dangerous game of nuclear chicken was underway. In fact, the game was nearly over. Western intelligence resources had determined that the Communist political and military leaderships were not posturing for war and, in certain instances, were going to lengths to insure recognition of that fact. Although Soviet Premier Khrushchev could not know how far Kennedy was prepared to go, he signaled that he considered it not worth his while to find out.

The missile crisis occurred when the capabilities of the U.S. intelligence establishment had begun to expand rapidly as perception of a more menacing Communist threat spurred huge investment in advanced technology and greatly expanded staffs to process, analyze, and disseminate the enormous volumes of data collected. The high altitude U-2 aircraft, vulnerable to antiaircraft missiles, was being supplemented and later largely replaced by reconnaissance satellites that provided coverage of military installations, research and development facilities, and other targets inaccessible to surface surveillance. Systems of that era, however, were relatively inflexible, and could undertake only missions of limited duration. The ground targets they could cover on a particular mission had to be predetermined in mission planning, and could not be significantly altered once the satellite was in orbit. Images captured were recorded on film stored in canisters in the vehicle. When they were full or the mission at an end, the canisters were ejected over the Pacific Ocean and their parachutes snagged by specially configured Air Force aircraft as they floated to earth by parachute. Later systems, substantially more maneuverable, collected their images digitally and transmitted them back to Earth soon after capture. This ability made them much more useful in tactical surveillance and, hence, for indications and warning of impending attack.

Growth in satellite imaging capability was paralleled by major expansion of signals intelligence collection and exploitation. Virtually all electronic devices emit signals which, if intercepted, can provide useful intelligence about their source. For example, a radar signal will reveal the make and model of the equipment generating it and, thus, whether it is military or commercial, airborne or surface-mounted. If it is military, electronics order-of-battle will reveal the types and classes of ship, plane, or vehicle in which that equipment is installed and, in many cases, the system intercepting the signal will be able to locate and track the emitter. At sea, the threat from deployed Soviet ballistic missile submarines spurred improvements in the network of hydro-acoustic detection and tracking installations established on the ocean floor to assist the Navy's anti-submarines warfare forces.

Intelligence collection and analysis was greatly facilitated by the advent of digital processors which enabled huge increases in volume and more sophisticated exploitation of intercepted communications traffic. As the computer age burgeoned, the Intelligence Community was at the forefront of customers for successive generations of processors, the latest ones so powerful and expensive that they were accessible only to Government agencies and not affordable to most of them.

From an intelligence perspective, dealing with a massive and powerful opponent is facilitated by the necessary size and complexity of his force composition and of the command and control apparatus needed to direct it. Changes in the status and location of component elements are difficult to conceal, in part because of the heightened communications and logistics activity attendant to them, particularly in the presence of the highly sophisticated intelligence collection and surveillance apparatus that the U.S. and its principal allies were continuously improving and expanding. The Soviets were unavoidably aware of their limited ability to conduct undetected military operations, and eventually ceased attempts to do so on a significant scale.

The term "intelligence failure" is generally taken to mean that the people and organizations responsible for obtaining and properly analyzing the information needed to prevent a catastrophe had not done so, subsequent investigation having shown the necessary intelligence to have been available. However, in the real world, catastrophes occur very rarely, and the likelihood is that the intelligence anomalies one is seeing do not foreshadow a worst-case scenario. Faced with the choice of acting decisively or waiting to see what happens, it is the exceptional watchman who will sound the alarm, particularly when the scenario posited has never occurred before. The great achievement of U.S. intelligence enterprises during the Cold War was essentially to eliminate this vulnerability by so reducing the ambiguity in our day-to-day knowledge of Soviet military activities as to make unwarranted complacency impossible.

In recent years, when international terrorism and narcotics trafficking became the primary threats to national security, the effectiveness of this huge intelligence establishment has been substantially reduced. The massive military forces and infrastructures that lent themselves to continuous photographic surveillance and communications monitoring gave way to small groups of individuals concealing themselves in the social and economic fabric of many of the world's nations. Intelligence collected became fragmentary and increasingly ambiguous because there was no established terrorist command and control infrastructure upon which to focus our surveillance and analysis resources. We knew who the leaders were, but it was not clear who they led and, most important, what specifically they intended to do. As terrorist operations erupted in various areas of the world, investigation showed them to be largely the work of local zealots acting on the inspiration of an Anwar al-Ghabrizi, perhaps with his financial and technical assistance, rather than his direct orders. While the arch-leadership was quick to take credit for virtually everything, investigators in the West could rarely find a direct chain of personal contact linking them to the perpetrators. Most disturbing was that the latter were usually not operatives smuggled into the country to mount the attack, but natives with established local ties and often decent economic prospects who had been persuaded that committing mass murder in the name of Islam was their just destiny.

What further complicated the war on terrorism and narcotics trafficking was that it required a paradigm shift of bureaucratic responsibility within the U.S. Government. The Cold War was a politico-military affair, which meant that virtually all intelligence assets were controlled by the Defense Department, the CIA, and the State Department. The Global War on Terrorism or GeeWot, as it is called in Washington, is, however, also a major law enforcement campaign centered in the Justice Department and the new Department of Homeland Security. Although constrained by law from domestic matters involving American citizens, the CIA and DoD own the bulk of foreign intelligence collection and analysis resources and began scrambling to make them relevant to the new threats and the altered bureaucratic structure.

Intelligence agencies are in business to collect and analyze information they then provide to their customers. Their grades and rewards depend upon success in alerting their clients to the capabilities and intentions of prospective adversaries: military, political, and commercial. While they jockey among themselves for attention, funding, and bureaucratic position, they are aware that a dreaded intelligence failure means that people who needed it did not get the correct word in time to effectively act on it.

Law enforcement agencies, however, are dedicated to catching and prosecuting lawbreakers, and their success is measured, literally and figuratively, by the number of people they put behind bars. Because of competition among federal, state, and local organizations to make the arrests that bring reward and recognition, sharing information with rivals was discouraged lest someone else grab up the perp and the credit. There have been examples of one police organization unknowingly targeting the undercover operations of another, eventually ruining both operations. Such dysfunction was most frequently experienced in counter narcotics operations in which law enforcement agencies at all levels were fully engaged well before counterterrorism stole the spotlight. Arguably, the threat to U.S. homeland security posed by the pervasive traffic in drugs is greater, if now less dramatic, than the GWOT, but the local dealer is far less fearsome than the unknown suicide bomber lurking in the subway, theatre, or shopping mall.

The World Trade Center catastrophe and subsequent investigations exposed the structural and operational weaknesses of the country's intelligence establishment, and contributed directly to creation of the Department of Homeland Security and the office of Director of National Intelligence. However well-intended these changes, their near term impact was largely opposite to the improvements required. A major bureaucratic restructuring within the Federal Government (probably within any government) requires years to sort itself out, as the newly ascendant organizations attempt to exercise their authority and responsibilities, while the losers seek to save what they can and delay giving up the rest. Observers of the Intelligence Community talk about "stovepipes," the vertical orientation of component agencies, which makes difficult cooperation and information sharing across bureaucratic boundaries. The law enforcement community, if anything, is probably worse. Mitigating this fundamental flaw was the primary purpose for creating the DHS and ODNI. However, it was not yet clear that the inevitable one step backward was complete, and that the two steps forward had begun.

Balthazar checked out of the Willard early Monday morning, and took a cab through a light rain to Union Station and the 8 AM high-speed train to New York City. He could have taken the air shuttle to LaGuardia, but wanted the more leisurely train ride to get himself focused on the tasks of the week ahead. He had visited New York many times on business, and knew Manhattan as well as a native. He liked it as well as he liked Paris, and looked forward to its amenities and to just wandering the streets. On an earlier visit, he had gone downtown to the site of the World Trade Center curious to experience his reaction. He was awed by the immensity of the melancholy site and the achievement of the hijackers in bringing the buildings down. Now, his employers expected his operations to surpass theirs, although both he and they knew that was virtually impossible.

Nothing equals the shock of the new, and no terrorist event after 9/11, no matter how spectacular, will have the same impact on the American people. There were many battles in World War II that produced more casualties and more lost ships and planes, but the impact of Pearl Harbor will last forever.

Balthazar arrived in New York in late morning, and took a taxi from the rank outside Penn Station to the Waldorf, where he stayed when in the City, and where they knew and treated him very well. The rain had ended and, as the cab inched through heavy crosstown traffic, Balthazar looked out at women hurrying along the sidewalks, perhaps to an early lunch. When he heard his satellite phone ring, he absentmindedly pulled it from a pocket of his raincoat on the seat beside him and answered in French. There was no response, and he punched the Off button disgusted with himself. He knew that he should not have answered.

The shock of Balthazar's voice caused everyone in the laboratory to jump. They had not really expected anyone to answer, and all of them stared at al-Ghabrizi's phone lying on a workbench. A moment later the word came through that the receiving instrument was probably located in New York City, and the chief of the Al-Ghabrizi Working Group rushed out to find Hannah. She was in her office staring at the Islamic wall hanging that Jerry had admired and thinking about the Sunday she had spent with Balthazar. They had wandered about the city, first to the Capitol, then down the Mall to the Washington Monument and beyond to the Lincoln Memorial, mingling with the early season groups of tourists, their members wearing the same caps or T-shirts for identification and esprit de corps. Although there was rain in the air, it held off, and a pleasant breeze off the Potomac kept the ubiquitous humidity at bay. After a rest, they walked on into Georgetown and, finally exhausted, went for an early dinner they lingered over for three hours. Then, it was a quick cab ride back to the Willard and to bed.

She had slept with him until the wake-up phone call came at 6 AM. They showered together and she watched him dress: the white shirt with long-pointed European collar, the gold cuff links, and patterned Hermes tie. He was a practiced traveler; it took him no time to pack, and suddenly he was gone. He told Hannah that he would be at the Waldorf for the next week, and asked her to come to stay with him, at least for the next weekend. It was that she was thinking about when the AGWOG chief burst in on her.

"It looks like one of the people on al-Ghabrizi's speed dial is in New York," he panted.

Coming back to reality was unpleasant. "Damn! Now, it is really in the fan," she exclaimed. "Who knows about this?"

"No one yet. But you'd better get to the Admiral before the Ops people do. I imagine he'll want to get to Bierschmidt and the President before the word leaks out."

Hannah rushed down the corridor to Bergen's suite. She knew that he was somewhere downtown, but figured that his secretary would know the best way to locate him. She ended up reaching him on his secure cell phone, and was relieved to learn that she was the first to bring him the alarming news. As anticipated, he decided to head immediately for the White House, and asked Hannah to meet him there. On the way out to her car, she stopped to phone Jerry, whom she located at his desk in John Cook's outer office. Hannah didn't tell him the news, but asked him to meet her in the Situation Room in half an hour. She did not want him to have time to pass the word on to others before the Director got downtown.

The White House was still at general quarters over the revelation that al-Ghabrizi was not the great catch the President had made him out to be. It was also disturbed and perplexed by the indications that the onetime terrorist kingpin had been betrayed to the CIA, presumably by people within his own organization. This news was not yet public, although media commentators were speculating on the oddity of the affair. It took no great leap of imagination to conclude that a new leader had forced al-Ghabrizi out and taken his place. The problem was that the country's community of counterterrorist agencies had no idea who that might be and what he might be up to. This failing did not inspire confidence in the President's leadership or his reelection prospects.

Tucker began shouting at Bierschmidt and Bergen as soon as they entered the Oval Office, evincing looks of gratitude from Cook and Norton who had been the sole targets until then.

"Why didn't we know about this, or at least suspect it, when we first caught the sonofabitch?" he complained.

"You'll recall, Mr. President, that we were, in fact, very suspicious at the time, particularly as it became more likely that the guy might really be al-Ghabrizi," Bierschmidt, The Director of National Intelligence, replied.

"Then how come I was allowed to make an ass of myself at that press conference?" The President was staring at Roger Norton, who was visibly squirming.

"I was led to believe that our intelligence was good, and that the bastard was who we thought he was," Norton stammered avoiding the fire coming from the eyes of the others standing before the President. Tucker did not miss the barely suppressed reactions, and told himself that he had probably saved Norton's life. He was realist enough to recognize that Roger was his creation, and could not be held solely responsible for the hole in which they found themselves, although that wouldn't prevent him from making the hapless aide's life miserable until things improved.

"Well, what do we do now?" Tucker demanded. "The media is going to start harping on the fact that we don't know who the new leader is, or if there really is one. They're going to start again with their damned confidence polls, and our ratings are going to slide rapidly back into the toilet. We need to do something preemptive now."

Norton responded with a sly smile, and Bergen and Bierschmidt knew that trouble was coming.

"I recommend," he started, looking only at the President and carefully avoiding the stares of the others, "that we put out the word that we were suspicious of al-Ghabrizi all along, but played along because we suspected that his organization was up to something, and wanted to get out ahead in preparing our countermeasures."

"And what would that something be, Roger?" Bergen asked incredulously.

Norton thought for a moment. "How about an attack here in the United States?"

Cook jumped in here. "That's ridiculous, Mr. President. We can't go conjuring up threats just to get peoples' attention off our screw-up. Remember when we raised the national threat level just to cover our asses? We got creamed!"

He looked to the intelligence directors for support, but they hesitated. "Actually, Mr. President, there is something new. That's why we came here today," explained the DNI. He looked to Bergen, who relayed to the group the information about the satellite phone call that Hannah had provided him with earlier.

"What does it mean?" Tucker asked.

"We don't really know," Bergen admitted. "On the face of it, it means that someone who has communicated with al-Ghabrizi often enough to be in his speed dial register is now in New York. There could be a non-alarming explanation, like the handset was stolen by an unwitting thief, but we, of course, cannot afford to take the chance."

"So, we need to visibly demonstrate that we are protecting the country," Norton proposed as the President nodded.

The President's Chief-of-Staff once again intervened. "We are going outside the purview of these gentlemen, sir. This is becoming a domestic law enforcement matter, and needs to be handed over to the FBI and the Homeland Security Department. There are also the state and local agencies to be considered. The public safety people in New York City are particularly sensitive, since 9/11, about being kept in the loop."

Tucker waved his hands. "Bring in whoever you believe needs to play, but keep them from trying to one-up one another. We can't afford to look stupid, particularly in New York."

"I believe the City has just begun its Fleet Week celebration. The people up there will be especially sensitive to anything we try to do while they're so preoccupied," Cook observed.

"But, it's also the kind of target that terrorists would give their eye teeth to strike," Bergen added grimly.

Norton's earlier pallor had disappeared, and he was smiling contentedly.

While waiting for the DNI and Admiral Bergen to come out of the Oval Office (or be thrown out), Hannah briefed Jerry on the satellite telephone episode in New York. He immediately called Assistant Director Detwiler who asked that he and Hannah come over to his office at FBI Headquarters the next morning. Detwiler had been content to keep the FBI out of the spotlight in the al-Ghabrizi affair, particularly when it blew up in the White House's face. He was happy to let the CIA and other Intelligence Community agencies take the flak, although the FBI, and virtually all of the Government's major departments, were also members. Each had its own intelligence element, some large others small, that participated in the interagency committees and other mechanisms intended to facilitate information sharing and other cooperative operations. However, the FBI and other law enforcement agencies traditionally did not believe themselves to be in the intelligence business, except as customers, and coined special descriptions to avoid labeling as intelligence information collected by their agents and other operations.

But, Detwiler could not ignore the satellite phone business, even if he wished to, because he did not want the CIA screwing around in Bureau territory. New York City was clearly a domestic venue, but the activities of the hijackers that culminated in the World Trade Center calamity had blurred the boundary between foreign intelligence and domestic law enforcement and, thus, between the agencies responsible for them. While whatever was to be done in New York would be led by the FBI, all they had to work on, thus far, was a vague implication of a possible threat from an unknown source provided by the CIA. He also knew that the City people believed themselves capable of running their own show without Washington's interference. Rick Caplin would not be happy to hear from him.

On Tuesday morning, Omar Khalid got to the Tremont yard early, only to find his four guests already there. They had climbed the fence and forced the door of the office, and, when he found them, were happily watching a cartoon show on the television set. He was furious. Had they been spotted by a passing patrol car, the whole operation would have been blown. But, he had nothing to keep them occupied and concealed while they waited, and was grateful that the TV set absorbed their attention and kept them out of trouble. There was a set in the room Khalid had rented for them, and they had spent Monday afternoon watching soap operas. When they came back to the yard after Anna had gone home, they peppered Khalid, in Arabic, with questions about the characters and plots. Initially, he tried to explain them, but quickly realized that neither he nor they knew what was going on. So, he made things up that appeared to satisfy the men and amused him. But, he was relieved that he would have to do it for only five more days.

Anna continued to be a concern: her dislike and suspicion of the sudden visitors was becoming unrestrained. They, in turn, glared at the office bungalow while puttering about the yard, particularly when they thought she was looking out at them, which was most of the time. Khalid went to extraordinary lengths to keep them separated, in part against the possibility that Anna might tip off the police or the FBI, but mostly because he liked the old woman, notwithstanding that she was a pain in the ass.

He was both concerned and annoyed that it was already Tuesday and he had not yet heard from his contact regarding the coming operation. It had occurred to him that perhaps something had gone wrong and the operation would not come off, and he had been surprised to discover that he was not sure that he cared. This bothered him increasingly. Why would one undertake such a dangerous venture for a reason in which one no longer believed? He could end up in prison for the rest of his life or even die. Khalid also wondered idly what he would do with the four soap opera lovers, if there was to be no operation.

Anna always arrived at the yard punctually at 9 AM, so Khalid made sure that the men were out of the office before then. He had just shoved them out of the building when the phone rang. Answering, he recognized the voice immediately.

"Good morning, Mr. Khalid."

"Where are you?"

"I am in midtown Manhattan. Are you prepared for our undertaking?"

"You must decide that," Khalid replied. "Only four of the six men have arrived."

There was a momentary hesitation. "I had forgotten that you were not told. The other two encountered an unfortunate problem about which I will tell you later. We must proceed without them."

Khalid was incredulous. "How can we do that?" he protested. "They were the ones who know how to drive the ship."

The voice did not hesitate. "That is easily overcome. You will make the crew pilot the boat."

Balthazar continued: "I want to meet with you to go over the plan. In honor of our cooperative venture, I will treat you to dinner at perhaps the finest Moroccan restaurant in the world, including even Morocco. It is called The Mediterranean, and it is on West 58th Street between Fifth and Sixth. I will meet you there at 8 PM."

"How will I know you?" Khalid asked.

"I will recognize you." Balthazar responded. "By the way, if you need to contact me, here is my cell phone number..."

After Balthazar hung up, Khalid stood frozen in place, not noticing that Anna had come in and was staring at him.

"Has someone died?" she asked.

"Perhaps, I have," he responded. Then, seeing the startled look on her face, he assured her that he was joking. But, he wasn't. The failure of the two ship handlers to appear meant that he had to go on the boat. He had not planned to do that, nor did he want to. As he looked out the office window at the men puttering about in the yard, he began to search for a way out.

CHAPTER FIFTEEN

FBI Headquarters is a hugely unattractive building occupying a full block on Pennsylvania Avenue in downtown Washington. Whatever the original intent of its architect, its fortress-like design fortuitously facilitated the anti-terrorist security precautions that were implemented after the infamous truck-bombing of the U.S. Marine barracks in Beirut, Lebanon in 1980, expanded following the Oklahoma City bombing, and again after the World Trade Center disaster.   Streets around the White House and Capitol had been closed permanently after the latter, and hopefully impenetrable barriers installed around major monuments and office buildings to prevent explosives-laden vehicles from approaching close enough to inflict significant damage. Effort was made to prevent the city looking like it was under siege (for example, steel beams sunk in the pavement were concealed inside graceful bollards) and, eventually, the public became used to the restrictions, which were absorbed into the tribulations of everyday life.

The Pennsylvania Avenue entrance to the FBI building was closed and barricaded, as were all but two of the other accesses. Each of those was protected by uniformed guards carrying automatic weapons and accompanied by explosives-sniffing dogs. Visitors were subjected to airport-style inspection and required to wait in a garage-level room until someone from the office they were visiting came to pick them up. On Wednesday morning, a small group of people met in a conference room on the 7th floor, called Mahogany Row by insiders because it was the floor on which the Director and other senior officials had their paneled offices. Assistant Director Detwiler sat at the head of the table, Hannah on his left and Jerry Ogden on his right. Six special agents, five men and a woman, completed the assembly.

James Detwiler was a prominent example of the successful FBI careerist, rising over the course of twenty-three years from rookie agent fresh out of college to his present eminence. He still had the crewcut, collegiate look prized by the Bureau, but was having difficulty with his waistline and the fit of his suit coats. The body strap of his fine leather shoulder holster, a gift from his parents when he graduated from the FBI Academy, was straining at the outermost hole. When it was new, the fifth hole was needed to keep his weapon from flapping against his side.

There were a number of Assistant Directors, most of whom were assigned to oversee specific aspects of the Bureau's operations and administration. Detwiler, however, was dedicated to covering the Director's backside in matters of particular interest to the White House and the national media. He had picked Jerry Ogden from the pack, and sent him to John Cook's office to be his eyes and ears, not only because of the young man's operational achievements, but because he looked and comported himself as an FBI special agent should, that is, as Assistant Director Detwiler believed he himself did.

After receiving Jerry's call, Detwiler had put out an internal levy for the five agents now at the table. He asked for the most capable people available, preferably with operational experience in New York City. He had also alerted the New York Field Office, one of the Bureau's largest, the major preoccupation of which with fighting organized crime was increasingly shared with counterterrorism. Normally, the case would be assigned to

New York with, perhaps, reinforcement from Washington. But, Detwiler felt instinctively that this one would be different. The White House was completely engulfed by the al-Ghabrizi fiasco and was hypersensitive to any indication, however tenuous, that something else was going on about which it did not know. The flimsiness of the satellite telephone business disturbed him, particularly since it relied on information from CIA rather than from an FBI source, the reliability of which he could better assess.

Creating a fuss in New York City was always problematical because, playing on a grand stage, it became magnified, frequently out of proportion to its ultimate significance. The City's public safety and law enforcement people, a number of whom were ex-FBI and ex-CIA, resented what they considered to be Washington's interference in their business, most especially Federal agencies' refusal to fully share intelligence and to provide compensation for staff-hours expended on their behalf. When Deputy Mayor Caplin had queried the Washington intelligence and homeland security communities several weeks earlier about potential threats to New York's impending Fleet Week, he had been told that none had been detected. Now, Detwiler was faced with having to say otherwise with virtually nothing to back him up. Bureaucratically, the expedient thing to do would be to tell the head of the New York office to call Caplin or the Police Commissioner and tell him about the cell phone intercept, offer Federal assistance if they requested it, and promise to keep them informed of further developments. That way, responsibility would be shifted to New York and a big fuss avoided over what would likely turn out to be nothing.

But, it was precisely that line of reasoning that gave Detwiler pause. The rationale for downplaying and, thus, ignoring this incident was too strong. Given that everyone involved had other things to do, it is likely that nothing beyond a couple of phone calls would ever take place. Did the intelligence in hand, as fragmentary as it was, deserve a stronger reaction? How, he wondered, could he hedge the probability that there was nothing to this by doing something that could alert them in time that their belief was erroneous?

Detwiler directed everyone in the room to identify themselves to the group and to give a synopsis of their backgrounds and experience. The newly assigned agents knew Jerry, at least by sight or reputation, but were surprised when Hannah identified herself as a CIA officer. That was noted by Detwiler as he began to brief the group.

"To the extent something develops from the information we now have in hand," he told them, "it will be a joint operation including the CIA, perhaps other intelligence agencies, as well as other law enforcement agencies in the Department of Homeland Security. Being that the focal point of activity appears to be within the United States, the FBI will be in charge of any investigation or operation. But, we will be working with state and local agencies that may very well have greater insight to the case than we do. Since we are talking New York, this could turn out to be a very big deal whether it needs to or not. All of us need to work hard to keep the situation in hand."

Having gotten, in advance, permission to brief at a lower security classifiecation level, Hannah told them about al-Ghabrizi's satellite phone, the tests the Agency had performed, and the location in New York of one of its speed dial correspondents.

"How do we know it's the same phone and that it was in New York?" one of the new agents asked.

"When you use your cell phone anywhere in the country, Hannah explained, the telephone company knows that it's your phone, for billing purposes, because every instrument has a unique identifier that goes out with the dial-up when you make a call. The satellite phone system is the same, only worldwide.

The phone company also knows the specific antenna towers sending and receiving your cell phone transmission, and can pinpoint your location very precisely by triangulation. The similar capabilities for a satellite phone system are located in the birds. They cannot geolocate as well as GPS, but well enough at least to determine that you are in a particular city. The information collected regarding who's calling whom and where their phone terminals are located is downlinked to the company's computers for billing and system management purposes. We catch it on the way down."

"How do we know the phone wasn't stolen by someone who has absolutely nothing to do with al-Ghabrizi?" another agent asked.

"We don't", Hannah replied, "since we have no idea to whom the phone being called belongs. We checked with the phone company, and learned that the service subscription is registered to a company in Damascus that, as far as we can determine, does not exist. We are hoping to find out who is paying the bills, but so far no joy."

Detwiler intervened: "Let's look at the big picture and see what we know."

Jerry took over at this point.

"What we've got," he began, "is a long, very thin thread linked to Anwar al-Ghabrizi. When he was captured in Karachi, he was meeting with two young men to whom he was supposed to give expense money and send on to a rendezvous in Paris. The men are Egyptians who had just finished terrorist recruit training and were being sent on their first, and probably last, mission. We sent them to Cairo for interrogation and, if they knew anything, we would now know it also. They didn't, and the only thing of possible use we got out of it is that they are both seamen, ship handlers from the Red Sea."

Hannah continued: "We believe that the mission they were intended to participate in was important, if al-Ghabrizi himself went to brief them, even if subsequent events have shown that he is not the big wheel he once was. So, if two and two can be put together, we might conclude that the operation in which the two were to participate involved boats or ships and is to take place in a maritime or riverine location."

"If there was such an operation planned," one of the agents asked, "how do we know that it wasn't cancelled when the sailors didn't show up?"

"Good question," Detwiler interposed.

"It is a good question," Hannah admitted. "We don't know, but we can't afford to drop it until we've checked out the possibility to a higher level of confidence."

"How will we know when we've reached that higher level?" the agent asked. "It seems to me that, if we don't come up with some hard intelligence, we're operating on gut instinct alone."

"Let's continue," Detwiler ordered.

Jerry resumed: "The Agency has done extensive analysis of the traffic to and from the satellite phone that was captured with al-Ghabrizi. He apparently didn't use the phone very much for initiating calls; most of his calls were incoming from locations around the Middle East. The actual subscribers he talked with are, as you would guess, untraceable. Some of the numbers he called, a number of them on speed dial, connected through a relay switch in Damascus. We believe it was one of those numbers that rang in New York."

"The only other thing to be added," Hannah concluded, "is that I interviewed al-Ghabrizi the other day. He told me that he didn't know anything specific about the operation the seamen were to participate in, and was tasked only to use his eminence to impress upon them its importance. He said that he had gotten his directions in Karachi over the phone from someone he refused to identify. I believe that he was likely telling the truth, or most of it, and may very well have known the person who sent him to the meeting only through business contact rather than personally."

"Why do you say that?" the female agent asked.

"Because we have very good indication that whoever sent al-Ghabrizi to the meeting ratted him out to the Pakistani police and to us. I think that he would have been reluctant to do so, if al-Ghabrizi could identify him to revengeful friends."

"Might this be someone who intended to replace him as top dog?"

"Quite possibly," Hannah responded. "But, that may be the final daisy in our chain. While this unknown person may have betrayed al-Ghabrizi in order to replace him, it is also possible that it was done as a diversion to confuse and distract us, which it has surely done. From that perspective, the willingness to sacrifice so iconic a personage could attest to the importance of the planned operation. It would also indicate that the United States, at home or overseas, is the target."

She turned to look at Detwiler, signifying that was all. He looked around the group at the table to see whether anyone had something to add. At first, there was silence, then the first agent who had spoken added hesitantly: "I'm not sure it makes sense that someone who was planning such an important operation would hurt its chances by sacrificing the Egyptian seaman, who were apparently so important to it."

Detwiler looked at Hannah, she shrugged. He sat staring at the far wall for a long interval, then he shrugged as well and spoke to the group.

"As you have all pointed out, this is very tenuous stuff, and there is probably nothing in it. But, these are extraordinary times and strange circumstances and, I believe, that we cannot afford to ignore any possibility of danger, particularly to New York. I've ordered up a plane to fly us all up there tomorrow morning. Please present yourselves at our National Airport ramp at 0730, prepared for an indefinite stay. Thank you very much. That will be all."

He turned to Hannah and Jerry, as the other agents left the room muttering among themselves. The idea of a special mission in New York working for an Assistant Director appealed to them. But, they hadn't the foggiest idea what they were going to do up there.

"Admiral Bergen has asked that we include you in our party, Hannah."

"He told me, sir."

"Since I will not be able to stay up there full time, Special Agent Ogden will be in charge of the Washington party, working in conjunction with our New York Field Office. We are not going up to do street work, but to provide a direct connection between

Federal and local organizations, particularly with respect to intelligence support. We cannot allow something to happen because we failed to cooperate. To be entirely candid, for your ears only, I am ordering this expedition not so much because I accept the threat as real, but because I want to cover our asses in the event something does happen. With all of this al-Ghabrizi business going on, the public will lynch us, if we get caught as we did on 9/11."

"We understand, sir," Jerry acknowledged. Hannah nodded.

"On the way to my current exalted position," the AD confided with a rueful smile, "I spent many years in intelligence which, in the FBI, has not been a preferred career path. The aspect of it that fascinated me most was the transition from intelligence to operations, the point at which information and analysis become the basis for decision and consequent action. As both of you know, particularly you Hannah, that transition is often not clearly defined and the ambiguities of a situation, as well as the biases brought to it, lead to inaction or wrong responses. There are all sorts of considerations that occur to the decisionmaker, not all of them objective. The decision that we could not spare the agent staff-hours needed to check-out some Middle Easterners taking flying lessons makes sense only if it was tacitly assumed that they did not intend to crash planes into the World Trade Center or do some other evil deed, and that the prospect of getting an ass-chewing for going over budget was a more realistic possibility. At the time, these were not unreasonable considerations, but they proved disastrous."

Detwiler was now pacing the room, turning frequently toward Hannah and Jerry, who were fascinated.

"The problem," he continued, "is that we need a way to deal with the ambiguities, the competing demands, the professional risks, and all the other crap that can keep us from getting it right. But, there is no magic method, particularly when every situation is different. I believe the only thing you can do is to make your best, most objective assessment and then figure out how you can reasonably hedge the possibility that you are wrong. The available intelligence, such as it is, does not make a compelling case that a terrorist attack is coming or that it will occur in New York. You guys are part of my hedge. See you tomorrow."

CHAPTER SIXTEEN

Said Ghoravi stood at the window of his office looking out over the harbor and up the Hudson River shore of Manhattan. He did this every morning, sipping his coffee and thinking over the day's prospects. The spectacular view usually also prompted broader and grander thoughts about his life, family, and ambitions. He recognized that he and his wife were extraordinarily lucky to have made, with their families, so successful a transition from the revolution-driven chaos of Tehran to a more than comfortable life in America. As he looked down through the wispy morning haze that hung over the water, Ghoravi could think of nothing that might alter this pleasant state of affairs.

This morning, in the middle of Fleet Week, there was a lot more to see than usual. The full complement of visiting ships was arrayed below him, some tied up at piers others anchored offshore, all with colorful bunting strung from bow to masthead to stern. Visiting hours had not yet begun, but by pressing his face against the window, he could look down into the street and see the crowds already coming from the Staten Island Ferry slips at the Battery and fanning out toward the visiting entrances. Through his telescope, Ghoravi could also see the knots of policemen gathering on nearby corners, getting ready to man checkpoints throughout the downtown area, and to patrol the crowds looking for suspicion-raising people and suspect parcels and containers that might bear explosives.

As he watched, a Manhattan Island tour boat came into his field of view, moving rapidly from the East River, around the Battery, and up the Hudson to the pier at which it would pick up its first load of passengers. Ghoravi smiled at the thought that each of those loads made the Caspian Sea Trading Company richer. He made a mental note to visit Tremont after Fleet Week, and to give his manager, Omar Khalid, a bonus for handling the additional workload so well.

Ghoravi's secretary appeared in the doorway.

"There's a gentleman named Balthazar on the phone," she said, "who would like to pay you a short visit this afternoon, if you will be available."

"Do I know him?" Ghoravi asked.

"He says that he is the owner of Marseille International Corporation, one of your suppliers."

"I recognize the company name. Do I have time?" She nodded.

"Then I will see him."

After making the appointment, Balthazar left the drug store phone and began to stroll over to Times Square. He never made operational calls from his hotel room or even the lobby because of the possibility, however unlikely, that he was being watched. When he arrived in another city on an operation, he purchased a disposable cell phone using a false name. That was the number he had given Khalid. His satellite phone had a sterile number, but he regretted the slip he had made in thoughtlessly answering it in the taxi the other day. However, it was unlikely to signify anything, he concluded, since he could not be identified.

It was a gorgeous day. Balthazar circled Grand Central Terminal and headed west on 42nd Street, the sidewalks crowded with office workers headed out for an early lunch, to shop, or just to stroll along with him. He knew that there were trendier hotels than the Waldorf at which to stay, but it reminded him of the grand Parisian hotels, and he loved its quiet luxury and art deco charm. Balthazar's modus operandi was designed to avoid the international byways in which he or his activities might come to the notice of intelligence or law enforcement agencies. He never actively participated in either the preparation or execution of his operations, carefully employing people who could not be connected to him or his companies. In recent years, he had been instructed by his employers to structure his spectaculars as martyrdom operations, in which the actual perpetrators destroyed themselves in the course of execution. The intended martyrs were provided to Balthazar, along with a considerable advance payment, at the beginning of preparations, and were conveniently not available for questioning afterward. Balthazar visited the sites of his operations early on, and developed the basic structure of the plan: the target, the strike scenario, the resources required, and the timing. Generally, he did this in response to a list of high priority targets provided by his employers. Since these were invariably cities that he often visited, he could arrive and depart not unnoticed, but unremarked. By the time an operation actually came off, he was demonstrably elsewhere.

New York City had been at the top of his list for a long time, but security conditions and the lack of a strong plan had kept kept him from taking action. Unlike previous operations, the idea for the current venture had come from Khalid and needed to be checked out, which Balthazar did, visiting New York while Khalid was awaiting a response. It was immediately evident to him that the proposal was a good one, requiring only a bit of his own special elaboration. When he called Khalid for the first time, it was from a phone booth in Grand Central Terminal.

Balthazar took the subway downtown, and walked from the station to Ghoravi's office building, detouring to the waterfront in Battery Park. He looked out at the beflagged ships anchored offshore, noting the guard boats circling them at a distance and the white patrol boats with red Coast Guard stripes darting about amidst the considerable traffic. Before heading to his destination, he watched a ferry from Staten Island, red, white, and blue bunting hung from the upper deck, pull into its terminal loaded with passengers eager to get quickly to the Fleet Week visiting piers.

Ghoravi was seated behind his desk when Balthazar was ushered into the room, and went immediately to the window, leaving his host in the midst of standing up to shake hands.

"You have an absolutely marvelous view, Mr. Ghoravi. I am envious," he said, turning from the window with his hand extended. "My name is John Balthazar, and I appreciate your taking the time to meet with me. I'm in New York on company business, and would like to compare notes with one of my good customers."

Ghoravi was puzzled, but also flattered that such an obviously prosperous and well-spoken man would be interested in visiting him. Perhaps, he was going to try to sell him more of whatever it was that he was buying from Marseille International. So, after his secretary had brought coffee and they had exchanged small talk about the weather and the Fleet Week crowds, he beckoned Balthazar to an easy chair and sat down opposite him.

"Your visit is a pleasant break in my day," he told him. "How can I help you?"

"It occurred to me," Balthazar replied, "that you and I have a great deal in common. We are both in international trade of fine foods, our parents were immigrants to our adopted countries, and we are both Muslims. You do still practice it, don't you?"

Ghoravi nodded, wondering how Balthazar knew so much about him.

"I am considering moving my home to the United States," Balthazar continued, and would be most interested in your views and experiences since you and your family arrived from Iran. I recognize that there are significant differences in our circumstances, but I particularly want to learn of your treatment as a Muslim, especially after the attack in 2001."

"Are you having discrimination problems in France?" Ghoravi asked.

"Not personal," his visitor replied, "at least not yet. My home and business headquarters are in Marseille, but I spend most of my time in Paris, when I'm not traveling abroad. As you know, there are large, poor Muslim populations in both cities, many members of which were born in France and are citizens of the country. I myself am one of them, but I have been able to escape the ghetto and create a successful life for myself."

"But, the vast majority of Muslims in France are underemployed and have limited opportunity," Balthazar continued. "They are fertile ground in which jihadist movements have taken root. The young people have progressed from overturning trash cans to burning cars to blowing up trains. And it is not simply to be blamed on extremist religious teachings. They are convinced that it is the only way to get attention."

Ghoravi grunted in disapproval. "Are you campaigning on their behalf?" he asked.

Balthazar looked momentarily surprised. "I would not do that," he replied after a moment. "It is characteristic of an extremist movement, whatever its persuasion, that its followers come to consider themselves deserving of success simply because they believe so strongly and clearly in their cause. For people like that, being given the opportunity to improve or to prosper is not nearly enough. They require surrender and revenge for past sins. I have no sympathy for people who will not take advantage of opportunity, whether offered or taken, and I shudder at the possibility that the jihadis will succeed."

Ghoravi was mollified. "I agree with you," he said. "Fortunately, we do not have that situation here in America, at least not nearly to the extent it exists in Europe and elsewhere. We have segments of society against which there is discrimination. But, they are not persuaded that the way to salvation is through blowing things up and mass killing. There are individuals and small groups at the extremes who will attempt terrorist acts, but the interesting thing is that the masses they claim to represent will not support them or provide them cover. Most foiled terrorist adventures have resulted from information being provided to the authorities by members of the community in a position to observe and become suspicious of what was happening in their apartment buildings and neighborhoods."

"Is this true also here in New York City?" Balthazar asked. "There are so many people, with so many different nationalities and religions, not to mention political beliefs, that I would imagine it is difficult for the authorities to keep track of them all. I can see, for example, that the security precautions for Fleet Week are very extensive. But, do you think the police and the FBI have any idea whether or not there is a terrorist plot hatching somewhere in Brooklyn or The Bronx?"

"I certainly hope they would know," was the response. "The City is still a primary target, the more so now that it is on guard and will present a greater challenge. I would assume that, if some group does try it again, they will try for something even more spectacular than 9/11."

Balthazar frowned sympathetically. "You sound very concerned," he said.

Ghoravi stood up abruptly, and went to the window. "I moved into this office about this time in 2001. Every morning that I was here, I stood as I do now looking out at Manhattan. Once upon a time, the World Trade Center was there, and it is not there now.

You are right. I am concerned."

Tom Keener was royally pissed. His assignment as CIA's Station Chief in Paris was supposed to be a secret, concealed by his cover as Third Secretary of the American Embassy. In an allied country like France, the counterpart security services knew about Keener and, indeed, there was continuing cooperation on intelligence matters, particularly those relating to terrorism. But, no one else was supposed to know. His safety and ability to do his job depended on it.

Yet, he was waiting on a Metro station platform on his way home that evening, when a man came up behind him,

174

shoved an envelope into his pocket, and made off into the crowd. In an earlier time, on a more dangerous assignment, Keener would have reacted more quickly and, perhaps, collared the man, certainly gotten a good look at him. But, this was his last posting before retirement and part of his consternation came from the realization, thus far suppressed, that he was past it. All that he had been able to tell was that his assailant was short and, perhaps, partly bald.

The envelope contained a single sheet of paper with two lines of writing in French: "I can identify the person responsible for betraying Anwar al-Ghabrizi. The price will be three million dollars US." This was followed by an EMail address at one of the free Internet services that blanket the world. Keener had gone immediately back to his office to see what he could learn about the EMail address without having to tell the French about the anonymous offer. What he learned was both enlightening and discouraging.

It is possible for literally anyone to open an EMail account using a false identity and postal address. Since the service is free, no credit card numbers or monthly checks need change hands, and there are no ties between the service and its subscribers. The EMail account, resident in a computer maintained by the service, is in effect a dead drop, with one extraordinary difference: it is essentially impossible to apprehend a person coming to the drop to pick up messages. Given a password created by the subscriber, the account can be entered from any place that offers access to the Internet, which is, increasingly, everywhere. The authorities can monitor the account to detect access attempts, and even trace such attempts electronically back to the computer or cell phone from which they originated, but they can't react to that discovery fast enough to dispatch agents or officers to catch the perpetrator in the act of sending and receiving. The astute user will log on at a workstation in a public library, airport, or internet cafe, never use the same one twice or at the same time of day, and scatter accesses over a broad geographic area.

While determining all of this, Keener sent a flash message marked URGENT: DIRECTOR to Headquarters at Langley in which he quoted the offer received and requested instructions. His secure telephone began to ring within fifteen minutes. Headquarters, of course, wanted more information about the prospective source, and was forced to acknowledge that no successful effort toward that end could be mounted without bringing in the French. The possibility was considered of offering up a cover story to explain why the particular assistance was needed, but it was quickly exposed as too risky. It was likely that the EMail box in question would become the medium for communication with the informant. So, if the French services were brought in to help monitor activity to and from that address, they would quickly learn what was going on, and would be royally pissed-off by a lame subterfuge. It was decided to bring in the Sûreté and, when monitoring facilities were in place, Keener was instructed to send a message to the Email address asking for evidence that the source was in a position to provide the information offered. The message he sent was picked up later in the day by the account subscriber operating from a location in a distant suburb of the city. It was answered the following morning from a Starbucks in the street that runs in front of the American Embassy. The response provided the correct names of the Egyptians who were with al-Ghabrizi at the time of his capture, as well as the name of the Pakistani security police officer in charge of the raiding party.

After leaving Detwiler, Hannah and Jerry walked back to the White House, showed their passes to the uniformed Secret Service officer at the Pennsylvania Avenue gate, and went immediately to the Situation Room to check for new developments. There was nothing new, only a message for Hannah to call the Director's office at the Agency. She dialed the number on a secure phone, while Jerry went up to check his desk in John Cook's suite.

"Hannah, hold for the Director."

She was shocked and alarmed. They had only been away at the FBI for a couple of hours, and there was nothing on the board when they got back. What had she screwed up so badly that Bergen needed to talk with her about so urgently?   Bergen came on the line, and told Hannah about the news from Paris.

"What do we plan to do, sir?"

"I don't know yet," the Admiral responded. "I've got Paris Station trying to find out the identity of the informant and whatever background they can scrape up. They've given us 48 hours to respond to the offer."

"What would you like me to do, sir," Hannah asked.

"The most critical thing," he responded in a voice heavy with emphasis, "is that word of this not get out, particularly where you are. If it does, not only will it get leaked by you-know-who, but they will force us to make the deal. That could be a huge waste of money, and might open a can of worms even larger than the one al-Ghabrizi opened by getting himself captured."

"I understand, sir."

"I've briefed Al Bierschmidt and sworn him to tell not a single additional soul for the time being.   Until we can determine how to proceed, neither the DNI nor I intends to appear at the White House unless specifically summoned. It won't save us from getting our asses reamed, if we're found out, but I don't want to be put in a position of being asked 'What's new?' and having to lie about it."

Hannah understood. "Can I brief Special Agent Ogden?" she asked.

"That's why I called you," the Director responded. "I know that you are going up to New York with the FBI team, and wanted to make sure that nothing about this leaks to anyone up there. Until we know more about what's going on, I don't want this new thing to blow up the al-Ghabrizi business any further. The FBI didn't ask me, but I don't know that what we've got is worth rushing up to New York for."

"Aye, aye, sir," Hannah acknowledged her orders. As she turned from the telephone, Jerry came back into the room.

"Interested in doing lunch, Hannah?"

In the Operations Center at One Police Plaza, the shift change briefing had concluded and Deputy Commissioner Caplin asked the Fleet Week Coordinator, the Chief of Police, and the Port Authority representative into the private office reserved for him off of the main floor. The briefing, which occurred every day during Fleet Week, was timed to coincide with the end of visiting hours and dispersal of the large crowds thronging the ships. At that time, demand for police and other protective resources slackened somewhat and the staff of the Operations Center was relieved by people who would remain on duty through the night. Thus far, Fleet Week had gone extremely well: the crowds were huge, but orderly, and the challenges to safety and order the police had dealt with were largely confined to brawls among people jockeying for place in line. The presence of heavily armed police and National Guardsmen almost everywhere was very restraining, particularly since they appeared to be extremely jumpy.

On the water, the Coast Guard and Harbor Patrol had been required to deal only with the odd pleasure craft attempting to approach too closely to one of the anchored visitors. Usually, a blast of the horn or siren did the trick. But, the maritime security plan called for more units and more frequent patrols after sunset. The visiting ships were relatively more vulnerable at night when visibility was restricted. As the sun set, Caplin had made a quick tour of the harbor aboard a Coast Guard helicopter, looking out at the buildings of Manhattan as they settled into shadow and the twinkle of lights became noticeable.

"I've had a call from my very good buddy, Jim Detwiler, at the FBI. He and some of his folks are coming up to see us tomorrow morning," Caplin revealed.

The others detected the sarcasm in his voice, and he explained that Detwiler was FBI Director McGinnis's junkyard dog, who got sent into situations in which the Bureau's or its boss's rear end could be exposed. Most people, Caplin included, considered him a good guy, but standard FBI procedure was to assert Federal precedence and take over the running of supposedly joint operations. This was resented virtually everywhere, but particularly in New York City, which took great pride in the performance of its public safety organizations. The NYPD had more people on the job than did the whole of the FBI.

"He said that he would tell me what it's all about when he got here," Caplin continued. "Conceivably, it has something to do with Fleet Week, but we are almost halfway through it, and there's no indication of trouble. We should send the helicopter to pick them up at LaGuardia."

"The suspense is killing me", he concluded dramatically.

They all laughed.

CHAPTER SEVENTEEN

"New York City looks better on the screen, in Technicolor," Hannah mused as she looked out of the plane's window at the city stretching out below. She was reminded of the many romantic movies she had seen that were set in the City: busy streets, glamorous shops, and handsome people rushing to get to the best restaurants and trendiest clubs. Hannah enjoyed New York, but visited only rarely because she knew no one who lived there and had no one in Washington with whom she cared to make the trip north over a weekend. Now, John Balthazar was at the Waldorf, and the thought of being with him in the City was very exciting.

Detwiler directed the pilot to circle the harbor and lower Manhattan before landing so that they could get an idea of the disposition of ships visiting for Fleet Week. It was still early, but the surface of the water was marked by the curling wakes of many vessels moving in all directions between the shores and around the anchored ships. The Coast Guard reported that the overnight had been uneventful, and that the new day was dawning on a promising note. As the plane shadowed the East River on its approach to LaGuardia Airport, its passengers could see the already heavy traffic on the bridges and expressways that ran along the shore.

"Sure looks crowded," one of the agents blurted out, sounding a bit overwhelmed. "Every time I come here, it takes me a week to get used to it."

Detwiler was not happy to hear that, in part because it indicated that he had chosen his team poorly, but also because it reminded him that he felt somewhat the same. He believed that, to be able to cope effectively in New York City, one had to have grown up there or at least lived in the City for a number of years. If the latter, it also helped to be young. Detwiler was a native of the mid-west, and he was no longer young.

After a quick tour of Caplin's operations center, the visitors were ushered into his private office for the confrontation that had become standard when Federal government officials came up to New York to tell the locals how to do their jobs and, too often, to try to do it for them. Detwiler introduced his team members, only Hannah eliciting a notable reaction in the New Yorkers. Part of it was due to her being from the CIA, part because she was very good looking. But, their attention was really provoked when Detwiler identified her as Admiral Bergen's special assistant. This was clearly out of the ordinary, and their eyes fixed on the FBI AD, awaiting an explanation.

"The reason we're here, Rick," Detwiler began, "is that the Agency has come up with an odd bit of information that may be related to the al-Ghabrizi business." He looked over to Hannah, who told them about the satellite telephone episode and its background, after warning them of its security classification. Afterward, Caplin looked at his colleagues and shrugged.

"That is very interesting, and we appreciate your coming all this way to tell us, but what are we to make of it? At the extreme, it could mean that someone connected to al-Ghabrizi is now in New York. If that's true, it could mean that a terrorist plot is underway or that the phone belongs to one of al-Ghabrizi's many brothers and sons-in-law. What are we supposed to do with it?"

"We don't know, either," Detwiler admitted. "But, coming as it did during your Fleet Week, we thought you needed to know."

"Quite right," responded the NYPD Commissioner. "But, why does it take an Assistant Director of the FBI and a Special Assistant to the Director of the CIA to tell us?" His tone of voice conveyed suspicion, now shared by all of the local officials, that there was more to this than they had thus far been told. Detwiler was uneasy.

"I assure you, gentlemen," Detwiler   told them earnestly, "that is all we have at the moment. But, we are digging like hell for more and, when we know, you'll know."   Hannah thought about the event in Paris about which the Admiral had briefed her, and felt a small pang of guilt. But, by not telling Detwiler about the new development, she had saved him from having to lie to Caplin and company.

"Look, Rick," Detwiler continued, "to be completely candid, we came up here to cover our asses. I'm sure you've been following the al-Ghabrizi cock-up in the press, and will appreciate how pissed-off everyone is in Washington. The President may have lost his chance to be reelected, and screams at everyone who comes into his office. I hear that Bergen and Bierschmidt don't go near the White House unless explicitly summoned, and Roger Norton and his minions are rushing about looking for someone to blame and things to do that will restore Tucker's poll ratings. If some kind of event that could be traced to al-Ghabrizi was to occur up here, it would be the final straw. Frankly, if we couldn't prevent it, we need to be seen as at least having tried."

The New Yorkers were silent in the face of honesty. Finally, Caplin shrugged and asked Detwiler what he and his people planned to do while in the City.

"We plan to avoid getting in your way," was the response. "I would like my people to work with yours here in the op center, so that they will be aware of what's going on. That way, we will able to troll Washington resources, particularly the Intelligence Community, for information that could be useful to you. Instinct tells me that this al-Ghabrizi business isn't over yet, and there's no telling what might turn up."

Caplin looked at his colleagues, then at his visitors. "We welcome your help and your support," he said.

Balthazar left the Waldorf early on the morning after his visit with Said Ghoravi. It was another warm, sunny day and he had abandoned his business suit for chino trousers and an I Love New York T-shirt he had picked up at a souvenir shop the previous day. He took the subway to South Ferry and joined the crowd heading from the ferry slip to the Fleet Week visiting piers, spending the entire morning climbing between the decks of an aircraft carrier and visiting the sail lockers of a Danish training barque. Afterward, he took a taxi to the midtown terminal of the company that ran cruises around Manhattan Island, where he again waited patiently in a long line. It was mid-afternoon before his tour got underway.

The tour boats were small ferries able to accommodate several hundred passengers on two decks. On the lower deck was a snack bar and preparation facilities that catered to the refreshment needs of the passengers during the three hour tour. Balthazar stationed himself on the upper deck where he could observe the boat's operation while also seeing the sights. He had purchased two hot dogs slathered with mustard and hot sauerkraut, which he ate with great enjoyment, washing them down with icy orangeade. Doing this was a highlight of his visits to New York. When the tour ended, pleased with his day and himself, he took a cab across town to the Waldorf.

Admiral Bergen and Director of National Intelligence Bierschmidt were in a serious bind of their own making. The information provided by the would-be intelligence source in Paris had convinced them that they could not afford to reject his offer, even though they were exposing themselves to a serious scam, should the information for which they would be paying three million dollars turn out to be bogus or not operationally useful. It was not the money that most concerned them, intelligence operations were expensive and the available slush fund would easily cover the cost, but the embarrassment to be endured, if word got out that the nation's intelligence chiefs had been gulled.

The most immediate issue, however, was whether they could commit the three million as an attestation of their belief in the value of the source while continuing to keep the White House in the dark. If the promised intelligence was actually forthcoming, they certainly could not withhold it, and would have to explain why the President and his senior advisors were not informed earlier. Bergen and Bierschmidt consulted at length, and decided to instruct Keener to arrange for the exchange. Once that was set up, they would tell the White House.

However, it didn't work out quite that way. The EMail message that Keener sent was picked up almost immediately, but there had been no reply, and the Directors knew that they could afford to wait no longer. On Wednesday evening, they alerted John Cook, and were taken to see the President in the Residence at 10 PM. He was in his pajamas watching television, and was not particularly happy to see them. Fortunately, Roger Norton was not lurking in the background, because the President's Chief-of-Staff had helpfully neglected to tell him of the meeting.

"Well, gentlemen, John tells me that you have something new on this terrorist we've got." His voice betrayed a lack of expectation, and he did not invite them to sit down. "Hopefully, it's something that's not going to come back to bite us on the ass, like your last big coup."

Bergen and Bierschmidt looked at one another. They had agreed that the latter would do the talking. He recounted the Paris contact, the offer of information, and what had been done so far.

"What are the chances this guy is peddling a load of crap?" Tucker asked.

"Only an insider would know the things he told us," Bergen replied.

"But, that doesn't necessarily mean that we will get our three million dollars worth," was the rejoinder.

"I don't think we can afford not to make the bet, Mr. President," Cook interjected.

The President persisted. "It's not the money. What would we learn from knowing who ratted out what's-his-name?"

"It could be that whoever did it is the new al-Ghabrizi," Bierschmidt pointed out, "or works for him. We are currently operating at a major disadvantage because we don't know whether or not the organization that al-Ghabrizi fronted continues to exist or, if it has changed, how. Is this a sign of conflict among the jihadis? If so, what does it mean? As long as we don't know what's happened, we're particularly vulnerable to an unpleasant surprise, Mr. President."

"Okay, let's do it," Tucker decided, and turned back to the television set, indicating that the meeting was over. His visitors were talking in the anteroom when Roger Norton came running up, and was visibly distressed to learn that their meeting with Tucker had already taken place. The three exchanged looks that conveyed agreement that Norton needed to be told what was going on, along with strong warnings. Otherwise, he would learn it from the President, and feel free to use the information without restraint, which, of course, he might do anyway.

As the President's Chief of Staff, Cook carried the most weight with Norton of the three. "Roger," he began, "we've had a potential new development in the al-Ghabrizi business that we are going to tell you about only if you swear on your life that you will not leak it or reveal it in any way."

Norton nodded vigorously, but they could see that his mind was racing ahead.

"Roger," Cook continued very slowly, "should you leak what we are about to tell you, Admiral Bergen will assign a CIA assassin to track you down and cut your balls off."

Norton stopped nodding.

Upon returning to the Waldorf, Balthazar ordered a pitcher of martinis and some caviar from room service, then took a long, hot shower. The waiter was standing by when he emerged from the bathroom wrapped in the heavy terrycloth robe that all luxe hotels provide. Someone had told him once that the robes were so thick and heavy because that made it harder to stuff one into a suitcase, although that thought had never occurred to Balthazar. Seated comfortably, with glass in hand and a plate of hors d'oeuvres close by, he smiled contentedly.

Later, he dressed carefully, then walked over to the Mediterranean Restaurant to meet Khalid. He arrived a bit early and stationed himself across the narrow street from the restaurant. This was a game he played whenever he was to meet someone he had never seen before. He'd bet himself that he could pick the individual out of a crowd and predict what he or she would look like and how they would be dressed. It was a most useful exercise in more risky circumstances than tonight's, and Balthazar was rarely mistaken. Khalid, he predicted, would be of medium height, dark with a bushy mustache, and wearing an ill-fitting brown or dark blue suit. He was right, and Khalid was surprised when Balthazar walked up and greeted him without hesitation, as though he had known him all his life.

The opposite was clearly not true. Khalid had no prior vision of Balthazar, and was as surprised by his appearance as by his familiar approach. He had expected that someone with a senior position in the jihad would be more august and look more like, well, himself. Instead, the man who greeted him could not have been more than thirty-five, and looked more like a playboy than the representative of a great revolutionary movement. The English he spoke was not a second language, and carried an inflection that indicated it was also not his only one.

They sat side-by-side on cushions at a low table facing an open floor on which dancers would later perform. At the back, a small group of musicians played softly. Balthazar ordered for both of them in an Arabic that betrayed his Lebanese ancestry and made Khalid, also a Lebanese, feel less strange. The waiters began bringing a long succession of dishes, each of which Balthazar attacked with equal gusto.

"Coming here is the highlight of my visits to New York," he said, dipping his fingers into the array of dishes on the table. "I try to come at least twice each visit."

He noticed that Khalid was just picking at his food.

"Why are you not eating, my friend? Are you not well?" he asked.

Khalid did not turn to look at him. "I am concerned about the operation," he replied. "As it comes closer, my life becomes more disrupted."

Balthazar did not stop eating. "You have nothing to be concerned about," he said soothingly. "Everything looks to be in order. You have the men and the materiel. Your plan is brilliantly simple, and the Americans appear to be vulnerable, despite their security precautions. I visited the location this afternoon, and can see no reason why your plan should not work, if everyone does what he is assigned to do."

Khalid did not respond to the reassurance.

"Are you having problems with the men?" Balthazar asked.

"Not in the way you might think," came the reply. "They will do what is expected of them, when the time comes. But, I am having a great deal of difficulty with them in ways that surprise and disturb me."

It was now Balthazar's turn to be disconcerted.

"What do you mean?" he asked. "I do not know these people, but I was assured that only reliable men would be sent."

"They are very young, and completely obsessed with women and sex. I understand that hormones do not distinguish among religions, but I would have hoped that young men who are so dedicated to the service of God that they are eager to martyr themselves in his name would not spend their waking hours in naked lust. Today, I had to confine them to the office at the Tremont yard, to keep them from wandering the neighborhood looking for women to molest. I am afraid their activities will expose us to the police."

Balthazar smiled wryly.

"I am afraid it's because they are so dedicated to martyrdom that they behave that way," he assured Khalid. "To prepare them for the kind of mission they are to undertake, they have been kept separate from normal society and indoctrinated to believe that there is nothing in the temporal world to compare with the joy and rewards of entering heaven after dying for the jihad. They have been promised, when they get there, an obscene number of virgins dedicated to fulfilling their every wish. Your people have made their deal with God, and are simply preparing themselves to enjoy the fruits of it."

"But, they do not care about the consequences of what they are going to do or the people who are going to die because of it," Khalid observed somberly.

Balthazar shrugged. "Once you know that you are going to die soon, nothing that happens before or after is of any consequence. It is rare for an individual dedicated to achieving martyrdom to have second thoughts. That is why our operations are most often successful: they are subject only to occasional equipment failure and the, so far, inadequate efforts of the enemy security forces. This one will be no exception."

"What happened to the other two men?" Khalid asked. "Why are they not here? They were supposed to be the boat pilots. How can we go without them?" He was greatly distressed that Balthazar was unconcerned.

"The men," Balthazar replied, "were with al-Ghabrizi when he was captured. Fortunately, they did not yet know anything, but it was too late to replace them. As I told you on the telephone, we will go without them. The American crew will be made to pilot the boat."

"But, that will require more than four men," Khalid objected. "Someone will need to control the pilothouse while the others are below decks."

Balthazar's response was the one Khalid expected and dreaded.

"You will have to go on the boat. We have invested a large amount of time and resources in your operation. You must do what is necessary to insure that it succeeds." To emphasize his point, he stopped eating and stared at Khalid until interrupted by the waiter come to clear the table.

Khalid stared straight ahead at the tables across the room, avoiding Balthazar's eyes.

"I did not intend to actively participate in the operation," he said. "Virgins do not interest me, and I do not care to die before my time. Once the boat was underway, I planned to leave the city in my car for Detroit, where I have friends who would get me across the border to Canada."

Balthazar was now thoroughly alarmed. If Khalid did not go along to command the operation, it could not succeed. Worse, Khalid had seen him and could identify him to authorities, if captured.

"You cannot renege on your duty to God, simply because you are afraid of dying," he told his reluctant companion. Balthazar was not sure of the most effective tone of voice to use, stern to remind Khalid that he would be judged by higher authority or consoling to assure him that his trepidation was understood and would be excused...if he carried out his mission. He decided on some of both.

He waited until the waiter had finished placing an array of small dishes containing sweets on the table. Khalid and he were sitting shoulder to shoulder, and Balthazar could speak to him without fear of being overheard in the large, noisy room.

"Normally," he told him, "I undertake only those operations that our leaders assign to me, and I plan and supervise all aspects of them myself. Taking part in someone else's plan is very risky. Doing it in New York is, perhaps, the riskiest of all, because the police and the FBI are so highly motivated. Adopting your proposal and providing the resources needed to execute it showed that we recognized its brilliance, but more that we trusted your judgment and ability to carry it out successfully. It is unfortunate that the seamen could not be available as planned, but you cannot abandon us at this late moment. God will punish you for missing a glorious opportunity to strike a blow on his behalf that will be heard and praised all over the world...forever."

Khalid did not reply, and continued to stare straight ahead. Balthazar poured him a cup of coffee and placed a dish of sweetmeats in front of him. After a while, Khalid spoke, still without looking at Balthazar.

"How could it happen that the Americans knew where to find Sheikh al-Ghabrizi. Was he betrayed by our own people?"

"I don't know." Balthazar replied. "I am afraid that some of our people are very passionate, and sometimes fight one another as ferociously as they fight the enemy. As you know, this business has made our project more difficult. Perhaps, it is a test that God has devised for us." He looked to see how Khalid was reacting.

Balthazar was boiling with anger at himself as he walked back to his hotel. If Khalid ultimately refused to go on the boat, he would be blamed. He should have developed a backup plan when he heard that the seamen would not be available. For a moment, he wondered whether whomever was responsible for tipping the Pakistani police about al-Ghabrizi knew that the men with him were intended for the New York operation or whether, perhaps, he Balthazar was the real target of the betrayal. After all, he had been the old man's principal source of support the past five years and al-Ghabrizi, in turn, had provided Balthazar the cover that enabled him to travel around the world like a prince doing his lord's bidding.

By the time he reached the Waldorf, he had decided that he was becoming paranoid, and forced himself to the look ahead optimistically to the next critical days. It didn't, however, make him feel any better that what had started out as a very pleasant business and pleasure trip was rapidly turning to crap. Then, he reached his room and found a phone message from Hannah saying that she was in New York, and wanted to see him.

CHAPTER EIGHTEEN

Thursday morning found James Detwiler and Jerry Ogden on Upper New York Bay in a fast Coast Guard patrol boat being used to monitor waterborne traffic in the Fleet Week visiting zone. The FBI Assistant Director had decreed that at least one member of his team needed to be in the vicinity of the City's Operations Center at all times, so Hannah had gratefully volunteered to stay behind. The bobbing of small boats made her seasick, but she also wanted to be alone when Balthazar returned her phone call of the previous night. She rehearsed the cover story made up to explain why she was in the City after telling him she couldn't come. A problem had come up concerning the visas of United Nations personnel entering the United States, and Hannah had been sent up to New York to deal with it. She was staying at a midtown hotel that had a contract with the Government to house its employees, whose per diem payment could not accommodate the City's sky high hotel rates. This, in fact, was what the entire FBI team was doing. Her cell phone rang, its screen showing an unrecognized New York City number.

"It is good to hear your voice," he said.

"And yours," Hannah replied. "I'm flattered that you apparently couldn't wait to talk with me. It's not even 8 AM."

"If I hadn't gotten back to the hotel so late last night, I would have called you then. What are you doing here?"

Hannah recited her cover story, and was careful to emphasize that she did not know what demand there would be on her time and availability. It would not do to get her arrangements with Balthazar mixed up with the requirements of her real job, the extent of which were not knowable hour to hour. Fortunately, he was tied up all day, both Thursday and Friday, with company business, but looked forward to the evenings and the weekend. She did also, but was more circumspect about it. Hopefully, Detwiler would declare their mission ended at close of business on Friday, and she would be able to spend the weekend in New York unencumbered by duty. They agreed to meet at Balthazar's hotel for dinner, and he gave Hannah his cell phone number, in the event their arrangement needed to be altered.

A Coast Guard flag officer was aboard the patrol boat to escort the visitors, and to brief them on maritime security measures implemented for Fleet Week. Jerry found racing around the harbor exhilarating, but was glad he had taken Dramamine before embarking. Detwiler evidently had not, and was looking increasingly queasy, with the boat tacking to and fro as their escort pointed out items of interest. The craft had a crew of five, including two men manning light machine guns mounted at the bow and stern.

"Our job is relatively straightforward compared with that of the police and the FBI," he was saying. "We know the things we have to protect, the potential targets, and how to go about it. Take that carrier over there. If terrorists want to attack it, they can either ram something into it or drop something on it from above, or perhaps both. We've established a perimeter around the ship that's far enough out to preclude anything short of a warship from firing a gun or a missile into it successfully. The perimeter is manned 24/7 by armed units like this one, with a more heavily armed cutter on call nearby. All quadrants of the perimeter are always under observation, but we increase the number of guard boats at night and during periods of low visibility, like fog. The airspace overhead is patrolled at all times by a combination of jet aircraft, light propeller planes, and helicopters, with jet fighters standing by at Air Force bases outside the city. A no fly zone was established before Fleet Week began that serves the same purpose as the surface perimeter. We watch for aircraft approaching the zone, using both radar and visual patrols, and intercept those who appear to be coming too close. Thus far, all the bogeys have been pleasure craft with pilots who did not know they were heading into trouble. I have to work hard to keep our bored pilots from scaring the shit out of some Piper Cub driver showing off for his girlfriend."

Detwiler and Jerry nodded appreciatively.

"During the planning phase," the officer concluded, "we even considered the possibility of a submarine sneaking into the harbor from the Atlantic, but could find no intelligence indicating that al-Ghabrizi or his running mates have one. Nevertheless, the Navy's got a destroyer patrolling the lower bay, listening with its passive sonar."

Later, in the small officers' club at the Coast Guard base, the three sat sipping beer, while Detwiler regained his land legs.

"I'm impressed by the way the Coast Guard is handling Fleet Week security, Admiral," the FBI executive volunteered. "In fact, I'm impressed by everything I've seen and heard so far about how the City as a whole is managing."

"Thank you, sir," the officer replied. "We've tried to cover every possibility we could think of. As you know, there has been no indication that anyone is planning anything, and most of Fleet Week is already gone."

"You have sort of an advantage, if you can call it that," Detwiler observed. "Since 9/11, we take the serious possibility of a terrorist attack in the United States as a given. Before that date, it was possible for an FBI supervisor to be more concerned about exceeding staffhour utilization limits than about sending agents to check out odd goings-on at flight schools. That kind of thing is far less likely to happen again, not because we've become so much smarter, but because the range of threats we are now compelled to recognize has become broader and clearer, and we've been forced to expend the resources needed to deal with them. Also, the 9/11 experience has greatly reduced our improbability threshold, to the extent that we feel compelled to take precautions against potential threats that make the plots of special effects movies look tame."

The Admiral nodded in agreement. "It has gotten very, very expensive. I was here for Fleet Week in the Spring of 2001, then got transferred, and returned this year. The ramp up in security precautions, on land, sea, and in the air, has been extraordinary. But, our resources are still stretched thin, particularly during high threat periods like Fleet Week. We can't ever be positive that we have the right bases covered or even that we know what all the bases are."

It was Detwiler's turn to agree. "That's supposed to be where Intelligence can help. But, we're still having trouble in Washington getting our act together. It seems that, whenever we have what people call an intelligence failure, it turns out that the information needed to have prevented it was in hand, but didn't get to the right people in time or they didn't grasp its significance or they didn't choose correctly among available action options."

"Or all of the above," added the Admiral, smiling rue-fully.

"It's funny," Detwiler mused, "discussions like this remind me of the weeks before Pearl Harbor when everyone was trying to figure out what, if anything, the Japanese were going to do. I'm a student of that period and, as you know, a lot has been written about it.

The public memory is of a surprise attack, which resulted in substantial damage and loss of life because we were unprepared for it. In actuality, the cause and effect were not nearly so clearly cut. We were not unprepared solely because the attack was a surprise, but because we had made certain explicit and tacit decisions regarding the probability of occurrences, and they turned out to be wrong. The one that is, perhaps, best known was the decision to bunch the parked aircraft at Hickam Field and Ford Island so that they could be more easily guarded against anticipated sabotage by Japanese agents in the Hawaiian population. That, of course, never happened, but the planes were easy targets for the Japanese air attack. But, it is hard to call that a dumb decision, just as we can't say that any of the security precautions taken for Fleet Week are wrong, even if it turns out that one of them facilitates rather than discourages a terrorist attack."

"In the period before the Pearl Harbor attack," Detwiler continued, "naval commanders in Hawaii did, in fact, recognize that a Japanese attack would come from the sea, and increased long range air patrols. Unfortunately, there were not enough long range patrol aircraft available to cover all of the approaches to the islands. So, flights were concentrated in the south and west quadrants nearest Japan, in the belief that a carrier-borne attack would most likely come from those directions. Under radio silence, the Japanese strike force came, in fact, from the north."

Omar Khalid got to the Tremont yard later than usual on Thursday morning, just in time to prevent a serious confrontation between Anna and his prospective martyrs. He had drunk more at dinner with Balthazar than he was used to, and had a headache made worse by his continuing unhappiness with the prospect before him. The men had charged into the office to get to the television set only to find Anna watching a morning variety show from Times Square. Their English was not good enough to communicate to her what they wanted, but it would not have mattered. They were getting ready to shove her out of the way when Khalid came in and chased them out to the storage shed.

"If you wish to spend the rest of your lives in an American prison, continue to act as you have," he told them in Arabic. "God will punish you for failing the mission he has given you, and you will be tortured every day and made into eunuchs."

He had their attention.

"If that's what you wish...fine. But, I have no desire to be dragged away with you to prison. You must be careful of Anna, and not make her so angry that she will go to the police. You will not have much longer to wait for your martyrdom. I have been told that the operation will go off as scheduled on Sunday."

The men grumbled, but settled down. Khalid realized that a good deal of the problem was boredom. After almost three weeks locked in a shipping container, then almost a week of being hidden from sight in a storage yard, the young men craved the ultimate excitement they had been promised. Until their final departure, not only could he not let them out of his sight, but he had also to keep them amused or at least terrorized by the contingent wrath of God. At that point, Khalid realized that he had no option but to do what was expected of him. The undertaking was too complicated for him to delude himself that it could succeed without him. He considered himself a man of honor, and had committed himself to God, just as these men had.

"Later this morning, I will take you in the car downtown to see the city," he told them. They cheered and, for the moment, Anna and the fallen women of daytime serials were forgotten.

Khalid returned to the office, Anna watching him through the window.

"Mr. Ghoravi's secretary called," she told him. "He wants you to come downtown to his office at four tomorrow afternoon. I told him that you would be there."

Khalid was alarmed. The only time he had been to the main office was on the day he was hired. Ghoravi had never asked to see him before; what had he done to warrant the summons now? He looked searchingly at Anna, but could detect nothing in her face to indicate that she had complained about their four guests. What could he do? The men couldn't be hidden somewhere because he needed to keep an eye on them at all times. In any event, where could he put them? He began to think of a cover story to tell Ghoravi, if asked what the hell was going on up in the Bronx.

The men chattered excitedly as he loaded them into his SUV and headed for the expressway downtown. The horseplay stopped, however, when they caught sight of the skyscrapers ahead as the car moved toward them, as to Oz. Most of them had never seen a tall building or even been in a large city. When Khalid left the FDR Drive and entered the warren of narrow crosstown streets, the men opened the car's windows and craned their heads out to stare upwards looking for the sky. Their leader, slightly older and more contemplative, looked at Khalid with an awed expression.

"What is this place?" he whispered in Arabic.

Khalid had forgotten that the men had been told very little of their mission before being locked in the shipping container. Neither, he discovered, had they received much training beyond rudimentary instruction in handling light weapons and explosives. Their principal qualifications, it appeared, were a small knowledge of English and the willingness to endure unspeakable privation and an early death in the service of God.

"It is called New York," he replied. "It is one of the main centers of the West, one of the largest cities in the world."

The men looked at one another proudly, then out at the passing scene.

"We have been chosen to achieve martyrdom in such a grand city, among millions of infidels. It is the greatest of honors!" their leader cried.

Khalid was unhappy that he did not share their enthusiasm. It would make his impending death easier to bear. He wondered where along the way he had lost his unquestioning dedication to their cause. When was it that he had begun to wonder what, in fact, the cause was, beyond endless slogans repeated over and over by fanatical men with dead eyes. But, he could not deny these mesmerized children their entry into heaven, and it occurred to him that his would be, perhaps, the true martyrdom.

They drove around for another twenty minutes, then headed back to the Bronx to beat the evening rush and to satisfy repeated demands for pizza.

Hannah spent an uneventful morning in the City's Operations Center attending meetings as an observer and watching the staff take care of business. Nothing out-of-the-ordinary was occurring, and the heavily manned desks and computer workstations appeared as though the room was in a state of suspended animation. At midday, Richard Caplin took her to the Lower East Side for the best hot pastrami sandwich she had ever tasted. Racing through traffic in an unmarked police cruiser, red light on top and siren blaring, they covered the distance to the narrow, basement delicatessen in less than fifteen minutes, leaving the car in a No Parking zone out in front. Hannah felt all eyes turn to her, as they entered the store and went back to what turned out to be Caplin's usual table.

After lunch, Hannah used her secure cell phone to check in with the Director's office at Langley. The Duty Officer had a message for her.

"Remember that company you asked us about last week?" he asked. Hannah, at first, did not remember, then recalled last weekend with Balthazar. She could feel herself blushing as she acknowledged making the request, and was happy that this was not a videoteleconference.

"Well, the company checks out as legitimate," he reported, reciting a lot of information that Hannah had already heard from Balthazar. "But, the funny thing is that there is a flag on the file without an explanation." The flag was a red sticker that was affixed to a file cover to indicate that the contents were of particular intelligence interest. It had room on it for the name and telephone number of the analyst or case officer to be contacted in the regard to the subject company, but those lines were currently blank.

"What the hell," Hannah exclaimed. This could mean something or nothing, but she didn't want to think about it at this time. She asked the Duty Officer to track down whoever tagged the folder, and to have he or she call Hannah's cell phone as a matter of urgency. "Bloody hell!" she exploded as she hung up, then noticed the people in her vicinity staring at her. Richard Caplin was standing behind her looking amused.

"Bad day at the CI of A?" he laughed.

Tom Keener was becoming desperate. He had thought, once he had communicated the U.S. willingness to deal for the al-Ghabrizi betrayal information, that he would hear back immediately concerning arrangements for the exchange. He even arranged for three million in large bills to be withdrawn from an Agency account at the Paris branch of a Swiss bank and sequestered in his office safe at the Embassy. However, almost a day had past with nothing heard, and the phone calls from Headquarters were driving him crazy, given that Washington was six hours behind Paris and his superiors could harass him into the night without inconveniencing themselves. Finally, after a quick check with Langley, he went to see the French intelligence officer who was assisting him with the Email tracking. Would it be possible, he asked, for the French service to review its files and active surveillance cases to see whether they could identify individuals who might be in a position to hold the information being offered to the Agency. His contact was dubious, but said he would give it a try. When Keener returned to his office, he found a new Email message assuring him that the deal was still on, but that there would be a short delay. He gratefully sent that on to Headquarters, hoping it would keep them off his back for a while.

But, it didn't keep the President and his minions off the backs of Bierschmidt and Bergen. The tension reflected the fact that it was not yet public knowledge that al-Ghabrizi had been effectively turned over to the U.S. by people, or a person, within his own jihad movement. When that became known, it was likely that most people would assume that it reflected a power grab by one of his rivals, and a clamor would be raised about the Administration's and Intelligence Community's failure to identify the perpetrator and to anticipate the event. Worse, public concern over the prospect of a more powerful and unknown successor to al-Ghabrizi would undermine the Administration's most assiduously nurtured boast: that it was on the job protecting the American people and their homeland against international terrorism.

However, if the facts surrounding al-Ghabrizi's downfall could be obtained before his successor began appearing on CNN, the Government could claim that it knew of him all the time, but had to protect intelligence sources and methods. The best of all possible outcomes, of course, would be a determination that al-Ghabrizi was ratted out by some insignificant underling interested in a piece of the CIA reward money.

The Director of National Intelligence and the Director of CIA spent most of that day at the White House shuttling from office to office and meeting to meeting. At five-thirty, they got together in John Cook's private office, over single-malt scotch, to review the bidding. They decided that there was nothing more they could do, pending additional word from Paris or some other development elsewhere. This did not make them feel better, and they sat at first in silence staring into their drinks. Admiral Bergen was the first to speak.

"The thing that bothers me most about this whole damned business is the way it's dominated all of our time and thoughts, not to mention the efforts and attention of our agencies. If I had a reason to suspect it, I could easily believe that someone timed this business to divert our attention from something else."

The others nodded.

"To be logically consistent," the DNI observed, "it would have to be something big and directed at the United States, since all of this was apparently done for our direct benefit. The only thing that comes to mind is a major terrorist attack here in CONUS."

"But, where?" Cook asked. "I've seen nothing even hinting that something is in the works, let alone something big."

"We can't just raise the national Threat Level to Red on general principle. The last time we did that, people accused us of ass covering," Bergen complained.

"Which we were," Cook admitted.

The CIA Director summarized: "The only place where we have anything at all is New York City, and that is too vague to even be called intelligence. They are having Fleet Week up there, which could be a major terrorist target, particularly since it is New York. Mostly to cover our butts, the FBI sent a team up there under Jim Detwiler. I've got my special assistant, Hannah Crossman, with them. Reports so far indicate everything is normal, and the event ends on Sunday."

"What would tip us off that some kind of terrorist operation is being mounted?" Cook asked.

"Depends, among other things, on who the perps are," Bergen replied. "You can have operations developed and executed by people coming into the target site from outside, as in the case of 9/11 and the African embassy bombings. You can have them mounted and executed by people resident in the target city, as was the case in the subway bombings in Europe, or you can have a combination of the two, where specialists come in from outside to assist the locals technically, financially, and, perhaps, with planning."

"Which is the easiest to detect, relatively speaking?"

"It depends on how good your intelligence and law enforcement services are. When your terrorists are homegrown, domestic law enforcement organizations that keep careful track of suspect groups and individuals have a good chance of detecting and stopping attacks before execution. They need to get into the neighborhoods and be aware of patterns of activities over extended periods of time so that anomalies that could indicate terrorist involvement become apparent. Above all, they need to develop reliable sources of information within the community that can tip them off to those anomalies. That really helps when strangers come into the picture and begin consorting with the locals. Unfortunately, the master technicians and tacticians, such as the ones al-Ghabrizi sent out, never stayed around very long, and were always gone when the operation occurred. With a couple of exceptions, we've never figured out who they are."

"But, the biggest frustration," Bierschmidt interjected, " is that, when people come into this country legally or illegally, the job of keeping track of them cuts across Federal, state, and local government boundaries, usually involving multiple agencies which do not always work well together. In addition to the many law enforcement agencies, the intelligence agencies like CIA and NSA are involved, not to mention the intelligence outfits of our allies and Interpol. It's like a bamboo thicket: all the stalks grow straight up, and not enough grows across. We can't even agree on the definition of "intelligence." Part of it is obsolete legalese, the rest bureaucratic turf protection. We've often been al-Ghabrizi's best friend!"

He stopped, aware that he was preaching to the choir.

"Tell us what you really think, Al," Bergen commented wryly.

Bierschmidt stood up to leave. "Let's get together when we hear more from Paris," he said. Then, to Bergen: "Please double-check that we're covered in New York, and make sure that the City people are not kept too much in the dark.

CHAPTER NINETEEN

Detwiler and Jerry Ogden returned to the Op Center from their excursion in the harbor, their afternoon meeting with City officials confirming that nothing appeared amiss, with three days of festivities remaining. The other FBI agents who had come up from Washington with them attended, the first Hannah had seen of them. They were working with the NYPD out of the Bureau's New York Field Office, supplementing the flying squad that dispatched investigators to check out anything that appeared even remotely suspicious. Nothing out of the ordinary had come up, but they echoed Hannah's excitement at racing through Manhattan traffic with siren wailing and lights flashing, just like on TV. Detwiler and Caplin were going to dinner, and asked Hannah and Jerry to join them, but she told them that she had already made arrangements to meet an old friend who lived in the City.

Admiral Bergen called on the secure cell phone just as Hannah reached her hotel room to get ready for her evening with Balthazar. The Director reminded her of the matter he had briefed her on before she left for New York, then brought her up to date. He told her of his suspicion, which the DNI shared, that the al-Ghabrizi business might be a diversion for something else, and that everyone in Washington, meaning the White House, was waiting for the other shoe to drop. New York was the only blip on the radar screen, but there was still nothing to go to general quarters about. (Hannah loved it when the Admiral used Navy terminology, once she figured out or been told what it meant.)   Eventually, Bergen got to his main concern: that the local officials in New York continued to be less than fully informed, although at that moment he could not concede that they had a need-to-know.   He was quite unhappy about it.   Hannah reminded him that the FBI did not know about the Paris lead either, which made him even unhappier.

"When I was working in the Navy," he complained, "I never worried about covering my ass.   But, now that I'm the big deal CIA Director, that's all I seem to think about."

"Perhaps, it's because you have so much more to cover now, sir," Hannah replied soothingly, before realizing what she had said.

There was a long silence while Hannah reviewed her brief career.   Then, she heard a loud and very welcome guffaw.

"Hannah!   Remind me to make you a deputy director when you get back."

They arrived at a satisfying compromise.   The next morning, Hannah would take Caplin and Detwiler aside and brief them on the Paris business, saying that she had just been told about it.   They would not be permitted to tell anyone else at this time.   She would also keep them abreast of new developments, should there be any.

Bergen chuckled as he closed the conversation.   "Now that we both recognize that I have such a large ass to cover, I will expect your full attention and devotion to doing so.   Have fun in New York, Hannah!"

That's what she intended to do.   Freshly showered and scented, Hannah put on the favorite dinner dress that she had brought along in anticipation of seeing Balthazar.   Leaving her room, she first stuck her head out into the corridor to make sure that she was not seen by one of her colleagues, who were in adjoining rooms.   She was far too dressed up to be meeting an old friend.   Instead of taking one of the nearest elevators, she followed the corridor to another bank at the far end of the building. She saw no one she knew, and was immediately able to catch a cab to the Waldorf, feeling vaguely uneasy about having fun while in the City on such potentially serious business.

John Balthazar returned to his room after a full day of meetings with customers and suppliers, and found a message from Ghoravi inviting him to a Fleet Week event viewing and reception at the head offices of the Caspian Sea Trading Company on Sunday morning.   He smiled, and immediately dialed the number provided to leave a message saying that he would be very happy to attend.

They met in the bar off the Waldorf's main lobby, Balthazar freshly groomed and wearing an Italian silk suit that Hannah complimented even before saying hello.   Over cocktails, they ran quickly through a review of their respective days, Hannah prevaricating adroitly, then discussed the kind of cuisine wanted for dinner, after which they opted to make love in Balthazar's room.

Later that evening, Hannah again found herself once again deep in the folds of a thick, terrycloth robe sipping coffee. The remains of an excellent room service dinner from one of the hotel's restaurants on the table between her and a similarly enrobed Balthazar.

"This is getting to be a habit," she observed not unapprovingly.

"I certainly hope so," he responded.   "I'm going back to Paris next week, and you are most welcome to accompany me.

The rates at my apartment are more reasonable than they are here at the Waldorf."

"What would the State Department do without me?" she joked. "Half the foreigners in New York would be deported for having faulty visas."

"If you will come with me, I will surrender my passport this very moment," he offered with great flourish. He came around the back of her chair and put his arms around her, his hands sliding into her robe and around her breasts.

"You can't be ready to go already!" she exclaimed in mock alarm.

"Why do you think there are so many Muslims," he replied while undoing the robe.

Later, they left the hotel and wandered the streets of midtown Manhattan in the warm Spring night. Balthazar's face carried a very contented smile, in which Hannah took a certain pride. She called him on it, and he admitted to being happier than he had been in a long time.

"How could I be otherwise," he said. "I'm in New York with a woman for whom I care a great deal, my business is going extremely well, and the weather is gorgeous. The only downside is that it will be over soon."

"Must you go back so early?" Hannah asked, then recalled that she herself was not a free agent and could be called back to duty without notice. To punctuate her realization, the secure cell phone in her handbag began to ring. She had forgotten to turn it off.

"Aren't you going to answer it? Balthazar asked. "It might be your mother." Hannah had told him about her mother's crusade to marry her off.

"No, I'm going to let it go to voice mail. It might be someone from the office, and I'm having too much fun to be interrupted," she replied both cleverly and truthfully. If she had pulled the instrument from her bag, Balthazar would have recognized that it wasn't an ordinary cell phone. And, of course, she couldn't have talked with someone from the Agency in front of him. After six rings, it stopped, and Hannah reached into her handbag and turned it off.

As they continued walking, Balthazar realized that he should not be as contented as he was. Upon parting with Khalid the other evening, he believed the Tremont manager would do what was expected of him, and that the operation would proceed as planned. But, as time passed, Balthazar grew less confident and, at that moment, resolved to call Khalid on Friday morning. The decision did not make him feel better, but he was able to turn his attention back to Hannah, where he preferred it to be.

She had noticed his momentary preoccupation and, thinking that it might have been caused by the cell phone incident, rushed to distract him.

"Has your visit to New York been successful, so far?" she asked. "I mean business wise," she added, seeing his amused look.

"Why should it not be successful," he shrugged. "My companies operate efficiently, and don't require my direct supervision. I come to New York because it is one of my favorite places in the entire world. As you've noticed, I don't travel frugally, and the businesses support me in the style to which I am accustomed. Mostly, I visit different places to maintain personal contact with the people who run the companies I buy from and sell to. But, if I couldn't travel first class and stay at places like the Waldorf, I would not come."

Then, he rushed to add: "But, of course, now I have added incentive."

Hannah laughed. "I can tell that you wouldn't last long traveling as an American civil servant. The only thing my official passport does for me is keep the security folks from stripping me naked when I try to get back into my own country."

Balthazar favored her with an exaggerated leer. "You wouldn't get off that easily, if I was on the job." They laughed, and headed back to the hotel.

The first thing Tom Keener did after he got out of bed on Friday morning was to check his personal Email. It was his lifeline to the real world outside of the tense, little hothouse in which he lived. The Agency provided Email service to all of its overseas personnel using a State Department cover. It was an important morale booster, but was never to be used for business matters. Many people around the world had Keener's address. Some of them knew he was living in Paris, almost none that he was CIA's station chief.

Because of the time zone difference, his morning Email collection generally contained messages originated the evening before in the States, along with the odd offer to share with him a fortune hidden in Nigeria or to cure his erectile dysfunction. This morning, however, there was also a message originated from an address in France that he recognized as the one they were monitoring. So much for cover, Keener thought, and made a mental note to check his credit card statements more carefully. He opened the message and found a single sentence directing him to his front door, where he found an envelope that had been shoved underneath during the night. It also contained a note, the content of which caused Keener to throw on whatever clothes came to hand and to hail a passing taxi, which took him to the Embassy.

"The bastards want to do the swap in Karachi tomorrow, not in Paris as we had assumed," Admiral Bergen told John Cook, the President's Chief of Staff.

"Can we do that?" Cook asked

"We'll have to fly the money in, but otherwise we can do it," the CIA Director responded. "The problem is that we may very well lose our ability to watch the exchange and to find out more about the other party. The French are pretty good at that kind of thing, and are very cooperative. The Pakistanis are much less so, and you can never be sure for whom individual officials are working. My guess is that's the reason for doing the deal in Karachi."

"It's funny that Karachi is the city in which the whole al-Ghabrizi business began. I wonder if there's a connection?" Cook speculated.

"That's what Jed, our station chief there, said when I talked with him. He's the one who started the al-Ghabrizi affair, and he is hoping not be dragged back into it," Bergen responded. Cook rose to leave.

"I'll brief the President when he wakes up. He's not going to be happy."

"What else is new," muttered Bergen to himself, as left the White House grounds with his still yawning driver. "Why do

all unpleasant things have to come up in the middle of the fucking night."

CHAPTER TWENTY

Hannah left the Waldorf at three AM, and took a taxi back to her hotel. She hoped to get back to her room without being seen by any of her colleagues, but wanted more to listen to the voice mail message left on her secure cell phone. She assumed that the message would be a follow-up on the matter of the Marseille International file. However, the caller turned out to be the analyst at the Agency's signals processing lab in charge of exploiting the satellite telephone captured with al-Ghabrizi. He had also supervised the test in which one of the phone's speed dial numbers had been answered by an unknown party in New York City. After that event, the investigation had been broadened to include traffic flowing to and from that number, of which there had proven to be very little. It had determined, however, that the phone had been used in Paris, during the previous week, to call a New York number assigned to the Caspian Sea Trading Company of Manhattan. No conversation or data exchange had resulted. The caller said that he had been instructed by the Director's office to relay this information to Hannah.

She dialed the number left by the caller, then realized it was four o'clock in the morning and punched in the number of the Director's duty office that was manned 24/7. Bergen was in his car on the way home from the White House. He had just called in asking that a call to Hannah be set up for 0800, but since Hannah was available now, they would patch her through to the Director's car.

"You're up late, Hannah, or early, as the case may be." Bergen liked Hannah, and their relationship had become less formal with time.

"I was just following orders, sir," she replied smartly. "You told me to have fun in New York, and I am trying my best. I'm calling for permission to pass on the new information concerning that Caspian Sea company to the FBI and the New York public safety people."   Bergen had not yet heard about it, but readily agreed, after Hannah briefed him.   Fleet Week had three days left to go, and all was still quiet.   The intelligence about the Caspian Sea dialup was probably of no greater value than the original satellite phone intercept, but it would give the investigators something to do.   In casual conversation with staff members in the New York operations center, Hannah discovered a growing fear, based on no tangible evidence, that because things were going so well, something of importance was being missed.

"Actually," Bergen continued, "I called to update you on the Paris business.   He told Hannah about the switch to Karachi and its implications.   At a minimum, the exchange would take longer to play out and probably less would be learned from it.   And, of course, it was still impossible to gage the impact, if any, of the information for which they were about to pay three million dollars.   Hannah was instructed to provide Detwiler and Caplin the updated story, and to standby for further details.

She napped for an hour, then took a cold shower.   At 0700, Hannah called Detwiler's room, wanting to catch him before he went down for breakfast.   He was somewhat surprised when she proposed to come immediately to his room as a matter of urgency.   Hannah realized that it was particularly important that she brief Detwiler first, then allow him to tell the others. The intelligence being provided had been obtained by the CIA, which was forbidden by law to be involved in domestic matters. If the leads, such as they were, were to be pursued, it would have to be done by the FBI and local law enforcement agencies. More important, Detwiler would lose face, should the New Yorkers perceive that their information (and implicit guidance) was coming from a relative underling who felt free to one up an assistant director of the FBI.

Detwiler was grateful for both the information and the consideration. After the morning meeting at the Operations Center, he met with Richard Caplin and the Chief of the NYPD to brief them on both matters, omitting the details of the prospective swap of cash for the al-Ghabrizi information. The police would begin to check out the Caspian Sea Trading Company and the people associated with it, with Jerry assisting by querying Federal law enforcement sources, particularly for information concerning the company's overseas activities.

Hannah was tired, but excited. She recalled in detail her hours with Balthazar, stimulated further by the knowledge that they had tonight and the weekend before them. The information she had received from Washington also provided a lift. It would probably yield nothing, but it was good to have something to think about and investigate. If the individual who answered his satellite phone in New York was the same person who attempted to call the Caspian Sea company from Paris, it would indicate that he is either one of its employees or someone with a business connection to the company. Neither prospect would be surprising or suspicious, and became interesting only when added to the knowledge that the number of the satellite telephone used was contained in al-Ghabrizi's speed dial list. She asked Jerry to have the investigators on the case check to see whether any of Caspian Sea's people were in Paris on the date of the earlier intercept, and to query Customs and Immigration to determine whether any of them had landed in New York on the day of the later one. She also called back to Headquarters to double check that there had been no further usage of the suspect telephone.

After he called the FBI's New York Field Office to initiate action on the records search, Jerry joined the team of NYPD officers doing essentially the same thing in the state and City files. Until they obtained basic information about the company, its people and locations, no real investigative measures could be initiated. Should that data, as was probable, reveal nothing indicative of possible criminal or terrorist activity, there was little further they could do. Caplin and his colleagues would be only mildly interested in these very unsubstantial leads. Fleet Week was about to enter its climactic weekend, with planned activities and public attendance reaching a crescendo. Everyone at the Friday morning status meeting was eagerly looking forward to the closing ceremonies on Sunday afternoon.

At this moment, Omar Khalid was dealing with another crisis at the Tremont yard. The men had sullenly left the office when Anna arrived at the yard, but she had unexpectedly appeared in the storage shed an hour later while they were inventorying the materiel they had brought with them. They chased her out with a tirade of Arabic invective, and Khalid believed that she had not been inside long enough to have seen anything that could betray them. But, she had become nearly hysterical, and was again threatening to go to the police or the FBI. Khalid assured her, as he had before, that they would be gone when she came to work on Monday, and got her quieted down. Then, he went to the shed and warned the men, one more time, that they would suffer the wrath of God, if they screwed up the operation on the eve of its execution. This done, he returned to worrying about his forthcoming meeting with Ghoravi. He half hoped that Tremont's owner was going to tell him that he was aware of what was going on, and that the police were going to prevent Khalid from having to die.

Bierschmidt and Bergen were furious, and John Cook was embarrassed. The Associated Press, citing unspecified White House sources, had reported that U.S. intelligence agencies were checking out the possibility that Anwar al-Ghabrizi had been deliberately betrayed to the West because he was getting old, and was no longer fully competent to lead the worldwide jihad. All available sources were being queried to determine whether or not a successor had emerged and who it might be. The President, however, did not share their outrage over the leak, and defended Roger Norton, who stood behind him smiling smugly.

"I don't see why you are so excited," he complained. "He didn't leak anything about the Paris business. We can't just sit around on our asses waiting for something to happen. The way things are going, when something does happen, the odds are that it will hurt us." He waved his intelligence chiefs out without waiting for their response. As they left the room, Bergen turned toward Norton and made a slashing motion, then pointed toward his crotch. Norton blanched, and positioned himself more squarely behind the President's chair.

"Have we heard anything from Keener or Jed?" Bergen asked a waiting aide, as they left the Oval Office. He missed having Hannah by his side.

"Nothing, sir. But, the duty officer at your office wants you to call him as soon as you can." He handed Bergen a cell phone similar to Hannah's.

The Admiral looked at Bierschmidt, then punched in a speed dial number.

"What's up?" He listened, and became excited.

"Call Hannah in New York and tell her to get down there immediately. Send a plane to pick her up at LaGuardia or Newark. Keep me informed," he directed.

He rang off and guided the DNI and Cook into the latter's office, shutting the door after checking the corridor for evidence of Roger Norton.

"Al-Ghabrizi has changed his mind about talking," he reported. "He's been watching Arab satellite television news channels in his cell and caught Norton's leak. The monitors at the stockade say that he is totally pissed off about something, and wants to see Hannah. He says that she is the only one he will talk with. We'll get her down there ASAP."

The three men looked at one another in dismay. Cook was the first to speak.

"That son-of-a-bitch Norton may have done us a large favor. We may have to let him keep his privates, after all."

By early afternoon, the Operations Center had the basic information about the Caspian Sea Trading Company and its owners. Although the Ghoravis and their relatives needed to be checked out further, there was nothing, at first glance, that seemed out of the ordinary. The elder Ghoravis, who started the company in the 1980s, had relocated to California more than five years earlier, and would be checked out by the FBI field offices out there. Said Ghoravi, his wife, and two young children lived in an affluent section of Westchester County north of the City.

He appeared to be a solid citizen: belonged to the appropriate trade associations, and was a member of the Mayor's committee on the post-9/11 revitalization of lower Manhattan.   His wife, Rena, stayed at home with their son and daughter, Michael and Yasmin, who attended a local private school.   She was active in religious and social affairs attendant to a nearby mosque.   The only thing of note, from an investigative standpoint, was that Ghoravi traveled extensively overseas, including the Middle East, which would be expected of someone in the import-export business.

Caplin and Detwiler listened to the report, shaking their heads.   The next logical step would be to put Ghoravi, his home, and office under surveillance, but there was no probable cause, and they certainly couldn't expect to get a court order for wiretaps.   Detwiler sent one of his agents up to visit the Westchester County Police to see whether they had any indication of Islamic fundamentalist activity in their jurisdiction and to inquire casually and indirectly about Ghoravi.

At the end, they settled for sending a list of keywords to every police precinct in the City and surrounding suburbs.   On the list, was every name, place, phone number, and brand that had been turned up, so far, in the Caspian Sea inquiry.   If any one of them turned up in the course of the precinct's operations, the Ops Center was to be notified immediately.   As the meeting ended, the call came in from Headquarters for Hannah to hurry down to the Langley Air Force Base stockade to re-interview al-Ghabrizi.   A plane was enroute to pick her up at Newark Airport, and she was to stop in Washington to report to the Director on the way back to New York.   She arrived at the airport, via NYPD radio car, as the plane was landing, and hid in a quiet corner of the terminal to call Balthazar's hotel, knowing that he would not be there.   She did not want to try her new cover story on such short notice, and contented herself with leaving a note telling him that she needed to make an unanticipated trip to Washington, and would call him later.

Still mulling his cover story, Khalid walked to the subway station a couple of blocks from the Tremont yard, and took the train downtown. He had decided to tell Ghoravi that the men were casual laborers he had hired to speed up the handling and delivery of supplies to the tour boats during Fleet Week. By the time the owner found out the truth, it would make no difference. As the train clattered toward Lower Manhattan, Khalid mused bitterly over the convenience of having an end date certain, beyond which nothing mattered.

He arrived at the Caspian Sea offices to find Ghoravi tied up on a conference call, so he waited in the outer office. That room also had a window wall that looked out on the harbor and the Fleet Week celebrations still going strong. Khalid watched for a while, and saw a tour boat come downriver and pass between the visiting units tied up at the piers and those anchored in the stream. He noted that it appeared to be escorted by a small patrol boat, either Coast Guard or NYPD Harbor Patrol. If that was a standard procedure, there might be trouble trying to reach the target, Khalid worried, as he was ushered into the inner office.

Ghoravi was at the window, and remained there looking down for a few moments while Khalid stood uneasily behind him. Then, he turned and motioned his visitor to a chair, which surprised Khalid who had not expected to be asked to sit down.

"Thank you for coming in, Mr. Khalid," Ghoravi told him as he sat down behind his desk. "I wanted to talk with you about how you've been running Tremont, in particular the tour boat resupply account."

Here it comes, Khalid thought.

"I have been looking over the reports and invoices that Mrs. Mingkovsky sends in every day and have been very impressed. The Fleet Week volume of business has been much greater than we expected, and the increased flow of supplies in and out of the yard must have been very difficult to handle. But, you have done extraordinarily well."

Khalid tried to cover his surprise, while appearing modest.

"I called your office with a question one day," Ghoravi continued, "and Mrs Mingkovsky told me that you had four men helping you handle the additional workload. I am very impressed by your initiative and good judgment, which explain why we are doing so well."

He reached into a desk drawer and pulled out a check that he handed to Khalid.

"This is a bonus to show the company's appreciation," Ghoravi told him. "When things quiet down after Fleet Week, we will get together and discuss an adjustment to your regular salary. Thank you again. You have done very, very well."

The check was for three thousand dollars, more money than Khalid had ever received at one time. He walked to the station staring at it, and held it in front of him in the crowded subway car as he rode up to the Bronx. So startled was he by his reversal of fortune, even though the downside had only been imagined, that it escaped him for a while that the check was worthless to him. He could not cash it, the banks were already closed for the weekend, and by Monday he would be dead. When that realization came to him, he thought also of how he was repaying Ghoravi's appreciation. It surprised him that he cared at this point, and he thought of his wards who cared about nothing, now that they had dedicated themselves to God. He decided to endorse the check to Anna, and to put it in her desk, where she would find it next week.

When Khalid got to his station, he noticed several policemen on the opposite platform, and a number of vehicles with flashing lights in the street above. He saw a man he knew from the neighborhood in a small crowd of onlookers, and asked him what was going on.

"A woman went off the platform and under a train. Cops think she was pushed. They're trying to find out who she was." He was very matter of fact, as though it happened every day.

The Tremont yard was quiet when Khalid reached it. He found the men in the office watching television. Anna was not there. But, it was past her normal departure time, and she was, he thought, on the subway headed home. Then he noticed her handbag was still on the desk, lying open with its contents hanging out, as if they had been pawed through. The men noticed him looking at the purse, and stared fixedly at the television screen.

"What has happened here?" he shouted. "What have you done?"

The men affected ignorance and boredom, and it was not clear that Khalid's question would be answered. Finally, one of them turned to him and responded with a shrug:

"She was a lot of trouble, and we were tired of her shouting at us. What does it matter? She was an old woman and a Jew. In a few days, it will make no difference."

"It will make no difference", he repeated to himself. "Nothing makes any difference." Then, he thought involuntarily, "If nothing makes a difference, why are we doing this. Why did Anna need to die, and why am I forced to put up with these ignorant, arrogant pigs?"

To the men, he shouted: "You idiots! I was just at the subway station and it is crawling with police. They know that Anna was pushed off the platform, and they are investigating. If someone recognized whichever of you did this, the police could find their way here, and it would all be over for us. In any event, they are likely to canvass the neighborhood, so you will have to stay here, inside until it is time to begin the operation."

The men said nothing, but looked at Khalid as though he were crazy, and he knew that he would have to watch them at all times. He felt that he had lost control, but also that he did not care, and that scared him. He went out into the yard and dialed the number Balthazar had given him. There was a note of surprise in Balthazar's voice when he answered, after many rings.

"What is it you want?" he asked inhospitably.

Khalid took perverse pleasure in relating what had occurred. After their meeting, he had decided that Balthazar was an arrogant prick playing games with peoples' lives, in particular his. Now, he told him:

"I am seriously concerned that I will not be able to control the men when the time comes. They have committed a terrible crime. I want you to come here tomorrow to talk with them."

Khalid heard a sharp intake of breath, after which a long silence.

"Do you really think that will be necessary?" Balthazar finally replied. "I am very busy."

"It will take only a few minutes. You must put the fear of God in them."

Another long silence, then Balthazar reluctantly acquiesced. He agreed to take the subway up to the Tremont Avenue station, where Khalid would pick him up at about 10 AM Saturday morning. The latter could hear the distaste in Balthazar's voice and feel his annoyance and, despite himself, he smiled.

CHAPTER TWENTY-ONE

Hannah was met at the Langley Air Force Base operations building by the same Agency liaison officer. While they drove to the stockade, he filled her in on what had transpired. Hannah's direction, during her earlier visit, that the prisoner be given access to Arab satellite TV channels had borne fruit. Generally, al-Ghabrizi would stare impassively at the TV monitor, which was installed on a high shelf out of reach. Other than read the Koran and the Arabic language newspapers brought to him, he had little else to do. When the report began appearing in the Middle East that he had been given up to the CIA because he had become too old and incompetent, al-Ghabrizi started pacing his cell talking angrily to the TV set. Finally, he banged on the door and demanded to see Hannah.

After notifying CIA Headquarters that she had arrived, Hannah went immediately to al-Ghabrizi's cell. He was eating an austere dinner when she entered carrying a chair, since there were none in the cell

"You are kind to come on such short notice," he began courteously. "I do not like to use translators, and you speak our language very well."

"We are, of course, very interested in what you have to say," she replied

Hannah waited expectantly for him to begin. There would be no introductory small talk, and al-Ghabrizi was presumably unaware that Hannah knew of his reaction to the Al-Arabiya announcements regarding his expendability. He chewed reflectively on a last piece of bread before beginning to speak.

"When you told me last time we met," he began, "that you had evidence I had been betrayed to the Pakistani police and the CIA, I did not believe you. I could not see why anyone in a position to know where I was that night would do such a thing. I still do not believe it, but these recent developments have made me concerned."

"You think that one of your rivals may have done it to get you out of the way?" Hannah asked.

Al-Ghabrizi looked momentarily startled. "Oh, you mean the business about my being too old to lead the jihad? That is nonsense. There is no person waiting in the background to become the next al-Ghabrizi. It is much too late for that: the jihad has gotten too big and is moving much too fast for any single individual to suddenly appear on television to claim that he is the supreme leader. I was present at the beginning, when I and the handful of people with me were the jihad. Our task was to attract followers and resources so that we could mount spectacular operations that would bring us more followers and more money. You will agree that we have been very successful, so much so that the glorious movement has unfortunately escaped us, which is why, irony of ironies, I am here talking with you."

He had reminded himself of his ill-fortune, and looked very sad as he finished speaking and took a sip of bottled water.

It was Hannah's turn to be startled.   Why had al-Ghabrizi reacted the way he had, if he was not concerned about being replaced?

"I was told by the people in charge here," she told him, "that you asked to see me because you were unhappy.   If that is so, what is it that you would like us to do for you?"

He did not reply immediately, surprised that she had come to the point so directly.

"I have a problem that must be dealt with," he began, "but it is obviously impossible for me to do anything in my current circumstances."

"What is the problem?" Hannah asked

"It is one that I have been ignoring for the past three years," he replied, "since I began working with the people I told you about when we first met.   Confined to this cell, I have had nothing to do all day but think, and it has forced me to face a reality that I have been avoiding.   Watching my presumed colleagues and disciples perform on television has helped to crystallize my thinking."

Hannah was mystified and fascinated, as she was sure were the people in the monitoring room videotaping the conversation. She waited for al-Ghabrizi to continue.

He took another sip of water.

"When I moved from the mountains, eventually to Karachi, I did so because there was no longer any point to remaining there.   Communications were poor, the Americans and Europeans had frozen my financial assets, and I rarely got to see anyone other than the people who lived with me.   We would watch satellite television and see all manner of groups claiming to speak in my name and crediting me with masterminding attacks all over the world. The final straw was when one of them began sending the stations voice recordings, supposedly made by me, claiming great victories for the global jihad and promising all out war on the infidel.

I am not a vain man and, for a long while, I welcomed and cheered every operation, believing that a blow for Islam was its own justification, and that it did not matter who struck it and for what reason. It was during that period that some of these people approached me with money and flattery, saying that I was the true leader of the jihad and that they wished to support my efforts. I was foolish enough to believe them."

Hannah wanted very badly to ask who these people were and where they were to be found, but wisely refrained from breaking the thread of al-Ghabrizi's narrative. He had again assumed a sad expression, as he thought back to the period he was describing.

"Having taken their money and support," he continued, "I became their prisoner, in the sense that I could not direct operations on my own or even decide whether or not a proposal from a jihadist cell in one place or another should be supported. When my opinion was asked about some matter, I could tell that it did not count for much because what was done was frequently different from what I had recommended. I was asked to help with operations---the meeting at which I was taken was an example—but never in a key position."

Al-Ghabrizi again stopped to drink, and Hannah got the feeling that what he had said thus far was preamble. Western intelligence agencies had been bewitched by the al-Ghabrizi image and track record, and had invested a great deal in efforts to comprehend and counter his organization and leadership. The belief that there is linkage among terrorist activities around the world is a very attractive one, because it implies that, if the organizations and individuals comprising that linkage can be determined, carefully targeted counterstrikes could bring down the whole thing. Hence, the focus on al-Ghabrizi. If he could be captured or killed, his organization presumably would be seriously degraded and its operations halted or, at least, seriously delayed.

"What I came to find out is that there are many groups and individuals separately pursuing their goals and their businesses in the name of God and under the flag of jihad. And not all of their efforts are directed against the common enemy."

Al-Ghabrizi spoke in the very tired voice of a man reading the handwriting on the wall.

"They shout the same slogans against the Jews and justify their actions in the name of poor Muslims around the world who are being abused. But, some of them are wealthy businessmen and oil barons who are doing it to protect and further their own interests. Others have dedicated themselves to the impossible triumph of Islam throughout the world, while others, I suspect, are criminals looking for opportunity to make a lot of money, perhaps by selling out their fellow jihadis to the Western intelligence services, as I was."

"How do these people operate?" Hannah asked quietly.

"Almost always," he replied, "they have other people to do their work. There are specialists who, for a very large fee, will plan, organize, and execute a major operation in any location in the world. The customer need only supply the necessary martyrs, since these people are much too smart to sacrifice themselves. I don't know the details, but I suspect the two men I was interviewing when arrested were intended for that purpose."

"Why does all of this concern you so much?" Hannah wondered. "I assumed that you would believe that any strike against the infidels, particularly Americans, is to be cheered and supported."

Al-Ghabrizi looked at her sharply.

"At the beginning that was true," he replied. "I believed that, if we continued to hit the West all over the world, showing them that no one and no place is safe from our vengeance, they would eventually agree to our demands as the price of security. But, I had underestimated their willingness to resist and ability to fight back. I thought that our great victory in New York would be decisive, but it turned out to be the opposite, and the battle became larger as more and more Muslims, alone and in groups, joined. It is now very easy to achieve martyrdom virtually any place in the world by going to your local mosque and finding someone who will put you in touch with one of these organizations that profess to speak in my name."

He shrugged and took another sip of water.

"The operations are simple. You fill a vest, a knapsack, or a vehicle with an easily obtained or manufactured explosive, then a martyr takes it to a target of greatest impact and detonates it. If you can do that multiple times simultaneously, the effect is many times greater because it demonstrates a high level of planning and coordination. But, the costs are relatively trivial, and there are organizations throughout the Muslim world, and even in the West, that will gladly defray them."

"I believe that your description is accurate, Sheikh al-Ghabrizi," Hannah responded. "But, you sound as though you disapprove of these efforts, and I find that surprising."

"What you detect is more despair than disapproval. We are forgetting that the jihad must have a goal and an end. God does not sanction killing and destruction for its own sake. While we point to the existence of Israel and its support in the West as the root cause of our anger and outrage, much of the jihad involves Muslims killing other Muslims. We have never been a united people, and the extremes of our beliefs create a thirst for vengeance that could engulf our society like a plague. When it is over, we would be exhausted, but still have nothing."

At that point, an orderly entered the cell, accompanied by a guard. He removed the remains of the prisoner's dinner and left a large pot of hot tea, two mugs, and a plate of almond cakes and dried fruits and nuts that Hannah had picked up in New York. Hannah poured cups for al-Ghabrizi and herself, and extended the plate to him. He took a cake almost eagerly.

"You are very good at what you do, Miss Crossman," he smiled shyly.

"Thank you, sir," she replied. "That is a very great compliment coming from you. What you have been telling me will be of the greatest interest to my superiors. We see the same things you do, but from the opposite angle. It seems to me that the question for all of us is what do we do about it."

He paused, perhaps contemplating the prospect Hannah's statement presented. Then, he smiled wryly.

"Perhaps, I should be happy that I am here in your prison, where I no longer need worry about meeting that challenge. I am not willing to lend myself to your fight against my brothers."

"But, are they all really your brothers? Hannah asked. "They may all be Muslims, but brothers do not kill one another indiscriminately. You know what will happen: the jihad will become all about revenge, and the people will suffer, as they have suffered in Iraq, Afghanistan, Lebanon, and elsewhere. The Western countries will take control of the oil fields to safeguard their interests, and your people will be back where they were in the 1940s."

Al-Ghabrizi nodded sadly, then sipped his tea.

"Unfortunately, what you are saying is likely to be the truth. Once the madness begins, I do not know how it can be stopped until everyone is exhausted. Our people are poor, and hatred is to them a cherished luxury, particularly when it promises early entry into heaven."

"But, we can't just sit idly by and let it happen," Hannah protested. We should at least try to stop people who make a profession of terrorism."

"I agree with you," al-Ghabrizi replied throwing up his hands. "But no one has told me who these people are, and I don't believe that you will find them in one place or in a single organization. It has become relatively cheap and easy to become a terrorist mastermind, and soon there will be al-Ghabrizis all over the world. For your intelligence agencies and police forces, the agents of the jihad will become the same as drug runners and other gangsters: anonymous men sneaking around your cities and ports subverting the established order and robbing you of your peace and comfort."

His final words were spoken slowly and with great bitterness, and Hannah realized that she had forgotten that they were conversing in Arabic. The interview was clearly at an end, and she thanked him for his candor and patience. He reminded her that it was he who had asked her to come, and assured her that he did not regret it. As she left the cell, he was again staring at the television screen above the doorway.

Hannah left for her waiting plane as soon as she had determined that the monitoring room had captured the entire interview on videotape, and directed that it be sent electronically to the AGWOG at Headquarters ASAP. She called ahead from the plane to determine the whereabouts of Admiral Bergen who, it turned out, was at dinner at the Saudi embassy, and would not be available until later. Everyone else she called was gone for the day, it now being after 8 PM, so Hannah decided to go directly to New York. She would check in with everyone in the morning. Thinking back on her talk with al-Ghabrizi, Hannah concluded that the most compelling thing that had been learned was that he did not believe that he had been done in by a would-be usurper, and that, in fact, there would be no future al-Ghabrizis. That, she thought, might make President Tucker feel a lot better, except that he couldn't very well cite al-Ghabrizi as the source of his confidence. Before settling down for the remainder of the flight into Newark Airport, Hannah called the Director's duty officer at Headquarters on the secure phone, and was told that there was no news from Karachi. Jed, the Agency's station chief, was standing by, but had not yet been given a meeting site. Hannah sat back, and thought about getting to New York in time to meet Balthazar for a late supper.

Admiral Bergen called Hannah as her plane entered the landing pattern for Newark. She reviewed the meeting with al-

Ghabrizi for him, telling him what she was planning to do as a follow-up.

"It's still not clear to me why al-Ghabrizi asked for the meeting," Bergen complained.

"I think that he wants to find some way to strike back against the people who've ratted him out," Hannah responded. But, when we came right down to it, he couldn't face up to working with us. I suggest we give him more time to stew about it. I've left orders to allow him access to all the news channels and to provide him all the Arabic-language newspapers and magazines we can get our hands on. He's also going to get better food."

Bergen approved, and told Hannah to keep him closely informed as to what was going on in New York City.

At the Waldorf, John Balthazar was not nearly as contented as he had been at the beginning of the day. He had been fantasizing about his forthcoming evening and night with Hannah when he got the message telling him of her sudden need to go to Washington. Later, he had gotten the call from Khalid about his difficulty with the men. Balthazar did not want to see them, but could not take the risk of them screwing up the operation. He had come in contact with imminent martyrs in connection with earlier operations, and they gave him chills. He could not understand how rational people, many of them educated and with reasonable prospects, could allow themselves to be talked into killing themselves. From what he had been told by the people who worked for his employers, finding and preparing them was relatively easy, even in the advanced countries of the West. Some responded to the promise of a warm welcome into heaven by countless virgins, others to the opportunity to exact vengeance for perceived crimes against Islam. It interested Balthazar that these grievances were rarely personal or even local, but rather of a sweeping nature, testifying that the martyrs' sacrifices were not made for trivial purposes. That was, perhaps, the explanation, he mused. What attracted this unlikely band of people to self-destruction was the perceived opportunity for fame on a global, even celestial, scale as an instrument of God.

Balthazar smiled at the thought. If this was true, then how should the world view someone like himself, who accomplished what he did on a much grander and more spectacular scale without killing himself? Was what earned God's favor the blow struck in the name of Islam or the fact that the martyr was killed in the act of striking it? It could not be the latter, since suicide is contrary to the teachings of the Koran. At that point in his interior dialogue, Hannah called from a taxi. She was on her way to the Waldorf, and would be with him shortly. He smiled happily as he hung up the phone. Ultimately, he knew, it was all about vanity.

240

CHAPTER TWENTY-TWO

"We have two days to go, folks, and we're still looking good. Let's not slack off now that we're almost home free." Richard Caplin concluded the Saturday morning staff update in a packed Operations Center, with the Washington contingent present. Afterward, Hannah briefed him, James Detwiler, and Jerry Ogden on her visit with al-Ghabrizi the evening before. She was working on two hours sleep, but also a strong and very pleasant afterglow. If possible, she would get back to her hotel room in the afternoon for a long nap before joining Balthazar for the weekend. It turned out that Balthazar also had business to attend to this morning, so there were no explanations required when Hannah left him at 3 AM.

The New York people could not judge the significance of the fact that the men who were meeting with al-Ghabrizi were seamen. Even if it did indicate that a terrorist operation on the water was forthcoming, it said nothing about where or when. Detwiler pointed out, however, that there needed to be another factor in the calculus: that an operation, if there was going to be one, required a target that promised maximum shock effect.

"If you believe that there may be a terrorist attack forthcoming, then you've got to assume that New York is a likely target," Detwiler concluded.

"So, what do we do that we haven't already done?" the Mayor's Fleet Week Coordinator asked.

"The Army has had four helicopter gunships standing by at a base upstate," Caplin noted. "I'm going to ask that they be immediately brought down to Governors Island, which will put them in position to cover the entire harbor area. They can fly in by noon, while their support trucks come down the road under police escort."

Everyone nodded in agreement, and Detwiler assigned Jerry Ogden to work with the Coast Guard and the Army on coverage of the harbor area. The only other item on the screen at the moment, Caplin reported, was a homicide the afternoon before up in the Bronx. An elderly woman, on a crowded subway platform, had been pushed under an oncoming train while her handbag was being snatched. The perpetrator had escaped.

"Why should that be of note to us?" Detwiler asked.

"I don't know that it is," was the reply. "But, some of the witnesses reported that the guy who did it looked like an Arab. Of course, others said he looked Hispanic."

"Welcome to the Bronx," someone volunteered.

"We're going to need to check it out," Caplin continued. "Problem is that all of her ID was in the missing handbag. So, we have no idea who she was. But, she apparently had bad feet, because there were prescription orthotics in her shoes. They have a registration number on them, which we should be able to trace back to the lab that made them. But, it's Saturday, and we're having trouble getting in touch with people who can help."

"Aside from that," he concluded, "there is nothing active on the police blotter that suggests anything more than plain old crime or mischance. As you know, the Caspian Sea Trading Company inquiry has turned up nothing about the company or its people that would give probable cause to justify further investigation."

Hearing that name reminded Hannah that she had not checked back with the analyst at CIA Headquarters about Balthazar's Marseille International Corporation. Her contact informed her that there was nothing new, beyond the coincidence he had told her about earlier that the company and its CEO had business in most of the cities struck by major terrorist attacks. Since all of them were major commercial hubs, that could not be considered any sort of an indicator. In response to Hannah's questions, the analyst confirmed that there was frequent interaction among the firms Balthazar owned, again not unusual considering that they were all in complementary businesses. On a hunch, Hannah asked whether the Caspian Sea Trading Company was mentioned in the file, and was rewarded with the revelation that it was a long-term customer of Marseille International.

Balthazar took the subway up to the Bronx, and was met outside the station by Khalid, who drove him to the Tremont yard. He had wondered how to dress for the occasion, and settled on a very conservative black suit, white dress shirt, and a striped tie in the colors of Hezbollah. Khalid told him that the men had been sullen and incommunicative since he had confronted them the day before. Their leader had told him that they were now responsible only to God, and could do as they pleased as long as they carried out the mission that would get them into heaven. Balthazar would have a difficult time with them..

The men were watching television in the office, and did not immediately turn around when Balthazar and Khalid entered. Balthazar stood watching them for a moment, then signaled Khalid to turn off the television, which got their attention. He continued to stare at them until they began to be noticeably uncomfortable and resentful. Then he began speaking to them in Arabic, in a voice that Khalid found surprisingly restrained and matter-of-fact.

"Sheikh al-Ghabrizi has sent me to assure you that God is observing you, and is pleased with your service to him. The task he has chosen for you is a difficult one, but he is sure that you have dedicated yourselves to its completion. I have been charged with giving you this token of the reward that is waiting for you in heaven."

Balthazar then handed each of the men a large, very shiny, gold coin that he had purchased at a midtown numismatic exchange on the way to the subway station. The men were thunderstruck, and stood staring at the coins glittering in their hands. This was more gold than any of them had ever seen, much less possessed, and they looked now in awe on Balthazar as the emissary of the great al-Ghabrizi, who spoke for God.

Balthazar signaled Khalid, and they left the office, unnoticed by the men who were busy chattering among themselves and examining their coins under a magnifying glass.

"You will have no trouble with them now," he told Khalid.

"That was absolutely brilliant," the latter responded, despite his dislike of Balthazar. His expectation of a violent confrontation, at best a standoff, had been unfulfilled.

"The best $5000 I've ever spent," Balthazar assured him. "Are you ready to go in all other respects?"

Khalid realized that he could not now say no, that Balthazar had gotten around him as well as the men. "Yes, I am ready," he replied, surprising himself with the strength of his voice.

"Good." Balthazar looked relieved. "I bought an additional coin for you," he told Khalid. "I am happy not to need it, but I will give it to you anyway as a token of my admiration for what you are doing."

Khalid looked at the coin shining in the palm of his hand. Tomorrow it would be worthless to him.

Jed had grown weary of sitting in his Karachi office waiting to be contacted by whoever it was that had three million dollars worth of information on al-Ghabrizi to sell. He had grown infinitely more tired of the incessant phone calls and messages from Headquarters asking whether it had happened yet, and had finally gone down the street from his office to a falafel stall for a bit of lunch. He was standing near the stall eating when he became aware of someone standing unnecessarily close. Jed turned his head slowly, and found next to him a man he recognized, after a moment, as the officer in charge of the raiding party that arrested al-Ghabrizi. Seeing that he had been recognized, the officer (in civilian clothes) spoke softly, almost into Jed's ear:

"I have been told to give this to you. It is what you are waiting for."

With that, he slipped a small envelope into Jed's hand, behind the falafel wrapping, and moved off unhurriedly. Jed was on the telephone to Headquarters the moment he reentered his office. The envelope contained a small piece of torn notepaper with two sentences written on it: " Please wire the agreed amount to the account of the Islamic Global Refugee Fund at the

Bank of Granada. When the deposit has been confirmed, we will send you the information immediately."

Later, Jed was talking with his boss, the Agency's Director of the Clandestine Service, who wondered: "Why all the screwing around? They could have made the swap in Paris two days ago."

"Doing it the way they did was intended to give us confidence that we're not being ripped off. I don't think it was mere coincidence that the note was handed to me by the same police captain who led the al-Ghabrizi raid. It tells us that, if they had inside information then, why shouldn't they have it now. Very clever! That's why they changed the venue to Karachi."

"Why do you think they would be giving the money to charity, rather than keeping the cash we got for them," the DCS asked.

"We need to check out how real the charity is," Jed replied, "but they could be trying to tell us that this is not being done by some guy trying to make a bundle for himself by ratting out one of the big boys."

"Well, the Director's authorized the wire transfer, and it's in progress now. If they keep their word, we should have the three million dollar name by the end of the day."

"Then what?" Jed asked.

"I don't know," was the response. "It depends on what the name is. But we, sure as hell, need to get something for our three million bucks."

The DCS's estimate was accurate. Late on Saturday, Tom Keener in Paris received another anonymous Email, saying that the man who betrayed al-Ghabrizi was Safwan al-Mufti, a Lebanese currently living in France.

248

CHAPTER TWENTY-THREE

"Who the hell is he?" the President exploded. "I've never heard the name."

He was sprawled on a sofa in the Residence, resenting having his weekend interrupted. John Cook, DNI Bierschmidt, Admiral Bergen, and Donald McGinnis, Director of the FBI stood nearby, hoping to make an early retreat.

"We don't know yet, Mr. President," the DNI replied. "He doesn't appear on any of our lists of known terrorists and their supporters. We believe the French will know, but it is a weekend night in Paris, and we are not having success getting hold of someone who might be able to help."

"I'm kind of relieved that it turned out to be someone we've never heard of," Tucker volunteered, "because it means that there isn't another what's-his-name lurking in the bushes."

"That's not necessarily good news, Mr. President," his Chief of Staff gently contradicted. "It would be disturbing if there was anyone in the bushes we don't know about, particularly someone in a position to bring down an al-Ghabrizi."

"The way this was handled by our source indicates that this guy is not just a driver or household servant looking to make a buck," Bergen added.

"What about that charity?" the President asked. "We'll look like idiots again, if the media find out that we've given three million dollars to a terrorist benevolent society."

"It is a long-established Islamic charity that we've been watching for quite a while," Bierschmidt reported. "We have our suspicions, but have not been able to find any association with extremist organizations."

"It does not operate in the United States," the FBI Director added, "but money can always be gotten to it by international wire transfer, just as we did."

The President signaled them to sit down.

"However it turns out," he complained, "there never seems to be an end to this business. When we find out who this guy is, there will be another guy, then another. Sometimes they're working with one another, other times they're enemies, except when they're not. The only thing that seems certain is that every year there are more of them, and they are causing us more trouble. Can we do something to put an end to it, once and for all?"

His four visitors looked at one another until Cook took on the question.

"I'm afraid, Mr. President, that there is no once and for all," he explained. "Islamic extremism, in its current manifestation, is still young, and it's hard to tell how long it will last. We have, I think, two basic options. We can either try to destroy it, as we did German and Japanese fascism, or we can contain it and let it run its course, as was done with Communism. None of this, however, can be done overnight."

"That's very interesting, John," Tucker responded, "but I can't just tell the American people that they need to take the long view, and wait out the terrorists. "We need a visible plan of action that is explainable, one that shows enough progress to keep our political support from disintegrating."

Admiral Bergen entered the discussion.

"The Islamic extremist movement has one dominant characteristic that it does not share with the others. It has no unitary leadership and coherent organization. Al-Ghabrizi was no Hitler or Stalin. His ability to lead and control was limited and being continually nibbled away, as he himself has told us. More important, it's not just that the jihad lacks central leadership, it's that it has many would-be leaders who oppose one another as much as they collectively oppose the infidels. It is not unlikely that, if contained, the jihad would destroy itself as the various political, ethnic, and ideological factions battled for supremacy, particularly in Central Asia."

"At the beginning," Bierschmidt added, " al-Ghabrizi apparently believed or hoped that, if he could shock and hurt the West sufficiently with attacks like 9/11, he could get us to negotiate peace, with he as the representative of the Islamic world. The general terms would be that there would be no further attacks in non-Muslim countries in return for al-Ghabrizi's religious extremists being allowed free reign in Muslim countries. He was probably prepared even to negotiate a modus vivendi for Israel.

But there were two showstoppers. First, his share of the world would have included Saudi Arabia and the countries that hold much of the world's petroleum resources. Second, as al-Ghabrizi's recent fall demonstrates, his assumption that he could lead the Muslim world was false. Had he been able to get the West to buy his deal, no doubt every jihadi in the world would have shouted approval. But, their loyalty would have disintegrated while al-Ghabrizi was walking to the mosque to praise God for his victory."

The President had been listening impatiently. What, he asked, did containment mean? During the Cold War, it meant keeping the Communists from taking over more countries. Now, Bierschmidt responded, it meant keeping those countries that had Muslim majorities from becoming radicalized, particularly to the extent that they were willing to follow the leadership of someone like al-Ghabrizi. The number of countries in South and Central Asia, as well as in Africa, that could fall to extremist movements was substantial, and their populations were huge and mostly poor, with little stake in the status quo. There were already radical movements in almost all of them, but their governments were, thus far, able to control them, ironically through the use of authoritarian methods that we would normally oppose.

FBI Director McGinnis picked up from the DNI.

"We need to keep extremist factions, particularly those that would engage in active terrorism, from operating in safety and secrecy within the Muslim populations of Western nations. The most valuable resource we have in the fight against such groups is the informant within the neighborhood, the mosque, and local social groups who learns about something going on and tips off the police or the FBI. Some of these people do it for money, but most do it because they don't share the goals and hatreds of the extremists, and don't want to have their lives disrupted. If the extremists are allowed to get too strong, they will intimidate the people they are hiding among, and we lose those sources."

"What's the FBI's view on how we're doing here in the United States?" the President asked.

McGinnis looked at his colleagues for a long moment before beginning.

"I think we are doing well, Mr. President, but we can never be complacent. The leaders in the Muslim communities around the country are cooperating, as are individual members. We have a number of cases that have become public, and several that are still being worked, of small groups of men who decided to join the jihad and began preparing to blow something up along with themselves. None of them got very far, and there was no indication of outside support from al-Ghabrizi or anyone else. Compared to the homegrown terrorist operations in Europe, it was hard to take them seriously. The scary thing is that at least some of these people, all born Americans, were apparently willing to kill themselves and many others for a cause they had barely heard of before some storefront mullah beat it into their heads. If you really want to, it is still relatively easy to find a way to kill yourself and others here in the U.S. I'm afraid we're not going to be able to stop everybody."

"What about this guy al-Mufti. Where is he?"

The four answered almost simultaneously.

"We don't know yet, Mr. President. We have no record of him ever having entered the United States, and his name was not on any of our watch lists until a few hours ago. A check of Intelligence Community computer databases turned up nothing. We're hoping the French will give us a lead, and we've asked our people in Beirut to do some checking."

The President reacted angrily.

"I see now, John, why you said that having this guy turn out to be a total unknown isn't all that great. It would more comforting to have the next terrorist kingpin to shout and aim at, but all we've got is a mystery man, and we don't know where he is.

Thank you, gentlemen, for ruining my weekend. I hope you will have something useful to tell me next time I see you."

He quickly left the room, slamming the door.

Jerry Ogden was convinced that he was gaining his sea legs, after the better part of two days on the water. Or, maybe it was the Dramamine talking. Fortunately, it was a beautiful Saturday afternoon, with virtually no wind to roil up the harbor and Jerry's stomach. The small patrol boat he was riding carried the Coast Guard's scene commander, and had spent the day darting from one end of the upper bay to the other among the anchored and moving vessels checking on the positioning of the many guard boats stationed to protect Fleet Week visitors. The boat's crew had provided him with a blue jumpsuit to protect him from the spray, and a lifejacket like that everyone aboard wore at all times. Pressed, the boat was capable of 40 knots, and could turn on a dime, throwing anyone who wasn't hanging on into the harbor. Although there had been no need, thus far, for rapid maneuvers, Jerry made a point of hanging on.

He had been in touch by telephone with Hannah, who was in the Operations Center. She told him, as best she could over an unsecured circuit, that they had received the name of the person who had allegedly betrayed al-Ghabrizi. But, no one had recognized the name, and the Agency was flogging around trying to get the French to help. Jerry's boss, Detwiler, had been briefed, as had the New York City people. Other than that, she told him, nothing exciting was happening. Jerry asked her if she was interested in going to dinner on their last evening in New

York, but she told him that she had a prior engagement, which puzzled him.   Where had she gotten the time to make a prior engagement.

Jerry's musing was interrupted by an unpleasant drone, which grew steadily louder. He saw two pairs of helicopter gun-ships, painted olive drab with Army markings, sweeping across the harbor not more than a hundred feet above the surface of the water.   These, he realized, must be the birds that Caplin had called in taking a familiarization tour before sundown.   They stayed well away from the piers and anchored ships, eventually sweeping toward Governors Island off the tip of Manhattan. Jerry's boat would soon be going in for a crew change, and he decided to check in with Detwiler at the Ops Center before head-ing for his hotel room and a hot shower.   He liked being on the water, and made a whimsical mental note to check whether the FBI had a navy somewhere in which he could serve.

The Tremont Grocery Supply storage yard was normally closed on weekends.   But, during Fleet Work, demand from the Manhattan tour boat service was so great that Tremont sent a full truckload of supplies for the boats' snack bars every morning before the first boatload of passengers embarked.   The truck had come back from the morning's delivery, and Khalid gave the driver and crew Sunday off with pay as a reward for their hard work during Fleet Week. He and the men then loaded the truck with the cases of explosives disguised as foodstuffs that had come in the shipping container.   The next morning, just before de-parting the yard, they would supplement the load with the fresh foods that were normally supplied to the boats.

As they worked, Khalid kept looking at the windows of the office bungalow, half expecting to see Anna peering out at them with her usual look of disapproval and suspicion.   He looked at the men who, their moment of glory fast approaching, were horsing around with one another as they worked. Balthazar had been right about them. Periodically, one or another of them would pull out his gold coin and hold it up, tilting it so that the sun's rays made it glitter. The others would gather around him to look at it, talking to one another in serious tones. Earlier, Khalid had edged closer to overhear what they were talking about, and was surprised to discover that they were not joking with one another or congratulating themselves on their imminent acquisition of an untold number of virgins.   Rather, they appeared to be seeking reassurance in the shining of God's sun reflected in their faces that they were doing the right thing. As Khalid watched, he thought of Anna, and wished they had consulted God sooner.

CHAPTER TWENTY-FOUR

After the afternoon change-of-watch meeting at the Operations Center, Hannah decided to call it a day. Nothing was happening, and she wanted to do a bit of shopping before getting ready to meet Balthazar for dinner. She mentally reviewed the checklist of ongoing tasks and issues to make sure that there was nothing she needed to do before heading uptown. She had talked with the Director earlier when he called to make sure that everyone in New York had the word about al-Mufti. Still smarting from the al-Ghabrizi fiasco, the White House was extremely nervous at the prospect of an unknown person, who might be the new international terrorism kingpin, wandering around God-knows-where. Everyone in Washington was rushing to make sure the President was covered, and themselves as well. Bergen had chuckled when he said that, remembering his earlier conversation with Hannah.

Tonight and, perhaps, tomorrow would be the last opportunities that Hannah and Balthazar would have to be together, possibly for some long while. She had to be on the job in Washington Monday morning, and his worldwide businesses no doubt needed tending. Hannah had promised herself at the outset that she would not think about the future of their relationship or even about how much she cared for Balthazar or he for her.

It seemed strange that, except for their first meeting in Geneva, they had known one another little more than a week. Everything was moving so rapidly that Hannah could think only of today, anticipate tomorrow, and savor yesterday. Being with John Balthazar was exciting. There was something tingly in the shadows of their relationship that both knew was there, but neither cared to investigate. And the sex was magnificent.

Hannah lucked out at Bloomingdales, finding what she called a New York dress, meaning that she couldn't safely wear it in Washington. Back in her hotel room, she took a leisurely shower then dressed carefully, adjusting her makeup to the demands of the new dress. The results, she thought, were spectacular, and Hannah told herself jokingly that she was wasting her time at the CIA.

They met at a Japanese place on West 52nd Street which had contrived to craft cocktails and sushi that were so complementary that one could drink and nibble, and yet be able to go on to a full dinner. As they left to go over to the restaurant Balthazar had chosen, The Mediterranean, one of his favorites, Hannah was aware that she was being stared at, to the mock horror of Balthazar, who pretended to screen her from the admiring eyes. When they exited onto the sidewalk, a taxi screeched to the curb in front of them before the doorman even began to raise his arm.

"You are a huge success tonight, Hannah," Balthazar told her fondly after they had been seated in the restaurant. "To attract so much attention in Manhattan, a woman must be really special."

"It must be the dress," she responded archly. "Actually, it must be me," she corrected herself a moment later. " I know that it's the cocktails and the fact that I've had about two hours sleep in the past three days, but I feel spectacular. Ain't adrenalin wonderful?"

The adrenalin was still pumping several hours later back in Balthazar's hotel room. They were lying in bed, Balthazar smoking, Hannah's head resting on his chest.

"When are you planning to go back to Paris?" she asked.

"If my business here continues to go well," he replied, "probably Tuesday or Wednesday of next week. But, I may not go to Paris. I'm waiting to hear from some clients who want to meet with me." He indicated a laptop computer lying open on a table.

"But, I am very tired," he continued, " and would like most to go home and stay there, at least for a while."

"I know what you mean," Hannah responded. "It's the terrorism business, and it's becoming worse for people like me because it's becoming more and more complicated. Having to come up to New York turned out lucky, but it would have otherwise been a large scale pain in the ass."

"I'm glad it did, my love," Balthazar reacted, kissing the top of her head. "How do you think all of this will end?"

"At the moment," Hannah replied, "I'm not very confident that it will end soon or well, although I'm not sure I know what 'end' means Although all of the jihadis profess to know why they are blowing things up and killing people, they are far less clear about what it is that would cause them to stop, other than being killed or captured by their would-be victims. Each one wants something else, and they agree only that they all hate Israel and us for supporting it. One of the fundamental objectives of Hamas, for example, is the return to Islam of all the land it ever ruled, which would include a large chunk of Europe. How do you deal with that?"

"You seem very knowledgeable about this, Hannah," Balthazar observed.

"It's in the newspapers and on television here every day. Since it is affecting my life so directly, I thought I should know something about it," she replied quickly, berating herself for letting her guard down momentarily.

"What do you think?" she asked, hoping to move the conversation on.

"I pretty much agree with you," he replied, after a long hesitation. "But, I think your government does not yet realize, or perhaps doesn't want to accept, that it is not fighting a single, global war on terrorism, but rather many little wars, each requiring its own strategy and tactics. Many people thought that, if only al-Ghabrizi could be caught, the war would be won. Well, he has been eliminated, and all that has happened is that everyone is alarmed because they haven't yet figured out who will fill the vacuum."

"They say that al-Ghabrizi was deliberately betrayed to us. Do you believe that?" Hannah asked.

Balthazar shrugged. It was possible to believe that could happen, he recognized, given the character of some of the contenders for power and visibility within the jihad. But, there are so many of them that it would be difficult to point to one as the culprit. We should watch, he said, for the person who now begins to speak loudly in the name of God and Islam. He will be the one.

"Who do you think will be the new al-Ghabrizi? Hannah wondered.

"I've not yet figured out what happened to the old one," was the reply.

Said Ghoravi had fallen asleep in front of the television set. When he awoke, he discovered that his wife, Rena, had also fallen asleep in her chair. The silence in the house, broken only by Jay Leno's voice, told him that the children were asleep upstairs. Except when they had all gone to the mosque for prayers, the children had been banging about the house excited by the prospect of going downtown on Sunday to see the tall ships. In the morning, they would drive downtown to the Caspian Sea Trading Company's offices, from which a magnificent view of Fleet Week activities was to be had. Sunday was closing day, and special demonstrations were planned, including flybys of new and old model aircraft, which would be flying low enough so that those observing from Ghoravi's offices would see them passing below them. He had invited the owners and CEOs of his principal customers to attend with their families, and had arranged a catered brunch.

"I also invited a man named John Balthazar", he told his wife, "one of my overseas suppliers. He happens to be in town, and came to see me. He's an interesting man, a Lebanese Muslim who grew up in France, and has become a very successful businessman. We had a good chat. He says that he is thinking of relocating to the United States, and wanted to know how we Muslims are being treated here."

"What do you mean he says that he is thinking of moving," Rena asked. "Don't you think he was telling the truth?"

"He is a strange man," Ghoravi replied. "You will meet him. He is young, handsome, extremely well dressed, and financially successful. Despite his words, I did not get the impression that he was particularly concerned about religious persecution or that he himself was a devout Muslim. Rather, I felt that he wanted to meet me for another reason, and conjured up this emigration business in order to have something to talk about. He did not appear the kind of man who runs when things get a bit sticky."

"What could that reason be? You know that your description of him can apply to you as well," his wife noted.

Ghoravi blushed. "You are very kind, my love. But, I have nothing to hide. I can't imagine what reason he might have, except, perhaps, that he wished to assess his chances of stealing you from me."

It was Rena's turn to blush.

"The children are really looking forward to seeing the ships tomorrow. Now, I am looking forward to it as well. I will tell you my decision after I've seen your Mr. Balthazar."

Ghoravi pretended to be scandalized.

"This is very unIslamic behavior, Madame Ghoravi!"

"We are Americans now," she replied.

Khalid made the men spend their last night in the office bungalow at the Tremont yard. He could not afford to let them out of his sight, and planned to spend the night there as well. First, he covered the windows, so that the interior lights could not be seen from the street. The yard was surrounded by a high chain link fence, the gate to which was secured by a heavy chain and lock when the business was closed. But, the buildings were visible through the fence, and Khalid believed that he had seen the patrol cars of the local police precinct pass by more frequently than usual.   The men did not object to his demand, since the television was available and Khalid had laid in an enormous supply of junk food.   They did not plan to sleep this night, in any event.

Before returning to the yard for the night, Khalid straightened up his small apartment and wrote a note on his computer explaining why he needed to do what was planned for the next day.   He was glad that he didn't have a camcorder with which to make a martyrdom video, knowing that his face would not conceal the fact that he was not at peace with either himself or with God.   He printed the note, and left it on the kitchen table with his gold coin on top.

Richard Caplin had been to the theater, which let out just before midnight.   His driver, in an unmarked official sedan, picked him up outside the lobby and, on the way across town to his home, Caplin called the Operations Center to see whether any problems or issues had developed.   The senior officer on duty told him that all was still quiet.   The detectives watching the Ghoravi home in Westchester had reported that the lights had just gone out, and the family was apparently in bed.

One more day.

CHAPTER TWENTY-FIVE

It was still dark when Khalid woke the men, who were lying on the floor of the office propped against a wall. They had been up until the early hours praying and otherwise making their earthly peace, and Khalid had to restrain them from shaving their heads, pleading that it could attract police attention. Now, they began immediately to finish loading the truck, a large box model with the company's name painted on the sides, with perishable foods like bread and fruit from a large walk-in refrigerator in the yard warehouse. The requirements of Tremont's contract with the tour line company called for the four boats to be topped off each morning before they left their service pier on the East River to go around to the line's terminal on the Hudson River to pick up their first loads of passengers. This meant that Tremont's truck had to be at the pier by 6:30 AM to begin transferring its cargo.

After the loading was done, the men changed into the black trousers and white smocks worn by the Tremont people who manned the on board snack bars, and clambered aboard the truck. Khalid drove out of the yard, then got out of the truck to go back to lock the gate. He found that act bitterly amusing, since he no longer had to care what happened to the Tremont Grocery Supply Company.

They drove through still empty streets, it being Sunday, stopping at a 24-hour coffee shop to pick up two dozen fresh do-nuts. The men were now quiet and solitary, and left Khalid to his thoughts. He had stopped feeling sorry for himself, and had begun to visualize the coming hours and what needed to be done. It would be hell, if he sacrificed his life and botched the operation at the same time, even worse if he got caught and had to spend the rest of his life in an American prison.

The pier was long enough for two boats to tie up on each side, and held a small service building. Khalid drove out on to the pier, stopping at a point equidistant from the gangways of the four boats. Other contractors were already on scene pumping diesel fuel, cleaning up the debris of the previous day, and servicing the boats' mechanical and electrical equipment. A squad of National Guard soldiers in camouflage fatigues and helmets, armed with automatic rifles, was gathered near the service building drinking coffee. Khalid jumped from the truck and opened the boxes of donuts on its hood, shouting for all to come and partake, which they did with alacrity. This was Khalid's standard practice whenever he came to check on Tremont's operations. As a result, the people on the pier were always happy to see him.

The men began to disperse the contents of the truck among the four boats, careful to carry the boxes containing the explosives to the boat that would be leaving last for downtown. This was done to maximize the number of people likely to be in the target area when the boat arrived. Khalid asked the boat's captain if he could ride it downtown to see the Fleet Week ships, after which he would take the subway back to pick up the truck. He was invited to ride in the wheelhouse, which afforded the best view. Aboard the chosen boat, the men stacked the boxes of explosives in a large pantry at the back of the snack bar, filling it completely. They could be positioned anywhere on the boat, but it was important that they be concentrated in one place. As the other boats left, one after the other, for the passenger terminal, the men busied themselves getting the snack bar ready for customers. Two guardsmen assigned as security sentries hung out, waiting for the coffee urn to begin steaming and the sandwiches and cakes to appear on the counter.

Richard Caplin was in his car on the way downtown when he received a call from James Detwiler, who made an odd confession. Frustrated by the inability of the police to get a response over the weekend, Detwiler had sent agents, in the middle of the night, to the home of the owner of the laboratory that had made the orthotic recovered from the body of the woman killed in the subway on Friday.

"They scared the shit out of him, Rick, and I hope he doesn't think to complain to his Congressman or the Justice Department. But, we got the information we were looking for." He gave Anna's name, age, and home address.

"Why should we consider this special, Jim?" Caplin asked.

"Because Ms Mingkovsky worked for the Tremont Grocery Supply Company owned by one Said Ghoravi." Detwiler replied.

"Well done, Jim! I'm about fifteen minutes out."

Caplin signaled his driver, who flipped on the car's lights and siren, and then began ignoring all other traffic in his race down Broadway. The Deputy Mayor speed-dialed the watch commander at the Operations Center.

"Three things," he told him. "I want the tail on Said Ghoravi up in Westchester reinforced. He is to be followed wherever he goes, 24/7. Two, I want the precinct up in the Bronx that's got the Tremont Grocery Supply Company in its territory to send a couple of radio cars there immediately to check it and report back. The premises should be placed under round-the-clock surveillance. Three, find out which judge is available right now to approve search warrants. I believe we can now look at Ghoravi and Caspian Sea Trading more closely."

Hannah and Balthazar overslept and, with the addition of a bit of impromptu lovemaking, she did not leave the Waldorf until almost eight. She found rushing through the lobby of her hotel in the dress she had worn the evening before somewhat disconcerting. She was concerned about running into Detwiler, Jerry Ogden, or one of the FBI agents who had come from Washington with them, but in the event saw no one. In the belief that lovemaking creates a unique scent, Hannah showered quickly, dressed and was on her way downtown by taxi in twenty minutes. In the cab, she remembered to turn back on her secure cell phone, and discovered a message to call Director Bergen's office.

As she entered the Operations Center, looking for an unoccupied room to use as a phone booth, she was spotted by Jerry Ogden, who beckoned her over.

There was big news, and she was needed at a meeting in Caplin's office now, he told her. The meeting was just getting underway, with the entire Washington contingent present, in addition to all of the senior New York City officials. Caplin was speaking, then stopped when he spotted Hannah entering the room.

"New developments, Hannah," he told her, turning then to the group. "First, it turns out that the woman pushed off the subway platform on Friday night worked for one of Ghoravi's companies. If that doesn't give us probable cause, it comes close. I'm applying for search warrants for Tremont in the Bronx and for Caspian Sea Trading's headquarters here in Lower Manhattan. We've also tightened surveillance of him and the locations.

But, the really big news came from Washington early this morning. It turns out that the guy who is supposed to have ratted out Anwar al-Ghabrizi, the one whose name no one recognized, has been using another name. The French tell us that his current name is John Balthazar, and that he is a successful, international businessman."

Hannah froze. Had she told him anything she shouldn't have? What a marvelous CIA analyst she was! Did she love him? Unconnected thoughts raced like lightening through her mind.

Detwiler added to Caplin's revelation.

"The French also told us that Balthazar flew Air France from Paris to Washington on the Friday before last. Customs and Immigration say that he listed the Willard Intercontinental Hotel as his local destination. The hotel says he stayed there that weekend, then checked out Monday morning. We haven't the foggiest idea where he is now."

"He's in Room 836 of the Waldorf-Astoria." Hannah heard herself speak without recognizing her voice. Everyone turned to stare at her. Caplin nodded to the Chief of the NYPD, who rushed from the room. No one appeared willing to ask Hannah how she knew. Just then, a police sergeant entered the room and spoke to Caplin, who then turned to the group.

"Surveillance reports the Ghoravis on the move, probably toward the City. It appears that the Tremont premises in the Bronx is shut tight, but patrol says that a big box truck that was in the yard yesterday is not there now."

Caplin had no more news to add, but was unwilling to return to what they were talking about before the fortunate interruption. So, he reminded them that this was the final day of Fleet Week, after which they were home free. Don't let even the slightest inkling of something unusual pass by uninvestigated, he cautioned, and make sure that everyone knows what's going on. He then left the room as though it was on fire.

After Hannah left, Balthazar showered and shaved, then put on what he considered his most attractive spring suit and a spectacular silk tie he had picked up on Fifth Avenue the previous day. He decided to walk leisurely over to Central Park before taking a cab downtown to Ghoravi's office for the Fleet Week viewing later in the morning. Balthazar was on his way out of the hotel when Hannah revealed his presence, and long gone when the NYPD detectives and FBI agents sent by Caplin and Detwiler showed up at the reception desk. None of the staff in the busy lobby had seen him go, and the officers lacked a photo of Balthazar, which the French had not yet been able to provide.

As he walked, Balthazar reviewed the recent course of events and the plans currently unfolding. He could find nothing to be alarmed about at the moment, and this made him uneasy. Was it possible that Hannah's presence, both physical and constantly in his mind, had caused him to miss something? He stopped in a nearby doorway and dialed Khalid's cell phone number. After what seemed like an endless number of rings, he answered with a gruff Yes. He was at the pier, the boat was getting ready to go downriver, and everything was going according to plan. Balthazar smiled and continued his stroll.

"They've located him," John Cook told the President as he entered the Oval Office. "He's in New York. One of the Agency's people spotted him."

"Marvelous," the Chief Executive reacted sarcastically. "Are they going to arrest him or let him disappear again?"

"Well, they don't actually have him at the moment," Cook admitted. "They just know that he's in the City, and they're looking. There's no photo of him available yet, so they've got only a description to go by."

"What's he doing there? Do we have any idea? Tucker asked plaintively.

"He's an international businessman, and must have customers in New York," Cook explained. "It could be that he's in town on legitimate business or to take in a couple of Broadway shows. The FBI agents who looked into his visit to Washington tell us that he was seen around the Willard with a really good looking woman. We just don't know that much about him yet."

"Well, what's the worst-case scenario?" the President asked with a pained expression on his face.

"That he's in New York to blow up the fucking place."

The Ghoravi household was in turmoil as the family prepared for its trek downtown. The reception at the Caspian Sea Trading Company offices was scheduled to begin at ten-thirty, timed so that attendees could view the early Fleet Week events taking place below their vantage point. Said Ghoravi, the host, needed to be there earlier to make sure the caterer was performing properly and to greet early arrivals.

The children were racing around the house, eager to be off, and chafing at the delay. Their mother was putting finishing touches to her makeup and her dress. She had debated briefly whether or not to wear a head scarf, since a number of the guests at the reception would be Muslims. She decided to wear the scarf, but to be prepared to remove it, should none of the other guests be similarly observant. Her husband stood at the door to the garage saying again and again, each time louder, that it was time to go.

As be backed the family sedan into the street and set out for the expressway entrance, Ghoravi did not notice the unmarked car with two FBI agents following them. When they crossed the city limits, the two cars were joined by two unmarked NYPD radio cars as they proceeded downtown in growing congestion, with thousands of other people heading for the spectacular close of Fleet Week.

After the explosive ending of the morning meeting, Jerry Ogden found Hannah in a vacant office cubicle completing a call on her secure cell phone. The call last night had been to tell her what she had just heard from Caplin and Detwiler: that it was John Balthazar who had apparently betrayed Anwar al-Ghabrizi to the West. Hannah was incredulous. It was possible that she was so besotted with him as to be easily fooled, thinking with your vagina they had called it in training at the Farm, but there was a lot more to this business that needed explanation. What was Balthazar's relationship to al-Ghabrizi that put him in a position to accurately tip off the police in Karachi, and why would he have done so? If Balthazar knew about the meeting in Karachi, did he also know about the operation in which the two seamen meeting with al-Ghabrizi were allegedly supposed to participate?

If he did know, did that mean that Balthazar was also part of the operation? If he was, did his presence in New York indicate its location?

"Bloody hell!" Hannah exploded, startling Jerry standing behind her.

"What's going on?" he asked.

"Apparently," she told him, "I've been consorting with the enemy. According to Headquarters and its sources, the man I've been sleeping with is the guy who ratted out al-Ghabrizi."

Jerry now understood why the others had bailed out of the morning meeting so quickly.

"What are you going to do?" he asked.

"I suppose that I will hear about it from Headquarters eventually," Hannah replied. "But, in the meantime, I plan to help find him and discover what he's up to. Christ, I'm the only one around who knows what he looks like."

In the interim, Balthazar had ended his stroll with coffee and a bagel at a delicatessen on Broadway. He ate leisurely, then found a taxi to take him downtown, telling the driver not to hurry. It was the beginning of another of the marvelous Spring days with which Fleet Week had been blessed, and the traffic heading to lower Manhattan got denser, both in the streets and on the sidewalks, as Balthazar's cab moved southward. He found the lobby of Ghoravi's office building virtually deserted, it being Sunday, except for the usual security guards and two men standing near the revolving door, who looked like they might be policemen. Balthazar's name was on a list provided to the front desk by his host, and he was directed to the bank of six elevators.

In the Caspian Sea Trading Company offices on the 30th floor, he found that a number of guests had already arrived, and were sipping mimosas while gazing down on the festive scene below. Ghoravi was not yet there, but his office staff was busy introducing people to one another and providing them with food and drink. A display of the products provided to Caspian Sea by the firms owned by the guests, including Balthazar's Marseille International, was set up in the outer office and drawing proud attention.

Balthazar took a glass, shook hands when required, but stayed close to the large office windows. He knew what was supposed to happen, but he didn't know precisely when or where. Ghoravi had thoughtfully rented, for use by his guests, ten or so pairs of binoculars, one of which Balthazar appropriated. When the first tour boat appeared in his field of vision, turning the corner off South Ferry to head up the Hudson, he watched closely as it passed through the congested area that was the center of Fleet Week displays and activities, seemingly shepherded by one of the small patrol boats darting restlessly around the harbor.

The Ghoravis' trip downtown was being impeded by an accident on the parkway ahead of them, as reported to the Operations Center by the trailing surveillance vehicles. The detectives posted in the lobby of Ghoravi's office building had learned of the reception taking place in his offices, and it was now assumed that was where he was heading. The Ops Center informed them that warrants were expected momentarily, and that the plan was to question Ghoravi when he arrived, and to search his offices. Caplin outlined his intentions to James Detwiler and Hannah, and asked for their support. Afterward, Detwiler told Hannah that he had spoken with Admiral Bergen about her.

"I gather that I'm in big trouble," she told him. "I should have called Headquarters, and told them, but I couldn't bring myself to do it. How am I going to explain this, without appearing a mindless twit who can't keep her legs together?"

"No one in Washington had yet heard about your...er...difficulty when I called to talk with Admiral Bergen about it," Detwiler explained. "I wanted him to get a clear perspective on what happened, before he got it third hand through the reporting chain."

"How did he react?"

"He didn't explode, if that's what you mean. He believes that, if there's an issue here, it would be a security issue, not a moral one. And, he doesn't believe that there is a security problem. He said that he doesn't have time to take it up with you right now, but will see you about it when you get back to Washington."

"Wow," Hannah exhaled with explosive relief, not aware that she had been holding her breath.

"In any event," Detwiler concluded, "the Admiral recognized that, but for you, they never would have found out where Balthazar is. That information saved his ass at the White House, at least temporarily."

CHAPTER TWENTY-SIX

The tour boats each required a crew of only three: a pilot in the wheelhouse, an engineer down in the engine room, and a deckhand to handle everything else. Its twin diesel engines could move the boat along at a rapid clip, particularly when there were no passengers aboard, and were fully controllable from the pilot house. The engineer stayed in the engine room only as a precautionary measure when the boat was underway.

The last boat pulled in its gangway, and backed out into the river. It was normally a half hour run to the passenger terminal on the Hudson in midtown. But, Fleet Week congestion around the Battery added fifteen minutes to the trip. With a blast of its horn, the boat turned south, and headed downriver, Khalid standing outside the pilothouse, the breeze ruffling his hair.

Below, on the main deck, the men had finished stowing the boxes they had carried aboard, except for the last one, which contained four pistols with silencers and short-range walkie-talkie radios. Concealing their weapons behind the snack bar counter, the men looked out at the guardsmen and the deckhand who were sitting in the dining area drinking coffee and eating donuts. With a nod from their leader, they darted out from behind the counter and shot the guardsmen. The boat's crewman, who might be needed later, was thrown to the deck and bound with plastic handcuffs. It was all done in less than a minute, the noise of the shots unnoticeable. The men appropriated the soldiers' automatic rifles, one going off to take prisoner the boat's engineer while another climbed to the upper deck to signal Khalid that the boat had been taken.

"What was that about?" asked the pilot, who had seen the hand signal.

"It was one of my men telling me that we now control the boat. You will please do what I tell you," Khalid replied, without raising his voice. He had known this man as a friendly acquaintance for a year.

"Fuck that, Omar!" was the pilot's reaction. "What's going on here?"

Khalid pulled a pistol from his pocket and repeated the command.

"We have taken over the boat. The soldiers are dead, and the other crew members have been taken prisoner. If you wish to remain alive, Frank, you will do as you're told." He pointed the pistol at him for emphasis.

"What is it you want me to do?" the pilot asked.

"At the moment, nothing," Khalid replied. "Just continue on to the passenger pier as usual." He beckoned to one of the men, who had put on the uniform of one of the dead guardsmen and come up to assume the security sentry position outside the pilothouse. Kill him if he does anything different from what he is doing now, Khalid instructed the man, then left for a quick inspection of the boat. He looked off to the right and saw the Manhattan shore passing by, and could hear the horns of cars on FDR Drive impatient to get downtown.

Khalid returned from below carrying one of the walkie-talkie sets. He had checked out the engine room, where one of the men was holding the engineer at gunpoint. The latter was, at first, happy to see Khalid whom he had encountered on the service pier many times. Then, he realized that he was the enemy. Khalid told him that he was to keep the engines running and not make trouble, otherwise the grinning young man in the waiter's uniform would shoot him. With the guardsmen dead and the third crewman tied up, the leader of the men busied himself hooking up and activating the detonator for the explosives, while the remaining man donned the other guardsman's uniform and took the post at the stern that guards on the other boats occupied. The explosives were rigged with a cell phone detonator, the number of which was installed in the speed dial registers of the phones that all members of the party carried. It was Khalid's responsibility to set off the charge at the right moment, but any of the men could do it in an emergency. The boat passed the UN Building on the riverbank, the halfway mark in its journey downstream.

Jerry Ogden was back on the water, this time dressed more suitably for a day of patrolling the harbor. The boat he was on was assigned to roam about the bay checking waterborne traffic, and there were a lot of sudden course changes and high speed dashes. The surface of the harbor was, however, relatively calm, the sun's rays glinting off the wakes of the many craft crossing between the New York and New Jersey shores and among the boroughs of the City that bordered on the upper bay. In addition, it seemed as though every boat owner in the metropolitan area had felt an irresistible need to be out on the water to celebrate the grand finale of Fleet Week. The Coast Guard and

NYPD Harbor Patrol already had their hands full keeping them out of restricted areas, and it wasn't yet 10 AM.

Jerry called Hannah on his cell phone to ask how she was doing after the morning's shock. She told him about her conversation with Detwiler and his with Admiral Bergen. They had cleared the air, at least temporarily, and allowed everyone to focus on the situation at hand. At the moment, attention was focused on Ghoravi (Hannah called him the "import-export guy" on the open phone), who was apparently on his way downtown to his office. She had been told to join Detwiler and the NYPD people who were going over there to intercept him when he arrived. As yet, there was no basis for detaining Ghoravi personally, so the situation was going to be tricky.

"What about Balthazar?" Jerry asked. "Have we gotten a line on him?"

"Not yet," Hannah responded. "The lack of a photo is severely hampering the search. I met with a police artist to give a detailed description of Balthazar. The sketch, unfortunately, turned out to be the spitting image of George Clooney."

The tour boat passed beneath the Brooklyn Bridge, the last of the East River crossings before the river merged into the upper bay. Water traffic had become significantly heavier, and Khalid ordered the pilot to slow down. There had been a call from the terminal wanting to know when they expected to arrive. Khalid had allowed Frank to take it because his was the voice the people on the other end expected to hear. But, when the wheelhouse phone rang, Khalid had pressed the muzzle of his pistol against Frank's head, and warned him against trying to be a hero.   The pilot confined his response to reporting their location and estimated time of arrival at the passenger pier.

"What's this all about, Omar?" Frank asked after hanging up the phone.   "Where the hell do you think you're going with this scow?   The place is crawling with cops and Coast Guard.   If we get out of the prescribed transit lane, they're gonna start blasting away at us.   What are you doing this for?   Are you some kind of terrorist, Omar?"

"That's what I am," Khalid thought bitterly, "a terrorist. This operation was my idea, and I must see it through.   But, when it is over, I will be dead and that clever bastard Balthazar will go on to his next spectacular richer and more arrogant. When did God allow the jihad to become a business?"

The building housing the Caspian Sea Trading Company's offices was only a few minutes away from the City's Operations Center, and Richard Caplin, with Detwiler, Hannah, a retinue of police, and an assistant district attorney, reached it at the same time as the Ghoravis, who parked in the building's underground garage.   When they climbed the stairs to the lobby (garage access to the elevators being shut off on weekends), they found it crowded with police, some with automatic weapons, and official looking civilians.   All of them surged toward the Ghoravis as they exited the stairwell.

"What is this?   Is there a fire in the building?"   Ghoravi asked the nearest officer.

Caplin and Detwiler approached him and introduced themselves, to Ghoravi's highly visible surprise.

"Mr. Ghoravi," Caplin began, "we are investigating possible terrorist activity involving you and/or your companies."

Ghoravi appeared to stagger, and his wife rushed to his side, dragging along the children, who began to cry.

"Do you own the Tremont Grocery Supply Company?" Ghoravi nodded.

"You know that he does," his wife interjected with mounting exasperation. "What is going on here?"

"Are you aware that Anna Mingkovsky, who worked for you at Tremont was murdered on Friday night?" Caplin continued, again visibly shaking Ghoravi.

"I was not aware of it," he replied. "Have you talked with my manager Omar Khalid?"

"We've not been able to locate him. Do you know where he is?"

Ghoravi explained about the tour boat replenishment contract, and suggested that Khalid might be with the truck at the East River pier. A detective, who had been listening, stepped away and began calling on his radio.

"Is my husband under arrest?" Rena asked.

"No ma'am," was the reply. "He's free to go. But, we have a warrant to search your offices and your home. You are free to accompany us upstairs, if you wish, and to contact your lawyer."

Ghoravi protested. "I am having a reception now for my best customers and associates. If you come in now to search, it will ruin my business. Why can't you do it tonight or tomorrow?"

Caplin hesitated, then stepped back to consult with Detwiler. They had no concrete evidence to indicate that Ghoravi or his company was involved in criminal activity. The woman's murder had taken place in a subway station, and not on Tremont premises. And, Caplin acknowledged that, had he not said the word "terrorism" many times to a judge anxious to get on with his Sunday plans, he might not have gotten the search warrant. They had agreed to post a guard on the offices, then search it after the reception when Hannah, on a hunch, asked Ghoravi:

"Do you know a man named John Balthazar?"

He looked both surprised and relieved. So, Balthazar is what this business is all about.

"I met him only this past week when he came by unexpectedly to see me," Ghoravi explained. "I am a customer of his firm, but had never before met Mr. Balthazar or even talked with him on the telephone."

"What did he want?"

"I don't really know. We talked about our lives in general, and he said that he was thinking of emigrating to the United States, but somehow I didn't believe him. Throughout the meeting, I had the impression that he had come for some other reason, and was just making conversation. I have no idea what that reason might be."

Caplin then threw in the jackpot question: "Do you have any idea where he might be now?"

Ghoravi appeared a bit nonplussed. "Well, he might be upstairs. I invited him to my reception, and he said that he would come."

Everyone ran to push the elevator call button.

The tour boat had reached the tip of Manhattan Island, and begun a gradual turn to the north to enter the Hudson River. This was the heart of Fleet Week waterborne traffic, and Khalid had reduced speed even further while he scanned the area through the pilothouse binoculars. He spotted what he was looking for, and pressed the muzzle of his pistol into the pilot's ribs.

"Turn left now, Frank," he shouted and pointed. "Head for that vessel there, full speed!!" He pulled the throttle lever to the stop, and felt the engines begin to respond, the boat heeling sharply as it turned. Frank saw the target that Khalid was pointing at and tried to reverse the controls. Khalid shot him, and shoved his body out of the way as it fell.

Jerry Ogden was the first to spot the errant tour boat. Where the hell is he going, he thought, turning to look in that direction. The boat was now heading directly for a ferry, loaded with eager Fleet Week visitors, crossing to Manhattan from Staten Island.

His shout caught the attention of the patrol boat's commander, who put it on a course to intercept the tour boat. At the speed of which the patrol boat was capable, the distance to the tour boat closed rapidly, until one of the crewmen was able to hail the tour boat by loudspeaker to warn it back to its proper track. His hail was met by a barrage of gunfire that caught him in the torso and legs, and sent him crashing to the deck.

"Battle stations, man the machine guns," the boat commander shouted, while swinging the craft away from the tour boat to get out of range of the fake guardsmen who were shooting at it. "What the fuck's going on?"

"I don't know who these guys are, but we can't let them get to that ferry," Jerry shouted. The Coast Guard officer had already lifted the microphone of the boat's radio, selecting an emergency channel that all water traffic in New York harbor was required to monitor.

"Staten Island ferry enroute Manhattan this is the Coast Guard area commander. You will turn north immediately, and proceed upriver at your maximum speed. I will advise further later. Out."

There was no response from the ferry, but Jerry saw it slowly alter course and begin to head upriver. However, Khalid also saw the change, and altered his own course to intercept. The loaded ferry was a lot slower than the empty tour boat, and it was evident that Khalid would catch up quickly. The patrol boat commander switched his radio to another frequency, requesting immediate assistance.

"What are you going to do until the cavalry gets here?" Jerry shouted.

"We bought a little time by getting the ferry to run. Now, let's see whether we can slow the tour boat down by ramming it. But, we need to be very careful how we do it. He's a lot bigger than we are, and can sink us."

They put on the bulletproof vests that had been lying unneeded in a locker, and everyone aboard, except the wounded man and the one piloting the boat, took a weapon. They would not again be taken by surprise. Loading his AR-15 automatic rifle, Jerry recalled the familiarization lesson he had received during FBI training at its Quantico, Virginia academy. *If I ever get to talk to a trainee class*, he mused, *I can tell them how you never know when the shit you learn will come in handy.*

The tour boat was now running in the clear as other traffic scurried to get out of the way. Jerry's patrol boat was running parallel, its commander calculating the right moment to throw the helm over to dart in to ram. At that moment, Jerry's cell phone rang. It was Hannah calling for confirmation that there was indeed gunfire in the harbor. She and Detwiler were with the New York brass at Ghoravi's office building and were about to go up in the elevator when the detectives with them thought they heard gunfire. Now, everyone was waiting in the lobby to find what was going on. Jerry quickly sketched the situation for her, and recommended that everyone stay loose until the incident was over.

"I've got to go, Hannah. With luck, I'll talk with you later."

The speeding patrol craft closed the distance to the tour boat rapidly. It was not sufficiently large to inflict serious damage on the much larger tour boat, but could deflect it from its course and, hopefully, slow it down for a while. As it approached the tour boat, Khalid's men opened fire. This time, however, they were answered by the patrol boat's considerably greater firepower, its machine guns raking the upper works of the boat, killing two of the three men firing from there. Khalid was flattened on the floor of the pilothouse as bullets smashed the windows and penetrated the steel sheet walls. Between bursts, he raised himself to his knees to assure that the boat was still on course, the engines racing on uninterrupted. He saw the patrol boat begin its move, and guessed what it was about. Khalid counted to five, then spun the wheel to the left, turning the bow of the fast-moving tour boat quickly into the direction from which the patrol boat was coming. When the collision came, the patrol boat got the worst of it. Its back was broken and it began sinking. Jerry, intent on firing at the tour boat, was not braced for the collision, and was thrown overboard, striking his left shoulder on something along the way. The patrol boat was a wreck, slowly sinking as it floated away from the tour boat.

But, the primary mission had been accomplished. The tour boat was dead in the water, its engines stopped. With the shooting over, Khalid called on his radio, hoping that someone was still alive down below. He was relieved when the man he had posted in the engine room answered. The shock of the collision had caused the engines to automatically shutdown. The engineer crewman was restarting them now.

There appeared to be no damage to the hull.

It seemed to Khalid like forever, but the entire incident had taken little more than a couple of minutes, and soon the boat was again underway in pursuit of the ferry. Floating in his life-jacket, hanging on to the wreckage of the patrol boat with his good arm, Jerry could see the distance between them visibly shrinking. Then, he heard the same unpleasant roar he had heard the other day. He looked up as a pair of helicopter gunships passed close over his head, two more just behind. They quickly caught up and passed the straining tour boat, turning around beyond the ferry and starting back.

Khalid watched this happening and knew he had failed. He went out on to what remained of the pilothouse deck and pointed his pistol at the oncoming helicopters, firing at them until the clip was empty. The lead helicopters each fired two Hellfire missiles and the tour boat dissolved in a massive explosion that almost engulfed the ferry and the helicopters as well. The sound of it reverberated through the canyons of Manhattan for a full minute.

288

CHAPTER TWENTY-SEVEN

The explosion rocked the building causing the lights to go out, as the circuit breakers tripped.   The sound of falling glass breaking in the street could be heard in the lobby.   Everyone instinctively crouched down, fearing the building might come down on top of them.   Said Ghoravi shielded his wife and children with Hannah's help.   Then, there came a seemingly endless interval of dead silence, broken when the people in the lobby realized that the trauma was over, and the police officers among them rushed out into the street to help wherever they could.   Radios crackled, and the lobby was filled with the annoying tinkle of elaborate cell phone ring tones.

In the offices of the Caspian Sea Trading Company, the effect of the explosion was more dramatic.   At that height, the building sway caused by the shock wave was strong enough to knock most of the people attending Ghoravi's reception off their feet..   Although some of the large picture windows cracked, none shattered, and there were no significant injuries.   When the swaying and rumbling faded, everyone got up off the floor and rushed to the windows to view the compelling scene below. Balthazar was among them.

A huge pall of black smoke rose from the river where the tour boat had been.   At its base, wreckage was still burning furiously, a flotilla of police and Coast Guard boats surrounding it, looking for survivors and warding off sightseers and souvenir hunters.   Raising a pair of binoculars, Balthazar tried to see beyond the smoke screen to where the ferry had been before the helicopter attack, but was unable to do so.   He could see only that other vessels were rushing to that area, presumably to the ferry's assistance.

All things considered, Khalid had done very well.   The ferry had been the primary target from the outset, it being being more accessible and vulnerable than one of the closely guarded Fleet Week visitors.   At the peak of the festivities, the boats were crossing the bay from Staten Island and New Jersey with more than two thousand passengers each trip, and there was almost always a ferry in mid-crossing available to target.   "It was a pity Khalid had to die," Balthazar mused.   "He would have made a valuable addition to my staff."

At that moment, however, Balthazar saw the ferry break through the dense smoke screen, escorted on each side by a patrol craft.   He could see that it had been badly scarred by shrapnel from the exploding tour boat, but was essentially intact.   It was en route the slip at South Ferry, where medical assistance for the passengers and crew could be provided more readily.   Two police helicopters hovered overhead, and all of the boats in the vicinity fell in behind, as the ferry made its way slowly across the harbor.   As it passed, the fireboats dousing the still blazing tour boat wreckage turned from their task to honor it with high arcs of water from their high pressure guns.   It was like a parade, Balthazar thought, noticing that many people on the ferry's upper deck were waving at everything in sight.   It would make an inspiring clip on the evening's television news.

The electricity in the building came back on, and Balthazar left the office.   The others at the reception stayed on to watch the events unfolding below them, while feasting on the barely touched spread Ghoravi had provided. In the lobby, the Ghoravis were escorted on to one of the elevators by Hannah, an Assistant District Attorney and five uniformed policemen, Caplin and Detwiler having departed for the Operations Center after the ferry incident. Arriving at the 30th floor, the officers exited first, followed by Hannah. Turning to bring the Ghoravis into the corridor, she saw Balthazar standing in front of the door at the far end of the elevator bank. He saw her at the same time, but continued to look rigidly straight ahead.

"John, it's Hannah! I need to speak with you." She began to walk toward him, alerting the policemen, who had started toward the Caspian Sea offices in the opposite direction. Balthazar did not acknowledge her presence, as the door in front of him opened and he darted in, turning immediately to punch a button on the floor panel. Hannah reached the door just as it finished closing. She rushed back to push the call button, to no avail.

"Call the lobby," she shouted to the policemen, "and tell them a wanted man is on his way down in Elevator #6. Ask them to stop and detain him. His name is John Balthazar." Their sergeant immediately got on his radio.

Hannah turned to the Ghoravis.

"I must return to the lobby immediately," she told them. "These officers will stay with you until this business is sorted out. My guess is that there has been a misunderstanding, and there will be no need to trouble you further. I believe that your guests will be happy to see you." Without waiting for a response, she hurried into an elevator car that one of the officers was holding for her.

Hannah could hear the pandemonium in the lobby three floors before she got there. When the elevator door opened, she was met by a senior NYPD officer, who was the scene commander. He explained that Balthazar had tripped the emergency switch, stopping the elevator between the second and third floors. The police had then instructed the building custodian to freeze the elevator car at its current location.

Hannah explained to him who Balthazar was and who she was, dropping Deputy Mayor Caplin's name shamelessly. She called the Operations Center to report the news about Balthazar, and was rewarded with a return call from James Detwiler. He had agreed with Caplin that the FBI would take the lead in the Balthazar investigation, inasmuch as all available information in the case had come from Federal sources, and there was no hard evidence that Balthazar had violated City or state law. When Detwiler arrived ten minutes later, he told Hannah that Jerry Ogden had been fished out of the water with a dislocated shoulder and multiple cuts and bruises. He was taken to Bellevue Hospital for treatment, but would be all right.

What the scene commander had not immediately mentioned to Hannah was that Balthazar had a hostage, an elderly woman who had innocently boarded his elevator at an intermediate stop on the way down. He also had a knife. This information had been learned through contacting Balthazar via the emergency telephone in the elevator car. He reported that the woman apparently had some kind of medical condition, and was not feeling well.

No consideration was given to allowing Balthazar to use the woman to bargain his way out, but something had to be done to get her out of the elevator car before her condition became more serious. The car could be brought to one floor or the other and stormed, but Balthazar would be tipped off well in advance that something was happening and could harm his hostage, although Hannah secretly believed that Balthazar would not do that. A suggestion that the car be flooded with a gas that would render Balthazar unconscious also could not be executed quickly enough to prevent him from killing the woman. Even the simple tactic of waiting until Balthazar fell asleep from fatigue was impractical because of the concomitant delay in getting relief to the hostage.

Hannah suggested they see whether Balthazar would be willing to swap the elderly woman for her. Detwiler was, at first, reluctant to consider the proposal, in part because Hannah was not an FBI employee, and, therefore, not officially subject to his orders. She called Admiral Bergen, who spoke with Detwiler. The day's events in New York had really caused the shit to hit the fan in Washington. The President was on the verge of sacking FBI Director McGinnis, DNI Bierschmidt, and himself. Catching Balthazar could save them. Hannah was a capable and experienced CIA officer. If she believed that she could help, Bergen advised Detwiler to let her try.

Police technicians had altered the circuitry so that the telephone line to Balthazar could be accessed and monitored in the command post set up in a custodial room off the building's lobby. A watch officer rang the elevator car, and Balthazar answered immediately. He sounded tired to Hannah, but otherwise as she remembered.

"John, this is Hannah. How are you?"

"How should I be, Hannah? A bit cramped." There was irony in his voice.

"I never guessed you were a CIA agent," he continued. Fatigue or despair more evident now.

"That makes us even, John. I had no idea you were a terrorist," she responded.

He did not continue, so she pressed ahead.

"We would like to propose that I come in there with you in place of your present companion. She's not well, and I know you wouldn't want to deny her medical attention."

His approval was immediate, so much so that Hannah and the others listening to the conversation became suspicious. Balthazar was up to something, they suspected, but the proposal couldn't be withdrawn. Hannah's obvious objective, it was agreed, would be to talk Balthazar into surrendering, although there was little she could offer him as an incentive to do so. At this point, no one was sure what he could charged with and of what charges he could be proven guilty. They could not plea bargain, only to discover later that they had enabled Balthazar to get away with mass murder.

By agreement with Balthazar, the elevator car was brought down to the lobby level, and the doors opened revealing him standing against the rear wall of the car holding his hostage in front of him, an armed looped around her neck, his other hand holding what appeared to be an open switchblade knife. Everyone in the lobby, except for Hannah, had been moved away from the elevator entrance. To satisfy Balthazar's concern that she be unable to carry a concealed weapon, Hannah was wearing only jeans and a tee shirt, surrendered by a policewoman of her approximate size. Because of his concern about Balthazar's intentions, however, Detwiler insisted in providing Hannah a small pistol secured with masking tape to the bottom of one of two folding chairs that she was to take into the elevator car with her, so that she and Balthazar would not have to sit on the floor. The weapon was borrowed from an NYPD detective, who kept it in his sock as a backup.

When the elevator door opened, Hannah was standing five feet back from it, her hands clasped behind her neck. Even at this moment of extreme stress, Balthazar admired her beauty, and realized that he was happy to see her. She rotated slowly in place to show that there were no weapons on her person, then moved slowly into the car carrying the two chairs which she leaned against a wall. She stopped next to the hostage and turned around, so that Balthazar could switch his arm hold from her to Hannah, and give the woman a light push out of the car. The doors closed, and the car rose to its previous location between floors, another condition that Balthazar had insisted upon, so that he would have warning of an attempt to move against him.

Inside the car, Hannah and Balthazar stood facing one another in the dim light. She handed him one of the chairs, careful to keep the one with the pistol turned so that he could not see the weapon on the seat bottom. It was taped in such a way that she could grasp the butt and trigger, then tear the weapon free and bring it to bear in a single motion, which, unfortunately, she had been able to practice only a couple of times. Hannah pointed to a small, wireless microphone clipped to her shirt.

"You don't mind this, do you? she asked. "My superiors insist upon keeping track of me."

"Not at all," Balthazar replied. "It's a bit too late for keeping secrets."

They opened the chairs and sat down facing one another, he against the back wall of the car, she near the doors.

"It seems a long time now," he began. "But, it was only last night that we were in bed together. This morning, I awakened at the Waldorf-Astoria. Now, I am here."

"It's a big shock to me as well," Hannah responded. "Why did you run when I called to you upstairs?"

Balthazar shrugged. "Reflex action, I guess, when I saw the policemen. I must have a guilty soul. The elevator door conveniently opened, so I jumped in. I guess the tone of your voice warned me that this was not a chance social encounter."

"We had only just learned that you were here, and had come up to find you."

"Why were you looking for me?" he asked. "I was only attending Ghoravi's reception."

"Because they learned in Washington that your real name is Safwan al-Mufti, and that you were the one who turned in Anwar al-Ghabrizi to us," Hannah explained. "As you would expect, this raised questions, particularly when we found out you were here in the United States. I, personally, knew nothing of this until this morning."

Balthazar's face reflected both shock and indignation. It was the first time he had heard his real name spoken in many years. Hearing it from a CIA agent meant that the new life he had built for himself was being destroyed. Hearing it from a woman with whom he was in love made it unbearable.

He reacted angrily. "Who told you that I betrayed al-Ghabrizi? That is nonsense. I barely know him, and certainly had no reason to do him harm.   I was shocked when I heard he had been arrested."

"We found your satellite telephone number in the speed dial list of al-Ghabrizi's telephone.   If he rarely talked with you, why would he have your number handy?"

Hannah watched Balthazar's face carefully, as she threw the question at him.   His eyes flickered as he realized that he had been caught.

"All right," he said after a pause.   "Al-Ghabrizi and I worked for the same people, sometimes on the same projects. His task was to provide people with particular talents and experience for my undertakings.   On occasion, we needed to talk with one another about details and arrangements.   His number is also on my telephone's speed dial."

"What undertakings are you referring to?" Hannah asked, anticipating that Balthasar would refuse to explain.   He stared at the wall for what seemed to her to be forever, and then, to Hannah's great surprise (and the joy of those listening in), he began to answer the question.

"There are people in countries around the world, Muslim countries, who are pursuing goals and strategies that differ from those of al-Ghabrizi's jihad on the one hand and those of America and the West on the other.   These people are powerful in their own countries; most of them are very wealthy.   They are dedicated to preventing the extremist version of Islam, and those who represent it, from ruling their countries and the Muslim world. At the same time, they want just as strongly to keep the West, particularly America, from interfering with their plans and confusing the people with ideas of democracy that only cause trouble.   So, they have become adept at working on one side and then the other so that neither will triumph. On balance, the jihadis are a bigger threat to them than the crusaders, but they do not themselves have the strength to defeat them. So, they must have active assistance from the West..."

"And they stimulate this assistance by terrorist acts, in cities throughout the world, that get blamed on the al-Ghabrizis of the world" Hannah concluded for him.

"Precisely," nodded Balthazar. "But, there is a serious drawback. Over time, the impact of those operations can be so great that Muslims all over the world begin to believe that the fundamentalists will prevail, and that it is the will of God. Then, these people must act to counter that trend by causing harm to the jihadis."

"I have never met these men personally," Balthazar continued, "and know of them only from talking with their underlings. I have never heard mention of an organization, like al-Qaeda, that unites them, nor of a single leader. The principals, many of them highly visible, rarely meet, but operate through lieutenants and trusted emissaries who congregate in places away from the regions in contention. One such place is Paris, from which I generally have operated, although my businesses are located in Marseille. In addition to being easier to get to, the food and the women in Paris are much better." He smiled at Hannah, but with none of the panache to which she had become accustomed.

"The strategy you describe is very difficult to pursue over an extended period of time. Are these people satisfied with the way things are going?" Hannah asked.

Balthazar pondered for a moment. "I don't see how they could be," he said finally. "Support for the jihadis among Muslims is growing stronger in the countries of Central and South Asia, and even among immigrants and their children in Western Europe. This cannot be of comfort to those in power in Muslim states who wish to keep control of their countries and resources. It will force them to deal more harshly with the fundamentalists and to move closer to the West."

"Perhaps, that is why al-Ghabrizi and you were turned in," Hannah suggested. "Maybe, the two seamen who were with al-Ghabrizi in Karachi were intended to participate in today's attack."

Balthazar shrugged. "That may be so," he admitted. "But, the operation plan came from someone here in New York."

The last caught Hannah by surprise. "Are you saying that you were aware that the attack was coming, that you had a part in the planning?"

"I only provided logistical support," he replied "I can't decide whether it was a success or a failure."

Hannah was not sure she had heard correctly. Why would Balthazar admit that he had contributed to a terrorist attack? Surely, he knew that there was probably no one left to finger him, and that he had a shot at walking away from major charges. Turning in al-Ghabrizi, which Hannah now believed Balthazar did not do, was not an indictable offense. In fact, it was possible that Balthazar could have talked himself into a sizable reward. She pursued his revelation.

"Is that the kind of thing you normally did for these groups?"

"No," he replied, "this one was different and a lot easier." Generally, I plan the whole operation, provide the money and technology, and make sure the people involved know what they were doing. The only things I did not do was recruit the martyrs and hang around to push the button. Usually, by the time the operation came off, I was back in Paris. Al-Ghabrizi was working for the same people as me, but I don't think he could tell one group from another. They were all just voices on the telephone, the difference between al-Ghabrizi and me being that I didn't care. If they paid my fee, which was very great, and provided what I needed to do the work, I was their man."

Hannah could stand it no longer. She almost shouted at Balthazar, realizing only later how strange that must have seemed to the people listening in.

"John, why are you telling us this? You know now that I work for the CIA and that the police and the FBI are recording our conversation. Why aren't you clamming up and screaming for your lawyer? Until yesterday, no one in this country had ever heard of you. We would have a very difficult time prosecuting."

Balthazar smiled wanly, and thought about where to begin.

"You see, Hannah, it no longer makes any difference. I could, perhaps, escape these charges, but your government will not let me go. I would not do so, if our roles were reversed. Even if I had nothing to do with the al-Ghabrizi business, which I did not, your President needs to have something to show after all the recent confusion and embarrassment, underscored by today's attack here in New York. How would it look to have to say that we caught the master terrorist, but had to let him go? Perhaps, they would charge me with kidnapping the poor woman on the elevator, but they would find something on which to hold me for a long time."

Hannah had to agree with him. The Agency, the FBI, and every other Intelligence Community organization would be directed to scour heaven and earth for information that could be used to convict Balthazar of something. It would take a long time, even if a case was never made. Clearly, Balthazar was not going to walk out of the elevator a free man.

"Aside from that," he continued, " my ability to live in the style and manner I enjoy is at an end. As I mentioned, the fees I was paid for my services were enormous, and bought me a very comfortable and respected place in international business and society. It's that, rather than the money itself, that I would miss the most. My parents still live in Marseille, and follow my career closely. They live in a much better house now, and no longer need to work, all of this because their handsome, clever son became a success. Who is going to employ me now? I would be lucky, if they did not kill me at the first opportunity, thinking that I must now be a double agent."

"You've got your legitimate businesses," Hannah pointed out. "They can support your life style. I understand that they are very successful."

"Who is going to buy from someone everyone thinks is a terrorist?" he replied derisively. "When I travel, I will spend more time in airport interrogation rooms than with my customers."

Hannah felt herself beginning to feel sorry for Balathazar, which she decided was ridiculous. The man had committed murder many times, if by proxy, apparently with no thought to the victims. This, she decided, was the right moment for the obligatory proposal.

"Considering the gravity of the mess you've gotten yourself into, John, would you consider working with us? It would make your life a lot more comfortable."

Balthazar laughed. "You would be disappointed," he replied. "I know no jihadis of any importance, and they never told me anything I didn't need to know for the operation I was undertaking at the time."

"So, how do we get out of this elevator?" Hannah asked quietly.

Balthazar thought for a moment, but had obviously made up his mind earlier.

"I do not propose to spend the rest of my life in an American prison, to be paraded around in front of reporters and television cameras just to make your masters look successful. I would like you to kill me, Hannah."

She thought she had not heard correctly, and sat there staring at him. Her shock appeared to amuse Balthazar, who continued:

"I would do it myself, but all I have is this puny pocket knife, and the thought of stabbing myself to death makes me ill."

"How would I do it?" she asked, not believing that she was actually discussing the prospect with him.

"You could use the pistol taped to the bottom of your chair," he replied matter-of-factly." The FBI and NYPD officers listening to the elevator conversation in total fascination suddenly realized what they had just heard.

"Standby to bring them down to the lobby," Detwiler shouted. "When the doors open, storm the car."

Seeing Hannah's confusion, Balthazar explained that he had seen the weapon when the chairs were brought into the elevator.

"Go ahead and pull it free," he urged.

"I have no intention of shooting you, John," she replied That kind of thing is not in my job description. I obviously hate what you've been doing, but I don't want to kill you for it, certainly not here."

Balthazar did not appear to be surprised by her refusal. She loved him after all, he decided. But, aloud he said:

"If you won't kill me, I will attack you with this knife and force you to shoot me in self-defense or your associates to do so, when they come to rescue you."

For emphasis, he snapped open the switchblade knife.

Hannah pulled the pistol free of the tape and pointed it at him. Balthazar jumped to his feet knocking over his chair, the sound of which was heard in the monitoring room.

"Bring them down, NOW!, Detwiler shouted.

The lights in the elevator car went out, and it lurched downward throwing Balthazar toward Hannah. She fired three times before he landed on her, and they crumpled in a heap in a corner of the car. His body was lying on top of hers when the doors opened and the cavalry came charging in.

CHAPTER TWENTY-EIGHT

"We were very lucky," Hannah said to Jerry Ogden, as they stood at the ferry slip looking at the damaged vessel under the glare of arc lights brought in to cover the long process of evacuating the hundreds of wounded and treating them in makeshift aid stations set up on the dock and in the park outside. There was ambulance capacity sufficient only to take the seriously injured to hospital, while the remainder were patched up by EMS teams drawn from all over the City. Fortunately, only a handful of people had died when the tour boat exploded, and the number of seriously wounded was small relative to the more than two thousand people who had been aboard the ferry at the time.

Apparently, the strength of the explosives aboard, combined with the four missiles fired into it by the helicopters, had been sufficient to largely vaporize the tour boat, greatly reducing the volume of shrapnel that hit the ferry. The latter had been running from the tour boat at the time, so that it presented a stern aspect to the explosion, making it a smaller target.

"We hadn't the slightest indication of the attack plan, and were busy chasing the poor Ghoravis," she complained. "We lucked into Balthazar, but not until the attack was over."

Although it was warm, Hannah was huddled in an FBI windbreaker, her arms folded across her chest. Underneath, her clothes were stained with Balthazar's blood, but she had refused offers of a car to take her back to the hotel. Her mind was still in the elevator.

She did not believe, and had not believed then, that Balthazar would have stabbed her. When he jumped or fell on her after the lights went out, she had fired reflexively, just as she had been taught at the Farm. Balthazar had gotten what he wanted, but she regretted being the instrument of his death, and felt it dishonest to deny to herself that she had fallen in love with him.

"I think you're being overly harsh," Jerry responded. "The attack was designed to kill a lot of people on a ferry boat, figuring that we would be focusing security on the visiting Fleet Week vessels and the crowds at the piers. It didn't succeed in that objective because of the extra security precautions we took, namely ordering in the helicopters. We took them because of the intelligence provided by Washington that something was up, even though we didn't know what it was. In your experience, when was Intelligence ever able to provide everything you needed to know about a threat? Sometimes you can't connect the dots, and need to take action just knowing the dots are there. That's the really hard part, because you are ordering people about and expending resources on the basis of a personal inter- pretation or even a hunch. But, if more people had done so, many of our so-called intelligence failures could have been avoided."

"You sound like your boss, Jim Detwiler," she teased, then smiled at him. Jerry had rushed over from the hospital as soon as he heard about the elevator incident. His left shoulder was heavily wrapped, and he carried his arm in a sling. There were several bandages on his face and neck. Hannah had needed to get away from the scene of the shooting and its aftermath, and she and Jerry had walked, mostly silently, through the streets of lower Manhattan for hours, ending up at South Ferry.

Hannah's secure cell phone rang. Admiral Bergen was at the other end, apologizing for not calling her sooner. He had been tied up at the White House since word of the terrorist attack in New York reached Washington. In fact, he was still there, calling from John Cook's office.

"I'm sorry about the mess here, sir," Hannah told him. "We just didn't have the intelligence to provide specific warning of what was going to happen."

"Don't apologize, Hannah," Bergen replied. "What you did was heroic and, incidentally, saved my ass and Don McGinnis's at the FBI, as well. The President was set to fire the lot of us. But, when word came through that you had caught Balthazar, and it turned out that the casualty rate on the ferry was low, he changed his mind and fired only Bierschmidt. Because we had not prevented the attack, someone had to go, and Al was the obvious choice, since he was supposed to be in charge of all of our intelligence operations."

"I'm sorry about Director Bierschmidt, Hannah told him, "but glad that I don't have to break in a new CIA Director, that is if I've still got a job."

There was a puzzled silence. Then, Bergen chuckled: "Oh, that! Consider yourself suspended with pay while the security people check out the charge that you were consorting with the enemy. But, I need you back in Washington tomorrow. The President wants to shake your hand.

The meeting at Security Police Headquarters in Karachi had ended, and Jed, CIA's station chief, was making his way to the unobtrusive side door he normally used when visiting. The Pakistani government was generally friendly and cooperative, but didn't want its relationship with the CIA known to the populace, which sheltered a number of very difficult extremist elements. For his part, Jed was just as happy to hide behind his cover as a purchasing agent for an American textile company, an inspired device that allowed him to move freely about the country, ostensibly visiting factories that produced cloth and clothing for export. Since the Pakistanis needed the business, he was always welcomed and taken at face value.

As he neared the exit, he was approached by the Captain he had dealt with earlier in the al-Ghabrizi matter, whose name had turned out to be Ibrahim Khan. By now, the two were on less formal terms which, under different circumstances, could have developed into friendship. Khan knew what Jed's position and duties were and Jed knew that Khan was not just a run-of-the-precinct police captain. After shaking hands, the two repaired to Khan's office, where refreshments were waiting.

The Pakistani officer congratulated Jed on the capture of Balthazar and the valiant escape of the ferry from the terrorist attack, that had occurred the week before. The media had been encouraged to treat the latter as a major victory for American homeland security preparedness, and big play was given to Hannah's contribution, although her name was never mentioned and there was no photograph. Jed thanked him, but pointed out that much was owed to the intelligence concerning al-Ghabrizi and Balthazar provided by the captain and the Pakistani government.

"If you chose to inquire," Jed told him, "you would not find my government ungrateful."

Khan thanked him, but protested that he was simply acting for others.

"Although we had known of Sheik al-Ghabrizi's relocation to Karachi almost from the outset, it was not our choice to arrest him or to turn him over to your people. We knew generally what he was doing, but none of it was directed against Pakistan, so we informed him that he would remain safe so long as that continued to be the case."

"What changed your mind?" Jed asked.

"Nothing," was the response. "We were asked by certain people in other countries to do this as a matter of common benefit. So, we did."

Jed knew it was pointless to ask who these people were, so he asked the next best question: "For what purpose?"

Khan thought for a moment about how best to phrase his response. He began carefully:

"It was intended as a gift to you Americans, to get your attention. My principals are concerned that we are nearing the edge of chaos in relations between the Muslim world and the West.   I'm not talking about government to government relations, although they are not without problem, but rather the impact that your policies is having on the masses of Muslims in countries from South Asia to Turkey and Africa.   The extremists are telling the people that what you are calling democracy is a religion opposed to Islam, and they are beginning to believe it. If that belief prevails, leaders like mine, who try to steer a middle course in their countries, will be unable to survive, just as the Shah's regime could not survive in Iran.   Our strength today depends on the military and security forces, and theirs on intelligence and support quietly provided by the majority of the people.

Should the jihadis succeed in convincing the masses that we are tools of the infidel, our ability to rule will end and sectarian conflict will break out and spread throughout the Muslim world. No one would be able to stop such a catastrophe."

"I've heard people in the West speculate that, perhaps, such a conflict should be encouraged," Jed noted, "after the oil fields are secured, of course. The jihadis would exhaust themselves killing one another, and wouldn't have the resources or incentive to attack the West."

"I also have heard that argument," Khan added. "But, it was made by an imam claiming that it was the West's scheme for stealing Muslim oil. The point is that there needs to be some structure or framework within which both sides can find a basis for ending this gradual descent into chaos. The key question is who will represent the Muslim world."

"Strangely enough, from what he has told us, al-Ghabrizi agrees with you," Jed responded. "He says that, earlier on, he thought that he could be the leader you are talking about, but has since given up. He, too, is concerned about the growing anarchy within the jihad, for the same reason that you and your associates are." Jed had read the transcripts of Hannah's interviews with al-Ghabrizi and her elevator dialogue with John Balthazar that CIA Headquarters had sent to key posts.

Khan looked surprised, then shrugged. Jed could tell that he was wondering, if only momentarily, whether a mistake had been made with regard to al-Ghabrizi.

"If what you say is true," he said, "it is an illustration of what we have been talking about. How can peace be made between Islam and the West, if we Muslims cannot understand one another and cooperate."

"Balthazar also spoke of the goals and efforts of your friends before he died," Jed added.

Khan snorted dismissively.

"Balthazar was a mercenary, who would work for anyone who paid his outrageous fee. In New York, he was not working for us. Actually, we did not even know he was there. He was exposed deliberately by someone among his employers in Paris who asked us to pass it on to you, believing it would have greater credibility coming from us. I suspect it was done because they thought it was Balthazar who betrayed al-Ghabrizi. We looked upon it as an additional gift to help secure your cooperation."

"What is it your people would have the United States do?" Jed asked.

Khan paused before replying.

"Your country must stop acting as a crusader for democracy in the Muslim world and pay more attention to its more vital national interest, which is to keep its own people safe and prosperous. The way Muslim countries are governed, their laws and social structure are none of your business, and your loud condemnations do nothing but provide ammunition for the extremists who would remake our world in the Taliban image. When terrorists attack your country and others in the West, they don't do it in hope of somehow taking them over, but with the goal of causing you to abandon their own countries. It is possible for such a war to go on forever.

Seized with delivering his message, Khan rose to his feet and paced back and forth in front of Jed, who sat listening intently and making notes in a pocket diary.

"You Americans have a saying: All politics is local. Well, the jihad is also local, different from country to country. While the mujahedin in Indonesia is sympathetic to the struggles of fellow Muslims in, say, Lebanon, his focus is at home, and we must keep it there. The worst thing we can do is permit the creation of a worldwide conflict between Islam and democracy. American governments, for domestic political reasons, have perpetuated the illusion of such a conflict to bolster their public support. Anwar al-Ghabrizi was its personification. Now, we have given him to you...with the plea that you not reinvent him."

"But, Jed protested, "whatever you call them, there are men out there trying to kill our people and destroy our way of life."

"That is certainly true," Khan responded. "But, nothing I've said should be taken to imply that we work less or devote fewer resources to destroying them. On the contrary, if it becomes no longer necessary for your country to constantly burnish its self-image as the great champion of democracy, we should be able to work together more effectively and responsively. As you know, our main line of defense runs through the security services of the Muslim nations, working together with organizations such as yours. But, the U.S. is not in charge of us, and we should not have to be concerned about the image of your administration in the media. Nor are our goals and imperatives necessarily the same. If we fail, we will not survive. If you fail, you will write books and become television commentators."

Jed finished describing his meeting with Khan to his boss Sam Glover over the secure satellite telephone, and promised a detailed, written report immediately for Glover to give to Admiral Bergen.

"What do you think, Sam? Jed asked. "Is this going to fly?"

"It would certainly make our lives easier," Glover replied. "But, I doubt the White House will buy it. The war on terrorism has become a big part of American life, and justifies many of the things our government does and a big chunk of the money it spends. I can't see us being quiet about it just so we can prosecute it better. In fact, it wouldn't surprise me to discover that Roger Norton, Tucker's flack, is planning to hold a contest to name the new al-Ghabrizi.

This is an opaque war. It is very difficult for the average person to see clearly who the enemy is and what he really stands for. It's not enough to say that it is 'terrorism' without putting a name and face to it, preferably one that endures to the end, so that we will know when we have won. For a long time, that face was al-Ghabrizi's; now, we've got to find a replacement. I'm not sure that our friends have done us a favor."

"What did you think of the warning from Khan's people that the jihad could go on forever?" Jed asked. "Reminds me of the Communist concept of permanent revolution, and look what happened to them."

"But," Glover observed, "the Communists had no God. If you have a God, you can do anything in his name."

###